MW01148452

Cover Design and Interior Format

FORTUNE'S
BRIDES
BOOK
ONE

Never Doubt a Duke

REGINA SCOTT

To my dear Kristin, for all the years of support and encouragement, and to the Lord, for leading us down unexpected paths

CHAPTER ONE

Surrey, England, late January 1812

Becoming a governess was harder than fighting off Napoleon.

Jane Kimball sat with her hands folded in her lap as the rickety hired carriage rolled through the countryside away from London and toward her new life. Every inch of her felt tight, as if her black mourning gown was suddenly several sizes too small. But then, some state of nervousness was to be expected. She hadn't tried to pretend she was a proper lady for a long time.

"You are exactly what His Grace needs," Miss Thorn said from across the carriage.

Jane still wasn't sure how the owner of the employment agency could be so certain. She'd thought when she'd answered the ad in the *Times* from the Fortune Employment Agency, seeking a governess, she might meet with a stiff-backed gentleman who would frown down his nose at her and inform her she was fit for nothing. After all, she had little experience and no references.

Spending the last ten years following the drum didn't count.

"I'll do all I can to make you proud, ma'am," Jane said.

Miss Thorn inclined her head. Now, there was a lady. Jane didn't know the employment agency owner's background or why she seemed determined to help gentlewomen fallen on hard times, but she knew quality when she saw it. Everything from Miss Thorn's sleek black hair under the feathered hat to her elegant frame draped in a lavender quilted-satin redingote said she should be respected, admired. In comparison, Jane's thick brown hair seemed positively unruly, even wrapped in a bun and confined inside her plain straw bonnet. Her figure was solid; ample her husband Jimmy had called it. Her eyes were too dark a brown to invite confidences, and her navy wool cloak more practical than fashionable. Then again, Miss Thorn's pretty coat hadn't seen duty in Portugal.

"You're nervous," Miss Thorn said, gloved hand stroking the short-haired cat in her lap. Fortune, she'd named the creature, and apparently the employment agency as well. At times, Jane wondered whether the cat was in charge. Miss Thorn certainly went nowhere without her pet. She was a handsome animal. The dove-grey fur was tailored like a morning coat, wrapping around her back and head to leave a white blaze down her throat like a cravat. Great copper-colored eyes gazed at Jane unblinkingly.

"Very nervous," Jane admitted. "I'm glad I didn't eat breakfast this morning."

Miss Thorn raised a brow, and Jane sighed. She never had understood why everything she thought popped out of her mouth. It had been a terrible failing in the daughter of a country vicar, where diplomacy was key. Even Jimmy's colonel had been taken aback a time or two. She was only glad her late husband and his friends had found the trait amusing, endearing.

"Sorry," she muttered to Miss Thorn. "Habit."

Miss Thorn glanced down at Fortune. As if she'd received a command from her mistress, the cat leaped across the space to Jane's side and rubbed her head against Jane's arm.

Something inside her uncurled. "She is so sweet."

"Only with those of whom she approves," Miss Thorn

said.

"I've known a few horses like that," Jane said, stroking a hand down the cat's thick grey fur. "I'm honored."

Fortune blinked her copper eyes, and her small mouth turned up. It was as if she'd seen something grand inside Jane, something worthy of approval. Perhaps Jane could do this after all.

"I'm going to miss her," she said, returning the cat's smile. "I'm going to miss you both. I don't know what I would have done if you hadn't agreed to represent me."

Miss Thorn's gaze, eyes the color of blue lilacs, rested on her cat. "I cannot abide bullies. Being born to or otherwise acquiring power should not make a gentleman determined to wield it over others. It is my privilege to be of service to you, Jane."

Another employment agent might have said the same, but Jane had never heard of any that worked so tirelessly. Miss Thorn had listened to Jane's story without judging and promised to find her a position where she would be safe, valued. When Miss Thorn had learned the constrained circumstances under which Jane was living, she'd opened her own comfortable town house on Clarendon Square. After that time, Jane had never felt alone again. Fortune had been ever at her side and Miss Thorn at her back. Jane refused to retreat now.

Even if she knew next to nothing about being a governess for a duke's children.

"Ah, here it comes," Miss Thorn said, gathering up her reticule.

Jane peered out the window. They had been running past trees and fields above the south bank of the River Thames, the water glassy against a grey sky that threatened more of the snow they had seen earlier in the month. They appeared to have reached a side branch of the river, for the water was lower and murkier, ice crusting its surface. Ahead, twin gatehouses of a golden stone flanked the entrance to a gracefully arching bridge.

"Wey Castle," Miss Thorn said as the horse's hooves clattered against the stone span.

Jane stared at the looming walls, rising easily thirty feet above the crest overlooking the side stream. Rough stone blocks at one corner told of an older building on the site, while the smooth stone and gabled roof of the rest of the building gave testimony of a more recent age. Narrow windows reflected the heavy sky.

"That's not a castle," Jane said, sitting back and glad for Fortune's presence beside her.

Miss Thorn raised delicately arched brows. "No? The guide book describes it as such. I believe the tower at the southwest corner dates from 1360. But then, I suspect you have seen a few castles."

She had. Egyptian palaces dating back to the time of Christ, Flemish fortresses from when knights on chargers roamed the land, and Portuguese marvels that had survived earthquakes. Jimmy and his regiment had fought below, behind, and inside them. She'd seen the massive stones pink in the light of dawn and red with the fire of defeat. The Duke of Wey's home didn't seem nearly so grand.

The drive led up the crest and into a courtyard paved with cobbles, the house enclosing it on three sides. She felt as if a dozen eyes must be watching from all those windows. Funny how the windows looking in toward the courtyard were larger. Jimmy would have said the outer windows were narrow for protection, but it seemed a waste to be forever looking inward when a serene island and river lay just beyond.

A footman with an old-fashioned powered wig hurried to lower the step. Fortune leaped back to Miss Thorn, who scooped her up into her arms.

The butler, a regal fellow with thick white hair that was surely no wig, came forward and glanced between them. "Mrs. Kimball?"

Jane could understand his confusion. Miss Thorn certainly looked more like a polished, proper governess.

Miss Thorn inclined her head, the feather in her hat dipping just as respectfully. "I am Miss Thorn, owner of the Fortune Employment Agency. This is Mrs. Kimball. His Grace is expecting us."

The butler took a step back. "You are indeed expected. Her Grace will see you in her chambers."

Miss Thorn's smile was firm. "After we see the duke."

The butler's look was equally unforgiving. "His Grace is very busy. He leaves all matters regarding the staff to me and all matters regarding his daughters to his mother."

Interesting. She'd heard of wives taking such a role, but of course His Grace was a widower.

Miss Thorn regarded him. "And that, I fear, is why you have gone through three governesses in the last year."

"Three governesses?" Jane glanced to her benefactress. Why hadn't she been told? If three likely more-experienced governesses couldn't handle the post, what made Miss Thorn think Jane could? Even the supremely confident glow in Fortune's eyes couldn't stop the sinking feeling in her stomach.

The butler answered before Miss Thorn could, his voice dripping ice. "Be that as it may, His Grace has not instructed me to bring you to him."

"Then I suggest," Miss Thorn said, tones clipped, "that you consult with His Grace, or I will have no choice but to take my eminently suitable candidate back to London, where I assure you other noble houses are clamoring for her services."

Doing it a bit brown. Jane clamped her lips shut to keep from stating the opinion aloud. She wasn't all that suited, having only cared for Colonel Travers's daughter for the last year, and she sincerely doubted dukes and duchesses were coming to blows as to who had the opportunity to hire her next. But the butler glanced between them, and

Jane tried to look as qualified as Miss Thorn had described her. It didn't help that she came no taller than the butler's rather impressive nose.

Either she succeeded in looking proper, or the situation was more dire than she'd thought, for the man promised to return with an answer and left them in the courtyard.

"Is the duke so cruel a master that he'd refuse to speak with us?" she murmured to Miss Thorn as they waited.

"Not at all," Miss Thorn assured her. "I have it on good authority that he is even-tempered and fair."

Some could have said the same of Colonel Travers. They hadn't seen him after he'd overindulged.

Miss Thorn strolled back and forth across the cobbles, black boots tapping, as their hired coachman climbed down to see to his horses. The footman was eyeing Jane's meager trunk and worn saddle on the back of the coach as if wondering whether to port them into the house or heave them into the river with her alongside.

"His Grace can be remote," her benefactress continued, "but he is not the chief problem here. The previous governesses were weak-natured, timid creatures, unable to stand under the demands of the position."

Jane didn't question how she knew. Miss Thorn had been amazingly informed about Jane when she'd strolled into the coffee shop where they had agreed to meet the first time. She'd commiserated on Jimmy's death thirteen months ago and sniffed disparagingly at the way the colonel's wife had turned Jane out without a reference. Perhaps Miss Thorn knew the family here better than Jane had thought.

Or Fortune had met the previous governesses and disapproved of them.

The cat certainly wasn't sure of her surroundings now. Her head snapped left, right, eyes narrowing and tail lashing back and forth, as if she suspected each of the servants of some nefarious purpose. A ladylike growl came from her throat as the butler returned, head up as if he wanted no one to notice how quickly he walked.

"His Grace will see you now." He eyed Fortune as if expecting to be given charge of her. Neither looked amused by the prospect. Miss Thorn swept past him for the massive double-doors of the house, and Jane could only follow.

The entryway made her rethink her opinion of Wey Castle. The flagstone floor felt firm, determined beneath her boots. Dotted with bronze scones that had once likely held flaming torches and hung with tapestries in rich reds and vibrant blues, the walls soared three stories to a ceiling painted with the hosts of heaven riding into battle. The air hinted of beeswax polish and lavender sachet. It was all commanding with a touch of elegance. Her father would have been delighted to see her in such surroundings. He'd never understood why she'd run away to marry a cavalry officer. But then, for her and Jimmy, it had been love at first sight. They would have done anything to be together. She wasn't likely to find a match like that again.

The butler ushered them through another set of double doors on their left and into a large room that somehow managed to feel cramped. Jane stopped to glance around and up, hand clasped to her bonnet to keep it from sliding back on her hair. Every wall save the rear was lined with floor-to-ceiling bookcases, with more jetting out at right angles, giving the library the look of a maze. So many books! Someone could spend a lifetime and never read them all, but what a wonderful challenge in trying. Books had been hard to come by in the field, closely guarded and shared only with trustworthy friends. This was true wealth.

A mew from Fortune recalled her to her purpose. Jane lowered her head and made herself follow Miss Thorn and the cat deeper into the room. In the center of the space, surrounded by padded Moroccan leather chairs, stood an elegant teak desk with curved legs. She couldn't recall ever seeing the surface of the desks in the officer's quarters; they'd always been eclipsed by the sweep of maps, dispatches, and scrawlings of the battle to come. This one was so clean she could see the inlaid pattern of ivory in the shape of a unicorn, one leg extended and horn down, as if bowing to someone.

Very likely the man standing behind the desk. The light from the slim, north-facing windows made him seem no more than a tall shadow. Her first thought was that he didn't look like a duke. Dukes should be hard, ruthless. Like some of Jimmy's commanders, they would bark orders, issue demands. This one had broad enough shoulders, but there was a stillness about him in his navy coat and tan breeches, like a lion about to leap. His warm brown hair was swept back from a heart-shaped face, and his eyes, like jade, narrowed.

Oh, right. Wasn't wise to stare at dukes. Jane dropped her gaze respectfully.

"Miss Thorn, Mrs. Kimball," he said. His voice was precise, polished, like the shiny top of his desk. "How might I be of assistance?"

"It was my understanding you wished to engage Mrs. Kimball as governess for your three daughters," Miss Thorn said, one hand resting on Fortune's grey head as the cat draped along her other arm. "Surely you wish to speak to her first."

"It was my understanding that Her Grace would interview Mrs. Kimball," he said. Jane glanced up to find him smiling pleasantly. "She's waiting upstairs."

Very likely that was all it took. A gentle hint, a whiff of the power behind it, and everyone must do his bidding. Clearly, he expected the same from Miss Thorn.

Miss Thorn did not seem inclined to oblige. "So we were informed," she said with a tight-eyed look to the butler, who was gazing impassively at the nearest bookcases. "However, there must be some mistake. A gentleman will want to ensure that the woman hired to care for his heirs is suitable."

Something flickered across his face. Frustration? Regret? Dukes could not like being scolded, however veiled in polished prose.

He spread his hands, the movement controlled, effortless. "I have complete faith in my mother. She chose your agency, Miss Thorn. I accept Mrs. Kimball on your recommendation."

"A shame I cannot say the same for you," Miss Thorn said.

And Jane had thought she spoke her mind too often. Was Miss Thorn intent on making an enemy?

The duke drew himself up. "Do you doubt my word, madam?"

Said in that steely voice, the question begged heresy. The butler's nose was distinctly out of joint as well at the slight to his master.

Miss Thorn merely seated herself in one of the leather chairs, as if she were the hostess. "Do sit down, Your Grace. We have much to discuss."

Clearly bemused, he sat. Jane took the chair closest to Miss Thorn. Fortune was wiggling, and she held out her hands to the cat. Miss Thorn released her hold, and Fortune arched up.

Right onto the duke's desk.

Jane tensed. This was it. He'd order them from his castle, or worse, confine them in the dungeons. All good castles must have dungeons. She edged forward on the seat, ready to bolt and take Miss Thorn and Fortune with her, if needed.

Fortune stalked up to the duke and paused, tail lashing. The duke stared back, unmoving. Jane counted off the seconds. Fortune rolled over on her back and offered him her belly. Her purr echoed against the bookshelves.

"Yes," Miss Thorn said, "I believe you will do nicely for

Mrs. Kimball. Shall we begin negotiations?"

Negotiations, the woman said, as if she would settle for nothing less than unconditional surrender. Alaric, Duke of Wey, had never met anyone like her, but he began to hope Mrs. Kimball had similar confidence.

She was certainly sturdier looking than the last three governesses. He'd only glimpsed them on occasion. They had been willowy, elegant things, not unlike Miss Thorn, but with decidedly more submissive demeanors. The only thing remotely submissive about Mrs. Jane Kimball were her large brown eyes, reminding him of the little does that wandered the island on which the castle was built.

She'd have to have more cunning than a doe if she was to deal with his mother. Despite his admonitions, Her Grace persisted on ruling over the nursery and schoolroom, as if no one could care for her granddaughters as well as she could. As she had not been a particularly doting mother, he found her sudden interest in the girls difficult to credit.

"I was informed my mother already agreed on salary and half day off," he told the formidable Miss Thorn, fighting the impulse to rub the belly the cat had offered him. "We have a suitable room prepared, as you requested. What more do you require?" That purr was infectious. He wanted to smile along with it.

Miss Thorn leaned forward. Mrs. Kimball was watching her as if she wasn't sure what the woman would do next. Alaric shared her concerns.

"Mrs. Kimball will be caring for your daughters," Miss Thorn said. "She will assess the situation and bring you a plan for their curriculum."

Mrs. Kimball started. Had she never devised a curriculum before? She seemed young for a widow, perhaps a few years his junior. Had her husband been a great deal older or died in some accident? Not that it was any of his business.

"Furthermore," Miss Thorn continued as if his silence meant acquiescence, "she will report your daughter's progress each evening before retiring."

A logical suggestion. His daughters seemed to change each time he saw them. He was kept apprised of every other area of his responsibility, by his steward, land agents, solicitor in London, the directors of the charities he supported, the prime minister. Why not his children? His mother could relay anything of import.

"I'm certain Her Grace would agree with that," he said.

Miss Thorn's purple-blue eyes pinned him in place. "She will report directly to you. She will take her direction from you. Anything else leads to anarchy."

Mrs. Kimball blinked as if surprised by this revelation as well. Had the two women even discussed this situation? He had assumed an employment agency screened its clients closely. Perhaps he should be the one asking the questions.

He returned Miss Thorn's forthright gaze. There was something vaguely familiar about the woman, yet he did not recall dealing with the Fortune Employment Agency before. Most of the castle's staff came from the island, and his mother or Parsons, their butler, saw to the hiring. He wasn't entirely sure why his mother had placed her trust in Miss Thorn.

"And what about Mrs. Kimball's qualifications or experience makes it important that she deal directly with me?" he asked.

"I'd as soon deal with your master of horse," Mrs. Kimball put in helpfully. "But I doubt he'd know much about your daughters."

He sat back. He was used to determining the course of action, issuing orders, and seeing his will carried out. What was it about these women that so disarmed him? The cat slipped down into his lap and cuddled against his chest.

Of course, Mrs. Kimball might well have reported to

his master of horse. Very likely Mr. Quayle learned a great deal about the workings inside the great house from other members of the staff. Alaric did not like thinking how little he knew about his daughters. Each birth had seemed a miracle; the baby a fragile, precious life entrusted to his care. Evangeline had been adamant about his role.

"Fathers groom sons," his late wife had said, pretty mouth drawn up. "Mothers mold daughters. The nursery is my domain, just as the estates are yours. I'm sure you wouldn't appreciate me interfering with the tenants, dealing with the flooding."

That he had not been able to argue. His father had been preparing him for this role since the day Alaric had been born. But when Evangeline had died attempting to bear him a son and heir, taking the baby with her, he had had no idea how to deal with the daughters she'd left behind.

Did Mrs. Kimball?

He was petting the cat. He wasn't sure when that had started, but the movement of his hand and the purr rumbling out of her made his shoulders come down.

Mrs. Kimball smiled at him, the look bringing out her cheekbones, the light in her eyes. "Hard to resist, isn't she?"

He pulled back his hand and leveled his gaze on Miss Thorn. "If you tell me the only way Mrs. Kimball will accept the position is if she deals directly with me, then I must question the role you see her playing in this household."

Mrs. Kimball's smile faded, and he almost called back his words.

"You are entrusting her with the lives of the three people who must be most precious to you in all the world," Miss Thorn pointed out. "Inquisitive young ladies who have somehow managed to drive away every governess since their dear mother passed on. I know what I am asking may seem unusual, Your Grace, but if you continue doing what you have been doing, you will continue to see the same results."

She had him there. This constant upheaval wasn't good for the girls, his mother, or the orderly household Parsons demanded. Why not try something different?

"Very well," he said. "I agree to your terms."

Mrs. Kimball brightened, until he added, "So long as you win over Her Grace."

CHAPTER TWO

Meredith Thorn watched from the entry hall as the Duke of Wey and Jane made their way up the graceful curving stairs at the center of the house. Her hand stroked the cat draped along her other arm.

"You like him, it seems," she murmured. "Despite his father."

Fortune rubbed her head against Meredith's wrist.

"Yes, well, you always were a better judge of character. Though I still don't understand why you chose me of all people. There must have been others more suitable on Bond Street the day you followed me back to that wretched little room I lived in while we waited for the will to be settled."

Fortune twisted to regard her with her warm eyes.

"Do not look at me like that. I've been given a number of reasons to doubt my own worth over the years, and coming back here hasn't helped."

Fortune lay her head down with a sigh.

"I'm sure I'm a sad trial to you," Meredith commiserated. "But then, that is what Lady Winhaven always claimed. Sometimes I feel wicked for being glad she's gone. She gave me a place to live when I had none, but it was never home. I want something better for Jane."

The butler was returning. She swirled and focused her attention on the porcelain figurine of a shepherd with his sheep, resting on the half-moon table against the tapestry-hung wall. The peaceful scene hadn't been there the last time she'd visited, but then neither had the butler. Perhaps things had changed at the castle in the last dozen years. Certainly no one had recognized her yet.

"Would you care to wait in the sitting room, madam?" the butler asked.

Such condescension. It was one thing to have spent half her life as a companion to an elderly lady. She had still been considered a poor relation, a duty, an obligation. She was painfully aware that she had gone into trade now, and, by doing so, forfeited any right to the courtesies due a lady. But then, those rights had been stripped from her ages ago.

"The entry hall is sufficient, thank you," she said. At least that way, she could escape out the door if anyone in the household remembered her and questioned her reasons for returning now.

His Grace, the Duke of Wey, strolled along beside Jane, face as pleasant as the butler's had been shocked when the duke had agreed to Miss Thorn's outrageous demands. Reporting only to the duke? Developing a curriculum? The closest she'd come had been helping her father lay out a course for study for Bible lessons at the little village church where he'd served as vicar. But then again, her time with the regiment had taught her that the key to survival was initiative and improvisation. She had never lacked for either.

Though she was no doubt expected to be silent and submissive in the duke's presence, she was far less skilled at either of those traits. Might as well do a bit of reconnaissance.

"Miss Thorn said your daughters are ten, eight, and five," Jane said.

He inclined his head. "I believe that is correct."

He believed? Didn't he know?

"And what are their favorite courses of study?" she asked

as he led them up to the landing. On the wide gallery, his ancestors stared balefully from their gilt-edged picture frames as if not a little dismayed to find her here. Well, she felt the same way.

The duke clasped his hands behind his back. One of the colonels Jimmy had served under had done that. Biding his time, Jimmy had said, until he could figure out an answer. Military strategy ought to take a little thought. But his daughter's preferences?

"Lady Larissa, the oldest," he said at last, "is following the typical course of study for a young lady making her debut."

At ten? That seemed a bit young, but Jane nodded to encourage him as he turned the corner onto another corridor, this one with walls paneled in yellow silk. Already she wasn't sure north from south. It seemed the house was as much a maze as the library.

"Lady Calantha has demonstrated some proficiency for oration, I have been told," he continued.

Did that mean she liked to talk? "Commendable," Jane managed.

"And Lady Abelona is just learning her letters, if memory serves."

Once more she bit her lip to keep from speaking her first thoughts aloud. Larissa, Calantha, and Abelona? Who'd saddled the girls with such appellations? Little Abelona would likely have to learn the entire alphabet just to spell her full name.

He paused before a paneled door, hand on the gilded latch. "I have been told my daughters require gentle handling since the death of their mother. I have observed a certain reticence on their parts. I would council patience, Mrs. Kimball."

Jane raised her brows, but he swung open the door and motioned for her to proceed him through it.

This could not be the schoolroom. Sky-blue walls

held alcoves with Chinese vases and crystal decanters. Curved-leg side tables displayed porcelain figurines and tiny chinoiseries boxes. The three little girls in their high-waisted muslin gowns—white of all things!—looked like waxen dolls seated on a sofa patterned with blue and yellow irises.

"Mother," the duke said to the silver-haired woman seated opposite them in regal splendor on a tall-backed chair of cerulean blue. "Girls. This is Mrs. Kimball, the new governess."

My, but he sounded confident, even though he had said she must win over his mother. Perhaps it was all show, that noble bearing, that distant smile. Inside, was he quaking as much as she was?

For a moment, no one spoke, and she dared glance around at them. His daughters must have taken after their mother, for all had varying shades of blond hair. The biggest, very likely Lady Larissa, had the darkest blond hair and eyes somewhere between brown and green. The ringlets on either side of her long face were already losing their spring. She inclined her head just as slightly as her grandmother did to acknowledge Jane's presence.

The next biggest, Calantha, had far paler hair, thin enough that any curl had faded. She blinked big blue eyes and fidgeted. A look from Her Grace brought her eyes forward and her spine ramrod straight. Jimmy would have been impressed, if she'd been a cavalry officer.

The littlest, with golden hair curling all on its own and eyes the jade of her father's, stared at Jane, full lower lip starting to tremble.

Her Grace's lips weren't trembling. They were set in an unforgiving line as she eyed Jane.

"I'll leave you to it," His Grace said with a bow to no one in particular as he backed toward the door.

Coward.

Jane put on her best smile. "Your Grace, ladies, did you

have some questions before I settle in?"

It was by far the bravest thing she could have said. But if the duke could brazen it out for a moment, so could she. Only Calantha looked impressed.

Her Grace curled her fingers to beckon. "Come here, where I can see you better."

Jane moved around the side of the chair, half expecting to spot rheuminess in the woman's gaze. But no, by the way the duchess's head came up, she saw all too well. She raised a gold-edged quizzing glass to her right eye, squinting at Jane through it. Her look moved from Jane's feet to her head, as if studying every inch of her.

"Shall I turn in a circle?" Jane asked. "Or would you like to count my teeth?"

The duchess dropped the eyepiece. "Impertinent girl! Is that how you address your betters?"

"It's how I address anyone who behaves rudely, Your Grace," Jane told her. "I assumed you'd want me to serve as a model for your granddaughters. No one should look them over as if they were an overripe cabbage."

"Certainly not," the duchess agreed. Then she frowned. "Where was I?"

"About to ask my qualifications for the post," Jane assured her. "I worked for Colonel Travers, the hero of the Siege of Ciudad Rodrigo, looking after his only daughter. I was raised a vicar's daughter with the usual studies in Scripture, history, Latin, and Greek. I speak French and Portuguese as well."

By the way Her Grace's face worked, she was trying not to look impressed. "And you are a widow."

"Yes, Your Grace. My husband was an officer in the Twelfth Dragoons. He was killed on duty thirteen months ago."

At last her look softened. "I am sorry for your loss. My husband has been gone nearly eight years now, and I still miss him terribly."

Jane's throat tightened. "My condolences as well, Your Grace."

The woman rallied. "These are my granddaughters," she said with a sweeping wave that took in the three statues on the sofa, legs not reaching the carpet. "Lady Larissa."

Larissa inclined her head again. "Mrs. Kimball." She had a pleasant voice at odds with her narrow look.

"She will need work in deportment and dance," her grandmother said as if the girl was deficient in those areas.

"Reading, arithmetic, science, and history as well," Jane said. "After all, she'll have to lead a great house one day."

Larissa frowned. So did her grandmother, but she nodded to the girl's sister. "And this is Lady Calantha."

The towhead continued to stare.

"Sometimes I fear she hasn't an original thought or much else in her head," the duchess confided. "You'll need to work on that."

By the color climbing in the girl's cheeks, she knew exactly what was happening and had her own opinion on the matter. Jane offered her a commiserating smile.

"Then there's Lady Abelona," Her Grace continued.

The little beauty raised her chin. "I want a unicorn."

Jane blinked.

Her Grace sighed. "I expect you to quell those fancies." She aimed her frown at her youngest grandchild. "Ladies don't ride unicorns, Abelona. There's no such thing."

The girl's lip was trembling again. "There is! I've seen them."

Larissa snorted, then covered her mouth with her hand as if she had merely coughed.

"That is quite enough," the duchess said, glancing at the three of them. "What will Mrs. Kimball think of you?"

Calantha finally spoke up. "The last governess said we were willful and spoiled. The one before that called us monsters."

Her Grace drew herself up, but Jane had heard enough.

She took a step forward, met their gazes in turn. "I don't hold with name calling. My father always said you know a person by their deeds. You decide what those deeds should be, not anyone else."

"By your fruit you shall be known," the duchess mused. "Well said, Mrs. Kimball. Larissa, show your new governess the schoolroom and her quarters."

Larissa slid dutifully from the sofa, but Jane's heart soared. It seemed she'd won her place in the duke's household. She could hardly wait to tell him.

She pulled in a breath and knew it wasn't relief that fueled it. Jimmy was the one she'd shared confidences with. She shouldn't expect things to be that way with the duke. She was a governess, nothing more. She needed to remember that.

Alaric strode down the corridor for the stairs, feeling as if a band of French cuirassiers rode screaming behind him, cutlasses drawn. He could stand before his peers in Parliament, make his case for or against a bill. He had seen to the release of men from debtors' prison. He had rescued tenants from the rising floodwaters of the Thames. He'd assisted friends serving under Lord Hastings to identify and stop aristocrats spying for France. He had helped nurse Evangeline through several illnesses. Why was it one moment with his daughters, and he wanted to bolt?

Miss Thorn met him as he came down the stairs. Her cat regarded Alaric from her arm. Those copper eyes seemed to see inside him. The twitch of her tail said she was disappointed in him. The look in Parsons' eyes as he excused himself said the same.

As if she had noticed, Miss Thorn offered him a smile. "If you need additional assistance with staff, I'd be delighted to help."

The footman standing by the door raised his chin

defiantly. Most of the staff he'd inherited from his father. He'd known them since he was a boy. Parsons was one of the more recent additions. Evangeline had hired him when Alaric had ascended to the title, claiming they needed someone more sophisticated and polished, as their butler. Only the nursery footman, Simmons, was truly new, having been introduced to the castle in the last year.

"Thank you," he told Miss Thorn, "but we're well staffed at present. Most of our people have served for years, even to multiple generations."

"That is a credit to your house." She gathered the cat closer. "I'll take my leave for the moment, then."

Alaric frowned. "Don't you wish to be certain Her Grace approves of Mrs. Kimball?"

She adjusted the cat against her chest. "Her Grace will approve. Like knows like."

The cat smiled as if to prove it. For some reason, he found it difficult to doubt either of them. It seemed he had a new governess, for now.

"I will, of course, return in a few days to ensure that everything is satisfactory," she said.

"A wise precaution," Alaric acknowledged. "Not every governess is suited to the role."

Her smile resembled the cat's. "It is not your satisfaction that concerns me, Your Grace, but Jane's. I expect a full report on my return. Good day."

She sailed for the door, cat peering around her elbow at him. The footman hurried to open the door and ran down the stairs to help her into the coach as well. She might have been the queen of England for the deference shown her.

Curious woman. What did his mother know about the redoubtable Miss Thorn that had made her reach out to a new agency? Or had the agency that had provided the previous governesses run out of suitable staff, and patience?

He retreated to the library and stayed there for the next while, waiting. The crowded space ever seemed cozy to him. The library had been a source of escape when he was a lad. Whenever his father was in London, he'd crawl into a corner and read—history, philosophy, even adventure novels, his father's only weakness. Now he used the room to oversee his holdings, a place to plan, to concentrate.

Not today. There would be an interruption any moment; he was sure of it.

But no stiff-backed duchess came sweeping down the stairs demanding a footman to throw the interloper out, and no dark-haired governess with speaking eyes went fleeing out the door in horror. Perhaps Miss Thorn was right, and Mrs. Kimball would last. Unfortunately, the previous three governesses had survived a week before giving up.

He rose and headed to the windows, which looked out onto the island. Beyond the buff-colored walls of the castle, fifty acres of Dryden land stretched out to the grey waters of the Thames. Across the bridge, several more hundred acres lay waiting for the spring planting. More than two hundred people depended on that land for income, sustenance. For most of his life, they had been threatened with spring floods, some years worse than others. Many of the worst years had been since he'd taken over the title from his father. If the new solution he'd fixed upon didn't work properly, he very much feared this year would see tragedy.

He knew what some of his tenants whispered. The House of Wey was cursed. Floods every spring, famines in the winter, fires ravaging the island last summer, his wife dying too young.

And no heir.

He glanced at the sky, but he couldn't doubt a merciful God. He had three bright, beautiful daughters. He was solvent; his tenants were getting by. He should not feel as if something was lacking.

Especially as he feared the lack was within himself.

Everything had seemed to run so much more smoothly when his father had been alive. When Father spoke, people jumped to do his bidding. His father's fierce intellect and commanding presence had assured as much. He had never understood Alaric's more quiet nature. And now Alaric had to fight against that nature every day so that his staff, his tenants, and England's finest only saw the next formidable Duke of Wey.

And none of them would have guessed the formidable Duke of Wey held his breath much of the afternoon. He could only be relieved when his mother joined him in the dining room, looking rather pleased with herself.

"Tolerable," she pronounced, and he knew she wasn't talking about the veal set on the long table. "This one has promise."

He wasn't sure whether that meant Mrs. Kimball would make a good governess or merely that his mother felt she could control the woman. He began to get a glimmer of an answer when Mrs. Kimball came to give him her first report that evening.

He had retired to the library to review the latest bill the prime minister had sent him. Parliament had started sessions earlier this month, but Alaric had remained home to make sure everything was ready for the spring rains. He was frowning over the almost accusatory language of the bill, which sought to remedy the cost of corn for the poor, when Parsons announced her, nose up and decidedly out of joint. The butler had served in London too long to ever be completely happy with his position in the country, no matter that he served a duke in a castle. He had expectations, requirements. Mrs. Kimball's access to the duke threatened the exalted position he strived to maintain.

If the new governess met Alaric's mother's and daughters' needs, Parsons would have to adjust.

Mrs. Kimball approached the desk and stopped a few feet from it, head high and gaze direct, as if she were a soldier reporting to her commanding officer. He refused to salute. She'd taken off the bonnet to reveal hair the color and thickness of melted chocolate, pressed close to her round face and wound in a bun behind her. She looked a little pale, but perhaps it was the lamplight barely reaching beyond the first set of shelves.

"Yes?" he encouraged her.

"I have had an opportunity to interact with your daughters this afternoon," she reported, gaze past him out to the night beyond the windows. "I expect their current curriculum to be acceptable except for four additions." She paused as if expecting an argument.

"Oh?" he asked.

"Yes." She took a step forward as if determined to make her case. He'd thought her eyes warm and sweet. Now they snapped fire.

"Exercise," she said. "It seems they never leave the house. A daily constitutional is required for good health."

He hadn't realized his daughters were under such constraints. Small wonder Calantha in particular always looked so wan in his presence. "I concur."

She drew a breath as if she'd fought her way through the first battle. "And I would like them to learn to ride, provided we can find a unicorn."

He shook his head, sure he'd heard her incorrectly. "A what?"

"A unicorn. Lady Abelona insists she will ride nothing less."

He leaned back in the chair. "Then perhaps Lady Abelona is too young to ride."

She frowned. "When did your father put you in the saddle?"

"When I was five, but that's hardly the same thing."

"I see no difference. Both ladies and gentlemen are expected to ride well."

That he could not argue. "Very well. Assuming you can

find her a unicorn, you have my permission to teach her to ride. I believe Larissa and Calantha have had rudimentary lessons in the past. Speak to my master of horse, Mr. Quayle, about suitable mounts. What else?"

"Art," she said. "They have no outlet for creativity. I thought we'd start with watercolors and move on to oils."

A bit ambitious, but he could see the value. "I approve."

She took another step closer, until her black skirts brushed the teak of the desk.

"Science and mathematics," she said, voice ringing with conviction. "Her Grace doesn't seem to see the value, but I assure you a lady who can tell the difference between nightshade and blueberries and can balance her household accounts is much more likely to find success in life."

What an innovative thinker. He had never heard the case made so clearly. A voice inside insisted that Evangeline would have disapproved. Surely the daughters of a duke had no need to determine whether a dark-colored berry was nightshade or blueberry. But he closed off the thought. His position required that he evaluate the recommendations of others. Mrs. Kimball had had sound reasons for each suggestion.

Aside from the unicorn, of course.

"Your plan seems wise," he said. "I will inform my mother that I approve."

She cracked a grin. "Better you than me."

Minx. He felt his own smile forming. "I'm glad you understand the workings of our household, Mrs. Kimball."

"I'm a cavalry officer's widow, Your Grace. I understand the value of scouting ahead, and currying favor with the general. I'll let you know tomorrow night how the search for the unicorn goes." With a nod to Parsons, she saw herself out.

For the first time in a long time, he found himself looking forward to tomorrow night.

CHAPTER THREE

The duke wasn't a bad sort. Jane smiled to herself as she walked back to her quarters near the schoolroom. Perhaps it was that cool green look, or the way he sat so still, like a catamount willing the deer closer. But she'd thought he might argue on the proper way to educate girls.

The duchess certainly had firm ideas, and not just on education.

"We cannot have boisterous behavior in the corridors," she had told Jane as she had led her and the girls to the schoolroom earlier that afternoon. "You will see that my granddaughters are cared for in their proper place."

The proper place had been up a narrow, dimly lit set of stairs at the end of the corridor. Jane had been a little afraid the girls had been confined to cells in the attics, but the top floor opened into a long, wide, room with sunny yellow walls and windows looking out over the courtyard and onto the island. Bookcases, miniature versions of the ones in His Grace's library, lined one wall, while the center of the room held a worktable surrounded by spindle-backed chairs. Crouched in one corner was a wooden rocking horse, color fading.

Smaller rooms opening along one wall held bedchambers for her and each of the girls. She didn't mind in the least that hers was smallest. The bed with its carved headboard and matching washstand was finer than what she'd made do with many times on campaign, and the walnut wardrobe along one wall would hold her meager belongings nicely.

"And these are your staff," the duchess had said with a regal wave at the three people who stood near the windows. She made no effort to introduce them, as if the two older women and younger man in the olive livery of the house were nothing more than additional pieces of furniture.

Jane broke away from the duchess to approach them. "Jane Kimball. And you are?"

The shorter of the two women, her light-brown hair neatly drawn back below a lace-edged cap, curtsied. "Betsy, ma'am. I've been nursery maid since Lady Larissa was born. Maud here came along when Lady Abelona arrived."

The larger of the two, in height and figure, Maud nodded her greying head. "And glad I was to join the household."

"That's Simmons," Betsy said with a look to the strapping footman. "He does for the nursery."

Simmons nodded, clean-shaven chin jutting out. He had hair the color of ripened wheat and eyes a steely grey. "Mrs. Kimball. I know the routine. You needn't worry about me."

Jane smiled. "Routines can change."

Larissa, who with her sisters had been avidly watching the exchange, shook her head.

The duchess drew herself up. "You will find, Mrs. Kimball, that we are traditionalists here at the castle. I have expectations, you know, for you and my granddaughters. See that you live up to them."

Jane knew what was expected of a gentlewoman— the ability to smile and nod while life tumbled around her, a good seat on a horse, accomplishments in piano, watercolor, and embroidery. Jimmy's stepmother would have argued that Jane had had all that, and it had availed her nothing. She'd been a disobedient daughter, an impossible daughter-in-law.

Now she knew what was truly needed in a lady—pluck and grit and determination. A willingness to see to the needs of others, no matter their ancestry or position. And the ability to protect herself. She would have loved to add drills with knife and pistol to the curriculum, but she fervently hoped the three little ladies in her care would never need those skills. After all, life at Wey Castle seemed rather predictable.

The scream as she started up the stairs now belied that thought.

It rent the air, terror lending it strength. Jane picked up her skirts and ran, barreling into the schoolroom and narrowing in on Calantha's bedchamber.

The little girl had squeezed herself between the double-doored wardrobe and pink, silk-draped wall. Hunched down and arms covering her head, she trembled violently. Jane squatted beside her, drew her close.

"What happened?"

Calantha shook her head, then buried it in Jane's shoulder while one hand pointed toward the massive box bed with pink and white chintz hangings that graced the center of the room.

"Did something frighten you?" Jane asked. "A nightmare?"

The little head on her shoulder shook a decided no.

Where were the others? The child had screamed loud enough to wake the dead. Larissa and Abelona should be crying out at the sound. One of the two nursery maids, Betsy or Maud, should have poked in a head. They shared a room just down the corridor, they had told Jane. And where was Simmons, the nursery footman? Shouldn't he be on duty?

With a shake of her head, Jane scooped Calantha up and rose, a bit unsteadily. The eight-year-old might look like a piece of eiderdown, but she weighed considerably more.

"Well, there's nothing to fear, now," Jane assured her. "I

won't let it harm you."

The girl gave a shaky sigh and cuddled closer.

A tall shadow appeared in the doorway. "Spider again?" Simmons asked. Earlier he'd been wearing the proper olive coat and breeches. Now his shirt was untucked, his feet in stockings, as if he'd thrown on his clothes or hadn't bothered to take them off.

Calantha shuddered at his voice.

"Ah," Jane said. "So that's it. Nasty things, spiders. I don't like them much myself."

Calantha pulled back to show a face puckered by fear. "Miss Carruthers said they'd bite me in my sleep if I didn't do my sums right."

Anger bubbled up inside her. "Miss Carruthers is mistaken. Spiders are more likely to go after governesses who treat little girls badly."

Calantha sighed again as she lowered her head. "Oh, good. That means you're safe too."

Jane nodded to the footman. "Check the bed, Simmons."

He straightened. "There's no spider. She's just scared." He nodded to Calantha. "Go back to bed, now, like a good girl."

Calantha sucked in a breath.

Jane held out the girl. "Very well, you hold her, and I'll check the bed. I probably know more about catching spiders anyway."

Calantha suffered herself to be transferred to Simmons's much stronger arms. "You do?" the little girl asked.

"Certainly I do," Jane said, shoving up her sleeves. "I've captured or killed spiders in Egypt, Flanders, and Portugal."

The footman scowled in obvious disbelief as Jane advanced on the flowing bed hangings. "Oy there! This is Lady Calantha's room, and you've no business skulking about." She grabbed the right bed hanging and shook the pink and white fabric. "Out! Out, I say." Not so much as dust drifted down. She turned to Calantha with a frown.

"No one there. Ah! I have it! The other one!"

She pirouetted in a circle and grabbed the other hanging, shaking it mercilessly. Simmons stared at her as if she'd gone mad, but Calantha giggled.

Now, that was better. Jane threw up her hands. "Not there either. How am I to catch a spider if it won't be found?" Calantha wiggled, and Simmons set her on her feet. "It's gone," she told Jane with conviction. "You scared it away." Jane cocked her head. "You sure? There are still two more hangings to check." She held out her hand. "Let's look together."

Calantha accepted her hand, little fingers cool in hers. Together, they shook and shouted, but nothing fell out of the material or scurried away from sight.

"What do you think?" Jane asked as Calantha crawled back onto the bed.

"I can sleep now," she promised, settling against the pillow and reminding Jane once more of a doll. "Thank you, Mrs. Kimball."

"It was my pleasure," Jane said. "Sleep tight. Don't let the bedbugs bite."

Calantha sat bolt upright. "There are bugs in the bed too?"

A quarter hour later, Jane followed Simmons out of the door and shut it behind her.

"Does this happen often?" she asked.

The fellow shrugged, muscles rippling. "Only once or twice a week. You'll get used to it."

Jane caught his arm as he turned to go. "No, I won't, and you mustn't either. What if it had been something serious?"

He laughed. "It's never something serious."

"It might be," Jane insisted. "If she screams, you move. I expect to see you there before the first shriek fades."

His face turned mulish. "Her Grace says we shouldn't encourage her. Let her cry it out alone. Why do you think none of the others came? She needs to learn to deal with her fears on her own. That's how my da raised me. No one came running when I was scared."

Jane put her hands on her hips. "The way to stop a child from being afraid isn't to make her *more* afraid. You leave the duchess to me. Those little girls are your future. Who do you think will hire butlers when they grow up?"

His eyes widened.

Jane reached up and patted his shoulder. "Good man. Now, get some sleep before the next scream sounds."

With a nod, he hurried off.

Jane made it to her quarters at last. Thank goodness Mr. Parsons had ordered her trunk brought up. She could only hope her saddle was safely in the stables below the castle. Right now, all she wanted to do was slip into bed and think. The duke had accepted her recommendations on the curriculum, but she still had to contend with the duchess and deal with Calantha's fears. She also had to find a unicorn.

A unicorn.

She smiled as she knelt beside the trunk, working the latch. She hadn't bothered to lock the thing when they had left London. No one at a great house was likely to paw through a governess's things. Now all she could picture was the duke's face when she'd mentioned Abelona's preferred mount. For a moment, he'd looked almost approachable. It was as if she'd found a friend.

Or perhaps not. Gooseflesh pimpled her arms as she saw her clothes tumbled together. Someone had searched her trunk. Looking for what? She had only one thing she truly valued.

Panic pushed up inside her. Out went nightgown, her spare chemise, the one dress that wasn't black. Where was it? *Please, Lord, don't let them have stolen it.*

The bit of gold braid lay shining on the bottom of the trunk. Jane snatched it up, hugged it close. Jimmy had been so proud the day the general had awarded it. She could still see his smile, the way the sunlight had caught the gold, as if reflecting the blond of his hair. Would he forgive her, when they met in heaven one day, for tearing it off his uniform before they buried him?

Something hot and wet dripped on her hands. Tears? Not now. Now she had a chance for a future, a home again. She might never find a love like she and Jimmy had shared, but she could still make a difference for someone.

The scoundrel who had dared to search her trunk would learn that it took more than that to scare Jane Kimball.

"A word, Your Grace?"

In the library, Alaric looked up the next morning from his pressed copy of the *Times* into his butler's implacable face. "Yes, Parsons?"

His butler allowed a sigh to escape. "It's about Mrs. Kimball, Your Grace. I'm not certain she should stay."

Alaric leaned back, foreboding dropping like a raincloud. "What's happened? Salt in her tea? Snake in her bed?"

Parsons went so far as to shudder. "Ladies Larissa, Calantha, and Abelona are far too refined to ever touch a creature like a snake. No, I fear she has countermanded Her Grace's instructions."

Interesting. He had only known one person who could get around his mother's edicts easily, and that had been his father. "Which instructions, precisely?" he asked, folding the paper and setting it aside.

Parsons drew himself up. "She comforted Lady Calantha over a spider."

"A spider." Alaric rubbed the bridge of his nose. "Forgive me, Parsons, but I seem to require another cup of tea this morning. Why is comforting a child over a spider a heinous crime?"

Parsons hurried to refill the china cup on the desk. "Lady Calantha is perhaps a bit unreasonable in her fears.

Her Grace advised us all to ignore her. Naturally, when Simmons heard her scream, he waited some time before responding. Mrs. Kimball had the effrontery to scold him for it."

Alaric set down his cup and rose. "Let me make sure I understand you. My daughter, the image of my dear, departed wife, screamed for help, and none of you responded?"

Parsons wilted. "Her Grace said…"

"Hang what my mother said." Alaric leaned closer. "If one of my daughters screams, I want every able-bodied man and woman who hears it to run to her aid. Run, do you hear me?"

"Yes, Your Grace. Of course, Your Grace." Parsons's hand was shaking, and he hurried to mop up the tea he'd dripped on the wood of the desk. "Then, Mrs. Kimball…"

"Was entirely right in scolding Simmons. You can tell him that if I had been there, he would have received more than a scold. Are the girls up yet?"

Parsons had recovered some of his usual dignity, for he straightened and looked down his nose. "They were up, dressed, and breakfasted before eight. She then took them for a walk."

By the sound of it, he considered that a heinous crime as well.

"Excellent," Alaric said, coming around the desk. "I feel the need to stroll as well. Send for me when Willard arrives."

He bowed. "Of course, Your Grace."

Alaric found Mrs. Kimball and the girls in his mother's garden behind the house. Sheltered on all sides by a stone wall, the space featured crossing paths among precisely sculptured shrubs. Now it was barren from winter's chill, but soon red and purple tulips would poke up their heads here and there, and the entire back wall would be braced by a bed of golden daffodils.

Mrs. Kimball had her navy cloak about her again, bonnet hiding the shine of her dark hair. Each of the girls wore a blue redingote, quilted and tucked. Funny—he had never noticed their outfits matching before. He knew a lack of funds wasn't to blame. Lack of imagination, perhaps?

Abelona sighted him first. "Father!" Breath puffing white in the cold air, she ran down the graveled path. Afraid she might trip, he scooped her up and held her close a moment. She smelled like warm, buttered toast.

"Your Grace," Mrs. Kimball greeted as he drew abreast of them. Calantha was staring at him, and Larissa was frowning. He set Abelona down.

"Your first constitutional, I see," he ventured.

Larissa sniffed. "Mrs. Kimball thinks it's good for us." She seemed to share Parsons's opinion of the matter.

"I quite agree," he told her. "I never realized you were shut up indoors so often. You should see the sunshine."

Calantha glanced up at the overcast sky. "Grandmother says sunshine ruins a lady's complexion."

Larissa nodded. "We'll get spots, like Mrs. Kimball."

Mrs. Kimball's fingers flew to her nose, but not before Alaric saw that Larissa was right. Delicate freckles arched over her nose, like cinnamon sprinkled on cream.

Another lady might have berated Larissa for her comment, but Mrs. Kimball laughed as she lowered her hand. "Just remember to wear your bonnet. That was my failing. Too eager to ride to fetch a hat."

He knew that feeling. There was nothing like being in the saddle, flying down the lane. A shame he had no time for such luxuries anymore.

"Mrs. Kimball says we're to go riding," Calantha informed him.

"As soon as we find a unicorn," Abelona reminded her.

"Ah, yes, the unicorn." He shared a smile with Mrs. Kimball, savoring the sparkle in her dark eyes. "How goes the search?"

"I found three," Abelona bragged.

"Three?" He couldn't help his frown.

"On the carriage, over the garden gate, and on the pavement in the center of the garden."

"Our crest," he realized. "Very good, Abelona."

She raised her chin and twisted from side to side as if thoroughly pleased with herself.

"But you can't ride those unicorns," Larissa protested. "They're just pictures."

"Which is why we must continue our quest," Mrs. Kimball said. "The knights of old considered it noble to seek a unicorn."

"A magical beast," he agreed. "Just the sort to prance among the daffodils. Perhaps Mr. Reynolds, our head gardener, noticed a suitable mount hereabouts. I see him through the bushes. Would you ask, Larissa?"

Larissa stood taller, as if pleased he'd singled her out. "Of course, Father." She started away, and Calantha trailed behind her.

"I better go too," Abelona said. "She might not ask the right questions." She toddled after her sisters.

Alaric took a step closer. He hadn't realized Mrs. Kimball was so short. She came just under his chin. A neat handful, his friend Julian Mayes would have said.

What was he thinking?

He focused on his purpose. "Thank you for seeing to Calantha's needs last night," he murmured. "I had no idea my mother had given the order to stand down, but I have made it clear my daughters' needs come first."

"Thank you." Her gaze remained on the girls as they approached the elderly gardener, who stopped his work to listen intently. "I wouldn't be harsh with the staff. They were only doing what was requested of them. As for Her Grace, I'm sure it takes a little practice to deal with a child in situations like that."

"I wouldn't know. I was never a child."

He'd meant it as a joke, but she shot him such as assessing look that he was forced to take a step back.

"I should go," she said. "We still have to find that unicorn. Until this evening, Your Grace."

He inclined his head, and she strode off to catch up with the girls.

Hands clasped behind his back, he returned to the house. Of course he'd been a child, raised in this very house until his mother had convinced his father he should spend a few years at Eton in the company of boys his own age. He remembered his time at the school fondly. Rowing competitions, fencing matches, races across the fields, the air damp against his cheeks. But over it all lay his duty. Never was he to forget he was the heir to lands that supported his family, his relatives, his staff, dozens of tenants, and their families. They were his responsibility. Every decision, every action, must reflect their best interests, not his.

Perhaps he truly had never been a child.

But that didn't mean his children were bound to the same fate. As daughters, unable by patent to take on the title, they could follow their hearts. He would make sure of it.

His steward, Michael Willard, had just arrived when he returned to the library. The sight of the big, fuzzy-headed man, tweed cap turning in his capable hands, brought Alaric's responsibilities crashing down upon his shoulders once more.

"Status?" he asked, taking his place at the desk.

Willard remained standing. "The lock has been installed on the western end of the canal, Your Grace, but the mechanism to open the gates is still sticking. We'll keep working on it."

"We must." Willard knew as well as he did what was at stake. His steward's house lay well below the rise of the castle. It would be one of the first to flood.

Alaric opened the center drawer of the desk and pulled

NEVER DOUBT A DUKE

out the plans, spreading them with his hands. "Show me the problem."

Shoving his cap into the pocket of his plaid trousers, Willard bent over the diagrams, thick finger pointing. "We think it's in this area here. The chain may not be long enough to wind around the capstan and completely open the gates to the river. We may get overtopping, which could bend down the gates and make them useless."

Alaric nodded. "Unwind the chain completely. See if the blacksmith in the village can add another link or two. I'll pay double for quick work."

Willard nodded as he straightened. "Yes, Your Grace. And I have lads stationed upstream. If the river starts to rise, we'll have a little notice to open the gates."

A little notice. It was more than they'd had before. But if they couldn't get the new lock system working in the next few weeks, he very much feared even a great deal of notice would not be enough.

CHAPTER FOUR

Jane felt rather pleased with herself as she approached the library door that evening. An entire day in the girls' company, and she was still standing. The duchess had made two surprise inspections but left each time with an elegant nod and a "carry on." They hadn't found a unicorn to ride among the horses kept close to the castle, but she still had hope. The one fly in the ointment was that she hadn't been able to identify who had searched her trunk and why.

It wasn't as if she didn't have suspects. Mr. Parsons glowered at her every time he saw her, as if expecting her to slide down the bannisters or howl at the crystal chandelier. Betsy and Maud cast her covert glances as they bustled about the schoolroom cleaning and tidying after the girls, as if wondering how much attention to pay her when she might not be in the position long. Simmons' lip had a decided curl. It seemed he remembered their talk last night with rancor. And one of her charges might have slipped in and looked through her things out of nothing more than curiosity.

Still, she could not be disheartened. She'd faced far worse along the way. Her mother and father might have thought Jimmy had hung the moon until he'd run off to join the cavalry, and Jimmy's father had considered Jane rousing good fun, but her husband's stepmother had made it clear how little she admired Jane. She had complained to Jane's

NEVER DOUBT A DUKE

parents about her lack of discipline. When she'd lost her earbob at the assembly, she'd intimated that Jane had taken it. She'd been certain the gate to the pasture had been left open by Jane in the middle of a ride, allowing their cows to escape. Simply put, in Mrs. Kimball's eyes, Jane was a disobedient, willful girl who would never be good enough for her Jimmy.

"And look at me now," Jane murmured to herself as she passed the Wey ancestors. She thought at least one looked impressed.

Mr. Parsons, however, gave her the evil eye as he let her into the library. She put on her best smile. Everyone knew that though you obeyed the colonel's orders, you'd better keep on speaking terms with his aide-de-camp, however snippy and full of himself he might be. She moved into the room, refusing to heed the beckoning call of the books, and came to a stop a respectful distance from the desk.

Which had become much more crowded since last evening. She raised her chin just the slightest, tried to make out the plans spread across the surface. Some sort of building, perhaps? Where was he intending to put it? The castle filled up every inch of the knob on which it was built, and the steep sides prohibited siting anything nearby.

Whatever his plans, he didn't seem too pleased with them. His muscular form was stiffer than usual, and that frown made him look rather forbidding. But he glanced up and nodded in recognition of her. "Mrs. Kimball. How did things go today?"

"Well, Your Grace," she reported, mindful of Mr. Parsons standing among the bookcases and glaring at her as if daring her to misbehave. "We are settling on a routine. Their ladyships are becoming accustomed to me."

"Excellent," he said. "And how did they take to the introduction of new subjects?"

Jane grimaced. "The constitutional met with consternation. I haven't broached the more difficult changes yet. One thing at a time."

He nodded again as if he thought that wise. "Did you have to do this sort of thing in your previous position?"

She tried not to flinch at the memory. "Not really, Your Grace. Colonel and Mrs. Travers had an established routine that made sense for their situation. I merely followed it." And she could only hope he'd leave it at that. "But I also worked with children at my father's church in Berkshire. We were always rearranging things to ensure everyone had a chance."

He leaned away from the desk. "Your father must be pleased to have you closer to home than the Peninsula."

"He passed on five years ago. My mother a year later." Her throat was tight again, and she swallowed.

"I'm sorry to hear that. I lost my father some years ago as well. His absence is still felt."

So, Her Grace wasn't the only one in mourning. "I like to think we keep a little of them with us."

His smile was tight. He glanced down at his plans again. Was he dismissing her? Why was that thought so depressing?

Jane took a step forward. "Have I offended you, Your Grace? Is that why you have so many questions for me tonight?"

He raised his brows as he straightened. "Not at all. I simply thought I should know more about the woman caring for my daughters."

"Probably should have asked before you hired me then," Jane said. "I could have made off with the silver and half the plate by now."

Mr. Parsons coughed, gaze on her in warning, but Jane couldn't regret her words. *Now* the duke thought to question her? Had he no more thought to his daughters? From what she'd gathered talking with the girls and the nursery staff, he hadn't ventured into the schoolroom very often.

"Parsons," the duke said, "inventory the plate. I

could stand to lose some of the silver, but Her Grace is inordinately fond of the Crown Derby. Word of warning, Mrs. Kimball."

Her frustration faded at the gleam in those green eyes. "What about the little fat porcelain pug dogs in the corridor?" Jane asked, fighting a grin. "I could get a quid or two for each."

A smile hovered around his mouth. "Well, you could safely take them. Never could stand the ugly things as a child. Parsons, kindly see that they are delivered to the schoolroom. I'm sure Mrs. Kimball could send them via the mail coach to London for sale. It stops at Walton-on-Thames."

Parsons glanced between the two of them as if he didn't understand what was happening. Jane had pity on the poor fellow.

"That's very kind of you, Your Grace, but I wouldn't want to deprive the rest of the household. Will there be anything else?"

He waved a hand, reminding her of his mother. "Not this evening, Mrs. Kimball. Good night."

Mr. Parsons showed her to the door, face settling into a scowl that was no doubt meant to put her in her place.

"I would cultivate a more professional demeanor, if I were you," he advised as she passed him for the stairs.

Jane glanced back at him. "I'd try, but I fear I haven't your experience or polished presence."

He thawed slightly. "Few do. Just mind your tone when addressing the duke and duchess. They aren't used to originality."

Neither was he, and she was beginning to think that was entirely the problem.

Lady Larissa certainly found it difficult. She continued to protest their constitutional the next morning.

"We have carriages if we need to leave the house," she complained as Jane led them down the stairs for the garden. "Besides, walking on gravel hurts my slippers." She stopped and raised a dainty foot for Jane's inspection.

"I see," Jane said, noting the scuffs on the kid leather. "Well, we can't have that. I'll ask your father for sturdy boots. You'll need them for riding in any event."

"I can ride a unicorn in slippers," Abelona insisted. "Unicorns don't mind."

Larissa merely rolled her eyes, but her laments resumed when they returned to the schoolroom.

"Why must we practice arithmetic? We have a steward to keep all the books."

"How will you know he's honest?" Jane countered, laying a slate before each of them at the worktable while the maids began cleaning the girls' rooms and Simmons went for more coal for the fire. "For that matter, how will you calculate the price of yardage for a new dress?"

Larissa wrinkled her nose. "I don't have to calculate yardage. I pick the dress, and Father pays for it."

Jane shook her head. "Someday you'll have pin money of your own. You'll want to know how far it can go. Lady Abelona, you can start by writing your numbers. Lady Calantha, show me the largest addition problem you can solve. Lady Larissa, perhaps you're ready for multiplication."

"Did your governess make you learn multiplication?" Larissa demanded as Calantha and Abelona bent to their tasks.

"I didn't have a governess," Jane told her, writing a problem on the slate for Larissa to solve. "My father was a vicar. I learned from him."

Abelona sighed, chalk squeaking on the number three. "I wish Father would teach us."

"He can't," Calantha said, rubbing out a problem and starting over. "He's very busy."

"That's the way with fathers sometimes," Jane said. "Mothers too. That's why you have me."

Larissa frowned down at the numbers on the slate. "How

much arithmetic did you know when you came out?"

"I never came out officially," Jane said, pointing at the slate. "I fell in love, married, and went off to adventures with my husband."

Calantha grinned.

Larissa looked appalled. "You never came out?"

"No," Jane told her. "Very good, Abelona. All the way to ten."

Abelona beamed.

Larissa pushed back her slate and rose. "I won't learn arithmetic from someone who never came out. I'm going to tell Grandmother."

Jane straightened. "Lady Larissa, sit down."

Calantha and Abelona exchanged glances. Betsy and Maud shut the door between the schoolroom and Abelona's bedchamber as if distancing themselves from the coming storm.

"No," Larissa said, backing for the door as if afraid to take her eyes off Jane. "I won't. You can't make me. You're a servant. You have to do what I say. I'm going to see Grandmother."

"No need," the duchess said, sweeping through the door. "I'm here."

Larissa ran to her. "Oh, Grandmother, you must stop her. She's forcing us to study things we don't need to know. Make her go away like you did the others!"

"But why must it go on my land?"

Alaric bit back a sigh. Every Tuesday morning, he made himself available to hear the concerns of his tenants. He knew other landowners delegated the task to their stewards or land agents, but the House of Wey had been treating the act as a sacred duty since before the Conquest. Still, he thought his ancestors might have had a more important litany of concerns to deal with—invaders from the north, perhaps, river pirates. His tenants had less to worry about. Sometimes it was cows straying from one side of the island to the other. Sometimes it was a suggestion of a needed improvement, a new well to be dug, hedges to be planted. At least once a month, Mr. Harden brought him a complaint. A middle-aged man with a craggy face and attitude to match, he always sidled in, hat in hand, and whined. Someone was fishing in his accustomed spot along the shore. Could His Grace forbid them? His roof looked thin—shouldn't it be replaced before the next rains? Why had his annual gift box been smaller than his neighbor's?

Today it had been the lock.

"A good quarter acre of my land," Harden insisted, yellowed teeth biting off the words. "Seems like I should be compensated."

"Preventing your fields from flooding isn't compensation enough?" Alaric asked.

Anyone else might have heard the danger in the tone. Harden merely worried his hands around the brim of his battered hat. "My fields always flood. Your father never minded. I was still fed."

Because Alaric's family saw to it. That had been the way of things. The spring floods were nearly as predictable as the river flowing along. The only question was who would be harmed and who passed over each year. His grandfather, his father had weathered each storm, rebuilt afterward, donated a plaque to the church in honor of those who had died.

He didn't want anyone to die. He'd been asking questions, reading engineering treatises for years, seeking a solution. Now Mr. Harden didn't want to be inconvenienced.

His father had dealt with such petty complaints with a gruff rejoinder, a stern command. Alaric had never quite mastered the art. At the moment, he was very tempted to tell Harden to find another duke to pester. But the last time a tenant had been evicted from the island, there had been months of unrest. He still remembered the fearful faces of the remaining tenants, the recriminations leveled against his father. A man, no matter his place in Society, should have confidence in his own home, his ability to contribute. He refused to evict anyone else without good cause.

"Pardon me, Your Grace."

He breathed a sigh of relief at the sight of his butler in the doorway. "Yes, Parsons?"

The fellow's back was straighter than usual. "It's Mrs. Kimball, Your Grace. She and the duchess are having words."

Another problem to solve. It was almost welcome. "Excuse me, Mr. Harden. I will think about how to resolve your complaint."

"All I ask is a fair accounting," his tenant said, though his worn look said he didn't expect one.

With a nod of dismissal, Alaric rose and followed Parsons up the stairs.

"What set it in motion?" he asked his butler as they headed down the corridor for the schoolroom stairs.

Parson's nose was particularly high, as if even the memory smelled distasteful. "A matter of curriculum, I believe, Your Grace. You should also know that Cook found the cellar plug open this morning when she went to select some cheese. We managed to close it before much damage was done to the other food stored there."

He almost made it sound as if that was somehow Mrs. Kimball's fault as well, but Alaric couldn't see how the governess could reach the old dungeon-turned-storeroom below the castle without being noticed or how she could have known that opening the heavy wooden plug would allow groundwater to seep in. She certainly didn't look like the sort to wish harm on her employer.

She was, however, the only person in the schoolroom as he and Parsons entered. She was standing by the worktable, wiping a slate with a cloth.

"Everything all right?" he asked.

As if Parsons expected a confrontation, he faded into the background.

Mrs. Kimball glanced up at Alaric. "Lessons have been cancelled by a fit of pique. I had the effrontery to introduce arithmetic. Her Grace is consoling them with tea and cakes."

She didn't seem angry, though she certainly had a right to be. In fact, she seemed a bit downcast. Her dark eyes were shadowed, and her usually upright frame slumped. He moved farther into the room.

"I approved of the introduction of that subject," he reminded her.

"You did. And I said I'd deal with Her Grace. I failed, at least for now." A smile crept into view. "Don't worry, Your Grace. This is no more than a skirmish. I refuse to surrender so soon in the engagement."

She could not know the armament arrayed against her. No one bested his mother. His father had chosen his bride well. His mother wore the dignity and grace of a duchess like a coronation robe and exerted her power as a scepter.

"Focus on the girls," he advised. "They are your calling."

She stacked the slate with two others. "If only I could convince Lady Larissa that there is more to life than her come out."

He pressed a hand to his chest in mock dismay. "No! How can you possibly say so?"

Her mouth twitched. "Perhaps because I've lived so much longer than she has."

"Yes, I can see that you are ancient."

She gave it up and grinned. "Takes one to know one, Your Grace."

No one talked to him the way she did. He liked it. But as he grinned back, she sobered.

"Truly, if she has the idea that the only thing of any importance in her life is her come out, what has she to look forward to beyond it? If that is the best she has to experience, I feel very sad for her future."

Put that way, so did he. "A come out is an important event, but I wouldn't want her to focus on it to the exclusion of all else."

"Too late," she said. "But we may be able to get through to her."

We? How surprising to meet someone who assumed he had a part in his daughter's lives. Evangeline had held them close, convinced him it was in their best interests. His mother had stepped smoothly into the void his wife had left. With his father held up as the very essence of a duke, he had attempted to fill the same role. He had never questioned his duty.

Perhaps I should.

Dangerous thought. The House of Wey was built on centuries of tradition. Every role, every action was codified in the hearts and minds of his family, his staff, his tenants. He had been proud to step into his father's shoes, for all he wondered about his ability to fill them. Perhaps that's why he hadn't argued against his arranged marriage to Evangeline. A duke's daughter herself, she'd known exactly how to fit into his world. At times, her rigid adherence to tradition had eclipsed his own.

But she was gone now. And nothing he'd tried so far has helped his daughters.

He offered Mrs. Kimball his arm. "What say we make the first attempt at persuasion now?"

She stared at him. "It was fairly clear I wasn't invited to tea."

"Neither was I," he said. "But they are my daughters, and they are your responsibility. It's time we made that clear."

She regarded him a moment more, then came to lay her hand on his arm. "Right beside you, Your Grace."

Why did he have the feeling that was right where she belonged?

CHAPTER FIVE

They found the girls, sitting once more like little dolls, with the duchess. Only Larissa seemed to be in her element, smiling beatifically and commenting on the weather. Calantha was frozen, as if fearing to make the least mistake in word or deed, and Abelona's fingers trembled on the cup that dwarfed her tiny hands.

"Wey," Her Grace greeted her son with a welcoming smile. "What an unexpected pleasure. We have no need of you at present, Mrs. Kimball. You may go."

Jane looked to the duke. He detached his arm from hers, and her heart sank. He was going to run away again, despite his brave words. She couldn't blame him. Anyone should fear a tyrant.

"I asked Mrs. Kimball to join us, Mother," he said. "I understand there's some confusion about the girls' course of study."

Her Grace sniffed. "There certainly is. I see no need to force them to do complicated calculations. They aren't studying to become accountants."

Larissa's smile was venomous. Calantha and Abelona shifted on their seats as if they wanted to escape.

"Perhaps I have a different definition of complicated, Your Grace," Jane said. "And a higher estimation of your granddaughters' abilities."

The duchess drew herself up, to deliver a scold, no

doubt, but the duke stepped between them. "Mrs. Kimball recommended a course of study, and I approved it. If you have an issue with the matter, address it to me."

My, but he was magnificent. His head was high, his carriage erect, and she half expected to see a flaming sword appear in his hand.

His mother regarded him with a frown. "Very well. I believe your daughters would be better served preparing for the most important day of their lives."

Larissa nodded emphatically. Calantha and Abelona fixed their gazes on their tea.

He cocked his head. "And what day would that be?"

"Why the day they come out, of course." Her Grace shook her head as if astonished he would have to ask. "You can have no idea of the pressure. The need to do every little thing with perfection, from appearing before the queen to executing the first dance at your ball. Everything depends on it."

Larissa drew in a breath, as if ready to take on the task now. Calantha had hunched in on herself as if fearing she would never measure up. Abelona had shut them out entirely, her gaze going to the window and the grey sky beyond. Jane wanted to reach out and gather them all close. Life was so much more!

"*Everything*," the duke drawled. "So, in all your…years, Mother, you have never done anything more important than your come out."

She smoothed her rose-colored skirts. "Nonsense. The come out was merely the beginning."

"Precisely. There are many more days of equal or greater importance."

"The day you wed," Jane suggested.

He shot her a glance and a nod. "The days your children are born."

All three of his daughters were watching him now.

"The day you learn you'll be alone," his mother

murmured.

Jane's heart cracked. She moved to the duchess' side and lay a hand on her arm. "We are only alone if we choose to be, Your Grace."

The duke joined her, setting his hand on his mother's shoulder. "You are not alone, Mother. But I'd rather Mrs. Kimball prepare the girls for all those days. I hope you can respect that."

She sniffed again, and this time the gesture held none of its usual disdain. "Certainly. When you explain it like that, it makes perfect sense."

Calantha nudged Abelona, smile popping into place.

Larissa's lower lip stuck out. "Then we have to learn arithmetic?"

"Arithmetic, science, history," the duke said. "Art and riding as well."

"I'm going to ride a unicorn," Abelona piped up.

Her Grace frowned, but the duke grinned at Jane. "So I heard."

Something fluttered in her stomach, as if Abelona's unicorn was prancing inside her. She had felt that way only once before.

The day she'd met Jimmy.

She stomped the feeling down. She was a widow. Jimmy had only been gone thirteen months. And His Grace was a duke. She was the governess of his children. Any feelings she had would only end badly.

"Very well," the duchess said. "The girls may return to their lessons. But I expect you to take an active role, Wey. No one sits a horse better than you do."

And a horseman too? One of the reasons she'd fallen in love with Jimmy, she was sure, was the way he rode neck for leather. She found it hard to imagine her controlled, purposeful duke pounding across the fields.

And when had she started thinking of him as *hers*?

He smiled at his mother, the familiar pleasant look that

made no promises. "I haven't had the opportunity to ride for pleasure in some time, Mother. There are matters that must be attended to. Speaking of which, I should return to my duty."

As one, the girls slumped.

Jane hurt for them. He'd cracked open the door, and they longed to push their way through but had no idea how. But she had a thought. As usual, it found its way out of her mouth.

"Perhaps you could spare us some time this afternoon," she suggested. "We've exhausted our search for the unicorn near the castle. I understand your farm down the island has other steeds available."

He quirked a brow. "Horses, yes, but unicorns…"

Jane jerked her head toward his daughters. "When it comes to unicorns, it's the quest that counts."

He looked to the girls. Could he see how they'd all perked up under his notice? The yearning on Larissa's face cut Jane to the quick.

Abelona climbed off the sofa and hurried to his side. "Please, Father? You could find me a unicorn. I know you could. You can do anything."

Calantha nodded.

He took a deep breath. "Not anything, Abelona. But if it matters so much to the three of you, I'd be delighted to join you on your search."

Abelona gave a little skip as she returned to her seat.

"Thank you, Father," Larissa said. Her nod was all polish, but Jane could see the glimmer of tears in her eyes.

"I'll meet you in the courtyard at two," he said. With a nod to the room in general, he turned and left.

Her Grace rose. "Go back to the schoolroom, girls. You should have time for a lesson or two before you change to go out. I'd like a word with Mrs. Kimball."

Jane's stomach tightened. Larissa gave her a sharp-edged smile, as if she knew Jane was about to receive an overdue lecture. Jane promised herself to be as pleasant as possible. The duke had won the battle for her. No sense losing the war over her pride.

"I do not approve of some of your behavior," Her Grace began, eyes narrowing. "Nor do I appreciate the impertinence that so often comes from your mouth."

"I am a sad trial," Jane acknowledged.

"That I am beginning to believe. The girls will require discipline. Do you have what it takes to be stern with them?"

Jane kept her face respectful. "Absolutely. Daily beatings and bread and water until they improve on their studies."

The duchess blinked. "No, no. You misunderstand me."

Jane frowned. "Did I? Well, perhaps a regimen of studies and exercise, opportunities to use their God-given talents and imagination, and a great dollop of love and kindness will suffice."

"Yes," the duchess said, looking a bit as if she'd come through a windstorm. "I suspect they might." She shook herself and raised her chin. "Let me be clear, Mrs. Kimball. I love my granddaughters, and I want the best for them, but I have high expectations of you."

"Wouldn't be the first time," Jane said.

The duchess's lips tightened, and she took a step closer. Jane had to force herself not to retreat. She'd thought she might have a moments' reprieve before the next battle, but it seemed Her Grace had rallied her troops.

She pointed a finger at Jane's chest. "You and I may never resolve our differences. But if you continue to advocate for my granddaughters, I will stand by you."

Jane stood straighter. "Thank you, Your Grace. May I go?"

The duchess narrowed her eyes. "One thing more."

Jane steeled herself. Would she spout more nonsense about deportment? Order Jane to dress more fashionably? Criticize her demeanor, her opinions?

The duchess's gaze was firm and implacable. "If you can make my son smile like that more often, I will support anything you do."

A quest for a unicorn. Alaric shook his head as he stepped out into the courtyard that afternoon. He had a dozen things that called for his attention—studying reports from his various agents on the state of his investments, inspecting the new chain for the lock, reviewing the local militia, sending suggestions of different wording for the bill the prime minister had provided—and here he was, preparing to spend the afternoon on a fool's errand.

All because a pair of speaking brown eyes had gazed in his direction.

Of course, he could not have ignored Abelona's plea, the looks from her sisters. Who would have guessed they sincerely wished for his company? Their eagerness was motivation enough to join them. But he knew the true reason for his choice had been the importunate look from Mrs. Kimball. Why did life seem sweeter when she smiled?

She was all business now. With the girls bundled in their matching blue coats, she helped them up into the waiting carriage—one of his smaller vehicles—then climbed in beside them. He joined them last. Mrs. Kimball sat facing forward, with Calantha on one side and Abelona on the other, leaving him to sit backwards with Larissa. It was a gentleman's duty to give the lady the better seat, but Larissa did not look amused by the arrangement.

"I should be sitting there," she declared, pointing at her governess's spot.

Mrs. Kimball shrugged. "Suit yourself." She rose, and Larissa slipped across the space, nose raised in triumph.

Mrs. Kimball settled next to him. "You don't mind, do you, Your Grace?"

He should probably point out that Larissa owed her older

governess respect. He should also be an example of putting service before preferences. But as the carriage started out and Mrs. Kimball bumped against him, he merely smiled. "Not in the slightest."

They rode out the gate onto the lane that led down from the castle to the island. The largest piece of property in the river for miles, the island was bisected by a single road north and south, crossed by a lane leading east and west. The farm that supplied the castle and held the other horses stood in the center. Fields lay fallow in all directions, dotted by copses of trees still dark with winter. Here and there a stone cottage jutted up. Most of his tenants were nestled inside, but the few who had ventured out in the cold raised hands in greeting as the coach passed. So much potential, so many lives, all in danger unless the lock worked.

He'd pinned his hopes on the structure after reading about how the Thames Navigation Commission had installed locks and weirs upstream and down from his lands. Those structures were used to keep river traffic moving expeditiously, but they'd had the added benefit of slowing the progress of the river in places. Working with an engineer his friend Julian had located, Alaric had developed a scheme to turn the side stream that ran below the castle into an overflow for the spring floods. It had been a bold notion, requiring his tenants to take time off during the busy summer months to dig out the channel, line it with stone to form a canal. While they harvested crops, he'd overseen the building of the lock gates, created from timbers massive enough to hold back the mighty Thames. They were so close to finishing. He was merely glad January had been more cold than wet. Who knew what February would bring?

"Just think, girls," Mrs. Kimball said beside him, "the next time you come this way, you could be riding."

Calantha nodded, but Larissa raised her chin. "We have had some lessons, you know. I'm sure I'll do quite well in the saddle."

"Very likely," he agreed with a smile.

"I'll ride well too, Father," Abelona predicted, "as soon as I have my unicorn."

"I know you will, Abelona," he assured her.

"Was their mother a good rider?" Mrs. Kimball asked.

Not in the slightest, but he didn't want to give Larissa a reason for refusing in future. "She wasn't fond of horses."

He turned his head to meet the governess's gaze. For a moment, it was as if she saw inside him, his loneliness, his loss. Then she looked away, and he almost spoke her name aloud.

Jane. Would she let him call her that? Impertinent to ask. Impossible to ask with three little girls watching.

"A shame." She turned her gaze to the window, as if seeing something more than the winter-frosted land. "There's nothing quite like being on horseback—the power beneath you, the freedom before you."

He knew the feeling. Even now, he could imagine giving his horse, Decatur, his head and flying over the fields until they reached the grey rolling waters of the Thames beyond. Instead, he sat in a coach as his daughters chatted, the sound surprisingly sweet.

They reached the farm easily and climbed out of the carriage in the stable yard. Two stable blocks stood at right angles, each block holding work, carriage, and riding horses. Another building housed carriages, from the big landau built for travel to the tiny gig Evangeline had used to tool around the island.

Alaric led the girls and Jane into the nearest block, where stalls ranged on either side of a center aisle. The air was thick with the scent of damp straw and rich earth. He did not spot his master of horse, Mr. Quayle, but one of the more seasoned grooms showed them around. He kept glancing at Alaric as if expecting a reprimand. Alaric had no cause. The place was well run, and the horses were fine

NEVER DOUBT A DUKE

beasts—he wouldn't have had them in his stables otherwise. Unfortunately, none seemed the right size or disposition for a little girl and her first horse.

"And not a unicorn among them," Jane said with a sad smile to Abelona.

His youngest daughter sighed.

"There's a nice brown one," Calantha offered. "It has pretty eyes."

"She certainly does," Alaric said, glancing at the sturdy farm horse. "But she might be a little large for your sister."

Jane was gazing down the aisle. The stalls on the left generally held work horses, mighty things that would be turned out to plow the fields come spring. The stalls on the right held riding horses, some not yet properly trained.

"Interesting," Jane murmured. "Excuse me a moment, girls."

Alaric frowned, but she was heading toward the end of the aisle, where a white horse stood in its stall, head bowed. A recent acquisition, if memory served, and one he hadn't been too sure of when Mr. Quayle had recommended it. The horse was big enough to work the farm, but she disliked being put into harness. Mr. Quayle was working with her.

"What's Mrs. Kimball doing?" Abelona wanted to know.

Alaric wasn't sure how to answer. At Jane's nod, a groom led the horse out by its halter, and Jane walked around it. By the way her lips moved, she was talking to herself.

Or to the horse.

Larissa tugged on his arm. "You see, Father? She does the silliest things. I don't want her for a governess."

Now Jane was stroking the horse's long mane, which had yet to be cut to the appropriate length for its duties. For a moment, he felt as if her fingers were sliding through his own hair, and he shifted on his feet to chase away the sensation.

Suddenly, she spit on her gloves and rubbed them in the

forelock. Calantha made a face. Larissa gagged. Jane took the lead and turned the horse to face them. At his side, Abelona caught her breath. "Look, Father! Look! Mrs. Kimball made a unicorn!"

So she had. The horse's forelock stuck out from its head like a horn as she led the beast toward his daughter.

"What do you think, Lady Abelona?" Jane asked. Abelona was hopping from foot to foot, and he thought she might attempt to scramble up the horse's legs. Instead, she threw her arms around Jane's skirts. "Oh, thank you, Mrs. Kimball. I love you!"

Jane's brows shot up. Something tugged at Alaric's chest. Calantha nodded. "Me too. I don't care if you do silly things and smell like dead flowers."

He had a feeling Larissa had made that second comment as well, for she was turning red.

"It's just an old horse," Larissa said. "It's not a unicorn."

Abelona released Jane to glare at her sister. "It is! You're just too old and mean to see it. Isn't that right, Father?"

All gazes swung to his, and only Jane looked the least contrite about putting him in this position. He had meted out justice as a magistrate in his corner of Surrey, negotiated difficult settlements with other landowners, offered terms on behalf of His Majesty to warring nations. Somehow, none of that seemed as important as what he did now.

"Pierce," he said to the groom, "saddle this beast. I want to see how a unicorn rides."

CHAPTER SIX

Jane stepped back with Abelona, Calantha, and Larissa as the groom hurried to saddle the horse. The flash of the dark eyes, the toss of that white mane, called to her. The horse was a bit tall for Abelona, to be sure, but the little girl would grow into her. Funny how the duke made the animal look fine-boned and delicate as he settled onto the saddle. He sat erect, proud, and the horse's head came up as if she knew the sort of man she carried. With a nod to Jane and the girls, he urged the horse out of the stable yard.

All the girls ran out onto the lane to watch him as he broke into a gallop.

"Unicorns can go fast," Abelona said, climbing the gate to the fields.

It wasn't just the unicorn. The Duke of Wey bent low over the saddle, as if he were whispering to the horse, and Abelona's unicorn stretched out, skimming across the fields. Jane wouldn't have been surprised to see wings unfold from her sides. She hadn't seen a man and horse so well attuned since…

She made herself smile as he cantered back into the stable yard.

"Unicorn is a fine mount," he said, swinging down from the saddle. "I'll have her and some of the other horses moved to the castle for your use. You may ride her, Abelona, when you have proved to Mr. Quayle that you can handle a horse this size."

"I'll do it, Father," she promised. "I'll be ever so good in the saddle. You'll see."

He lay a hand on Larissa's shoulder and another on Calantha's, the touch hesitant, as if he feared he'd break them. "All my girls will do their best to be good riders. They are Drydens."

Larissa ducked her head, blushing, and Calantha sucked in a breath and stood taller.

He released them and turned to Jane. "I should see about some work on the western tip of the island. Are you comfortable returning the girls to the castle?"

Their faces fell. But after the way his ride had affected her, Jane was more than happy to take the girls back alone. "We'll be fine. Thank you, Your Grace."

He nodded to the groom, who went to fetch a big-boned black horse. Very likely he was the duke's regular mount. The horse certainly seemed powerful enough to carry a knight into battle. As she and the girls moved toward the carriage, he mounted and rode out at a far more sedate pace.

But she could not forget the sight of him, silhouetted against the sky and flying.

She managed to escort the girls back to the house and the schoolroom, but it was clear Larissa was still smarting about her father's decision to support Jane's curriculum. Jane decided not to give her charges arithmetic but directed them instead to a history piece about the War of the Roses. Though Calantha and Abelona listened intently as Jane read, even tales of thrilling battles failed to amuse Larissa. Jane could almost see the thoughts percolating behind her hazel eyes.

Finally, she leaned forward and perched her chin on her hand. "We must be a terrible burden to you, Mrs. Kimball."

Calantha and Abelona straightened, frowning.

"Not at all," Jane assured them all. "I'm a governess. Caring for young ladies is my duty."

"But we've made it difficult," Larissa protested. "Grandmother can be so demanding."

"Miss Carruthers said she was a perfectionist," Calantha helpfully supplied. "I'm not allowed to say what Miss Waxworth called her."

"Her Grace wants what is best for her granddaughters," Jane said. "Quite understandable."

"But we're a trial as well," Larissa persisted. "Abelona will only ride a unicorn."

"I love Unicorn," Abelona said, gaze turning dreamily out the window.

"And Calantha is horribly afraid of spiders."

Calantha squeezed her shoulders so high her neck disappeared.

So much for a history lesson. Jane closed the book. "Here's the thing about spiders. They're squishy."

Larissa shuddered even as Calantha said, "Ew!"

"No, that's a good thing," Jane told them. "It makes them easy to kill. Scorpions, now, those are nasty. Luckily they aren't native to England." She rose and went to the bookshelf for a volume she'd spotted earlier. "Let's look up what is native to England, particularly the small woodland creatures."

Calantha and Abelona gathered close to her once more as she retook her seat and opened the book. Larissa pouted.

The duke's eldest didn't give up, though. She pointed out every little flaw in her sisters, from the way Abelona printed her letters crookedly to Calantha's tendency to slurp her cream of asparagus soup at dinner. As bedtime neared, the two younger girls shrank in on themselves more and more.

Jane beckoned them to the hearth as they waited for the nursery maids to turn down the covers and fetch them for bed.

"No one," she said, gazing at each in turn and especially long at Larissa, "is perfect. I don't expect you to be. I expect you to try your best and to keep trying. That's all."

Calantha and Abelona nodded. Larissa stared at the toes of her slippers.

"I know you've had several governesses. It's hard to get used to people when they leave so quickly. I don't plan on leaving any time soon. This is my position, my home now. You can expect me to keep trying my best too."

The maids came in then, and Jane wished the girls good night. Larissa gave her a narrow-eyed look as she left.

"I'm not sure your oldest likes me in the slightest," she told the duke when she saw him a short while later in the library. He had been standing beside a table and chairs nestled among the bookcases when Parsons had let her in. A fine marble chess set sat on the table, the knights riding high on their horses. His hands were clasped behind the back of his navy coat, fingers curled and thumb twitching as if beating time with his thoughts as he considered his next move, and she wondered who his opponent might be.

"I'm not sure Larissa likes anyone except her mother," he replied, gaze on the pieces. "Calantha and Abelona were nearly babies when my wife died. Larissa is old enough to remember. I suspect any woman would have trouble with her." He raised his head, pleasant smile firmly in place. "You seem to have won over her sisters."

"Amazing what a unicorn can do," she quipped.

"There wouldn't be a unicorn but for your quick thinking," he countered. "Though I shudder to think what Mr. Quayle will say if you have to spit on the horse's mane each time Abelona wants to ride."

"He'll accommodate," Jane predicted. "And eventually she'll love the horse so much it won't matter."

He waved her into the seat across the board and took the one nearest him. "Do you play chess, Mrs. Kimball?"

She nodded, gaze going to the pieces. "My father taught me. Looks like someone has you in a corner."

His smile warmed. "My friend Julian Mayes. Care to press his advantage?"

Jane rubbed her fingers together, noting location, the pieces still available. She grasped a bishop and slid it closer to the king.

He stroked his chin with two fingers as he studied the board. Such a strong chin—determined. And his lips…

Jane sat straighter. Better to think of something besides his lips. "You certainly put that unicorn through her paces today. Where did you learn to ride like that? I could see you leading a charge."

He moved his king to the right, out of the path of both bishop and the knight that had been threatening. "As a lad, I wanted nothing more than to join a cavalry unit. I trained for months in the vain hope I could persuade my father. In the end, he refused. I was the heir, you see, and there was no spare. Heaven forbid I die in battle."

"Fathers are like that," Jane commiserated, edging a pawn forward. "Mine wanted to keep me close as well. I suspect that's why Jimmy's father let him go. He had three older brothers at home."

She glanced up to see something spark in those green eyes. "Jimmy—your husband?"

Funny how it didn't hurt so much to talk about him. When had grief turned to acceptance? "Yes. He was something on a horse. He could do all manner of tricks—hang off one side, ride standing with the reins in his teeth while firing."

He quirked a brow. "That must have been something to see."

"Oh, it was. He might have ridden for Astley's, the equestrian show in London, if he hadn't decided to follow the drum. That was his dream as well. Took him two years to save enough for a commission."

He was watching her. "You must miss him."

She shrugged. "Not as much as I did." The truth of it struck her hard, and she dropped her gaze to the board. Why, she'd almost made it sound as if the duke had taken Jimmy's place!

"Forgive me, Your Grace," she murmured. "I'm here to report, not reminisce."

A noise behind her reminded her that Parsons was listening to every word. Jane raised her head, fixed her gaze on the bookcases beyond the duke's left shoulder. That's what Jimmy had said was the right way to report to a commanding officer—not too familiar, proper, respectful.

"We haven't found our rhythm yet as far as studies go," she admitted. "Calantha and Abelona seem interested in history and the natural sciences, but Larissa still doesn't see the need. Still, I live in hope. We'll try arithmetic again tomorrow and see how that fares."

He sat back, as if realizing the time for informality had passed. "Excellent. I look forward to hearing of your success."

Her success? She glanced directly at him. The polite smile had become warmer. It encouraged her to share confidences, dreams. But there lay the danger. She had no right to share anything with this man, except the progress his daughters made.

She rose and curtsied, and he stood and bowed as if she was a fine lady, an equal. The best she could do was escape the room before she said something to reveal herself further. Parsons saw her out and closed the door firmly behind her.

What was wrong with her? She shook her head as she started up the sweep of the main stairs. Twice in one day she'd let blatant sentimentality intervene. She should not be looking for encouragement of a personal nature from the duke. They had no personal relationship. Their professional relationship made it impossible to be truly friends. She had not come here seeking a husband. She'd had a husband, a wild, passionate, devil-may-care husband. She didn't want another. The duke didn't appear to be looking for a wife. And he certainly wouldn't go hunting for one in the schoolroom.

Besides, he clearly knew the importance of having an heir. Except in rare cases, dukedoms could not pass to a daughter. He'd have to marry eventually if he had any hope of begetting a son who would care for the girls' future. A woman who'd been married ten years without conceiving didn't sound like such a good choice.

Darkness settled over her as she climbed the narrower stairs to the schoolroom suite. She'd never understood why she and Jimmy had never managed children. They'd certainly given it a good try. Perhaps it was all the movement, the travel, the harsh climates, rough living conditions. Perhaps it would have been different if they'd stayed in England. It didn't matter now. He was gone, and so were her chances of holding his baby in her arms.

She'd told the duchess no widow had to be alone except by choice, but she certainly felt alone as she snuggled into bed that night.

That is, until the moaning started.

She hadn't even fallen asleep when the low, painful sound rolled through her room. Gooseflesh pimpled her arms. The castle was certainly old enough to have attracted a few ghosts over the centuries, and the late duchess might have something to say about how Jane was treating her daughters and admiring her husband. There was only one problem. She didn't believe in ghosts.

"Who's there?" she demanded, sitting up in bed.

The sound came again, slow and mournful, but rather high-pitched for any sort of manly ghost. She tried to pinpoint the source. The door?

"That's quite enough," she said. "Some people need their sleep so they can work for a living, you know."

"Goooo," the ethereal voice called. "You are not wanted heeeeree."

The wardrobe, then. Little minx must have sneaked in while Jane was with her father.

"You're not wanted here either," she informed her so-called phantom. "Now hush up and let me get some sleep." She plumped her pillow and lay back down.

The ghost was silent a moment, as if weighing her options. Then the wardrobe rattled. "Go, I say! You are in terrible danger."

Jane threw the pillow at the wardrobe. "Hush it, you! I'll tell St. Peter you escaped your bounds. Or worse, I'll tell the duke!"

Alaric tried not to sigh as Parsons approached him in the withdrawing room. He'd devised a strategy for beating Julian, thanks to the moves Jane had made. He'd listened to his mother lament the fact that she'd misplaced the cameo pin his father had given her and ordered Parsons to tell the staff to keep an eye out for it. He'd finished and franked his comments on the bill. He'd just stretched his feet to the fire for a few moments of quiet before retiring to bed.

"Yes?" he asked from the wingback chair.

"It's Mrs. Kimball, Your Grace."

Not again. Alaric straightened. "Mrs. Kimball and I have an understanding. I don't care what my mother says."

Parsons' face was tight. "Yes, of course, Your Grace. That's not the issue. She's causing a commotion."

Alaric frowned. "My mother? She's never made a commotion in her life."

"Certainly not, Your Grace. It's Mrs. Kimball. She's shouting."

"At whom?" he demanded.

"That's just it, Your Grace. She's in her room, alone, and shouting." He lowered his voice. "I fear she is unwell."

He rose and passed the butler for the door. "If a woman of Mrs. Kimball's character is shouting, man, there's clearly something wrong, and I wouldn't assume it was with her."

He could hear his butler puffing behind him as Alaric took the stairs two at a time. But very quickly other noises eclipsed the sound—thumps and wails and cries. He quickened his stride.

A crowd huddled around the door to the governess's bedchamber—the two nursery maids, the schoolroom footman, Calantha, and Abelona. The adults were mumbling among themselves, his daughters fairly hopping. He could understand why. The rattling coming from the room would have made the stoutest heart quail.

"It won't open," Jane was shouting. "You must have wedged something in the door. Push!"

"No! Go away!" Though muffled and drawn out, that was clearly Larissa's voice.

"Mrs. Kimball," he called through the door. "What's happened?"

There was a flurry of movement, then the door opened. Jane stood in the doorway, dark hair streaming about her shoulders, curves nestled in a flowing white nightgown. Her cheeks were flushed, her eyes bright. All he could do was stare.

"Your Grace," she said. "Just the fellow we need. Stand back, you lot." She held open the door, clearly inviting him in where no gentleman was ever allowed.

CHAPTER SEVEN

He hesitated. Jane could understand why. A gentleman did not enter the bedchamber of a lady not related to him by blood or marriage. A duke certainly didn't enter the chamber of his children's governess without good cause. She'd have completely agreed with the sentiment but for two things. They had an audience, and his daughter was trapped in the wardrobe.

She grabbed his hand and tugged him toward the tall walnut door. "If you please, Your Grace. Larissa is inside, and I can't get her out. I was about to demand Simmons's help when you arrived."

He pulled up short of the carved door. "You locked my daughter in a wardrobe?"

Gasps of shock echoed from their onlookers.

"Don't be ridiculous," Jane said. "That would be cruel, not to mention ineffective. Now, please. She's quite distraught. I've tried to pull the door open, but it won't budge."

He eyed the wardrobe so cautiously she might have thought it held an enraged lion rather than a frightened girl. "Larissa?" he called.

No answer.

"She's suffocated," Betsy predicted, and Maud let out a wail and covered her face with her hands. Calantha and Abelona clutched each other, eyes wide.

That galvanized him. "Larissa!" His tone could have ordered a regiment against the entire French army. "If you are in there, answer me."

"Yes, Father," said a wavering voice.

He frowned at Jane, then turned to the wardrobe again. "Can you push the door open?"

"I've tried. It's stuck."

His frown deepened, even as he backed away, cocking his head as if studying the wardrobe from all angles. "I know it must be dark inside, but can you tell me why it's stuck?"

Jane thought she heard a hiccough. "Mrs. Kimball's boot is in the way."

She made it sound as if Jane had put the thing there on purpose. Jane managed to keep her mouth as tightly shut as the door, even though Mr. Parsons showed up just then and added his glare to the situation.

"Can you move it?" His Grace asked.

The wardrobe trembled as she must have tried. "No," Larissa reported. "I wedged it in when she was trying to open the door."

The duke glanced her way again, as if completely perplexed by the turn of events. For once, she felt compelled to let the circumstances speak for themselves. As if he understood, he began peeling off his coat. Under the tailored wool lay a physique any footman might envy. Clearly His Grace had not spent all his time at his desk.

"Simmons," he called to the nursery footman, who shouldered his way past the maids to hasten into the room. "Position yourself there, at the side of the wardrobe. Don't let it fall over."

With a nod, Simmons braced himself against the wood frame.

The duke grabbed the handle. "Larissa, press yourself against the back of the wardrobe."

"Yes, Father." Something thumped as she must have obeyed.

"Ready?" he asked the footman.

"Yes, Your Grace," Simmons said, watching him. Muscles bunched under the lawn shirt as he lifted the door up and yanked it free. Jane's boot tumbled out onto the floor.

Larissa followed right behind. She threw herself into her father's arms. "Oh, Father, you saved me!"

"Huzzah!" Calantha cheered. Abelona echoed her, and Betsy applauded while Maud lowered her hands at last. Only Mr. Parsons looked less than pleased, and his gaze was on Jane. She swallowed the desire to stick out her tongue at him.

His Grace nodded to Simmons to stand down as he held his daughter out. "All safe, then?"

The tremor in her lower lip belied the brave nod.

"Good." He straightened. "Betsy, see Lady Calantha and Lady Abelona back to bed. I'm sure the rest of you have duties to attend to."

Amazing how quickly they moved when a duke spoke. In short order, it was only Jane, Larissa, and the duke, though likely Parsons was hovering not too far away. One arm around Larissa's shoulder, His Grace gazed down at his daughter. "Care to tell me why you were stuck in Mrs. Kimball's wardrobe?"

Jane waited for the answer. Would the girl make up a story? Lay the blame at Jane's feet?

Larissa searched her father's face, then dropped her gaze. "I was pretending to be a ghost."

"A ghost." He looked to Jane as if for confirmation. She nodded.

"Playing a prank," he surmised. "I'm not sure anyone appreciated it."

"Oh, I found it highly diverting," Jane assured him. "Until we couldn't get her out of the wardrobe."

Larissa cuddled closer to the duke. "I'm sorry, Father. I won't do it again."

"I imagine not. But I'm not the one you owe an apology."
She glanced up, first at him, then at Jane. She squared her
shoulders. "I won't apologize to her. She's nothing but an
old humbug."

Jane shook her head, but the duke straightened, dropping
his arm from around his daughter. "What's that supposed
to mean?"

Larissa put her hands on her hips, puckering the white of
her flannel nightgown. "She's not a proper governess. She
doesn't know anything about deportment. She's probably
never even been presented to the queen."

"Guilty," Jane said. "I never got myself locked in a
wardrobe either."

Larissa tossed her head. "I don't care. I'm a lady. You're
nothing."

"Larissa Mary Elizabeth Augustina," the duke said, tone
ringing once more. "You will apologize. Now."

Larissa shrank in on herself. "I won't. I want her to leave.
We don't need a governess. We need a mother."

A direct hit. The duke blanched. "Go to your room," he
said. "We'll talk about your punishment tomorrow."

She ran from the bedchamber.

Jane lay a hand on his shoulder, finding it tensed, hard.
"I'm sorry, Your Grace."

His smile was wry. "You have no need to apologize, Mrs.
Kimball. We disturbed your well-earned rest, invaded your
privacy, and called you names. You'd have every right to
tender your resignation."

Jane returned his smile. "Oh, I don't give up so easily.
Besides, where else would I have the opportunity to see a
unicorn?"

"There is that." His smile faded. "I'll speak to her in the
morning. I begin to see why the other governesses left."

"Cowards," Jane told him. "I've seen too much to be
frightened of a voice in the wardrobe."

"I'm glad, Mrs. Kimball." Suddenly he made a face,

making him much more human. "I wonder, would you mind if I used your first name?"

That fluttering feeling was building again. She ought to refuse, keep her distance. Her mouth opened before she could stop it. "Not at all, Your Grace."

"Thank you, Jane."

Why was it she felt as if he'd caressed her cheek? Her first name was only one syllable while her last name was two. He was probably just being efficient.

"And on behalf of my entire family, I apologize." He swept her a bow as if to prove it. "You have been like a summer breeze through this place, clearing out the cobwebs and chasing away the dark."

How beautiful. Once again, she clamped her mouth shut against the words building behind it.

"And perhaps we can dispense with the 'Your Grace' business," he suggested.

Jane fidgeted. This was dangerous ground. The maids and footman were just down the corridor. Parsons had to be waiting. But still she felt as if the world had come down to the duke and her.

"I don't know your first name," she pointed out. "And I imagine Mr. Parsons would have apoplexy if I used it. Perhaps Wey? And only in private."

"I will settle for Wey. I'll leave you to enjoy the rest of your evening. Thank you, Jane, for not giving up on us."

She saw him to the door, closed it behind him, and leaned her back against it. She had never been the type to give up. She was more likely to ride the extra mile, take the high hill. She had fought against Jimmy's stepmother to marry him, fought for her place at his side in the field. She had never let anything stop her from achieving her dream.

But when it came to her growing feelings for Wey, she knew an impossible dream when she saw one.

"Then Larissa demanded a mother," he concluded when the duchess requested an explanation for the disturbance of the previous night. She had joined him in the breakfast room on the south side of the ground floor for the first time in years. Never one to lounge in dishabille, she was wearing a lavender-striped walking dress well flounced and bedecked with lace, her hair elaborately curled.

She took a sip of the tea Parsons had poured for her. "Are you surprised? It is high time you started looking again."

He buried himself behind the newspaper. It was his duty to sire an heir, a son who would carry on the proud traditions of the House of Wey. But his first marriage had been a sham. Evangeline had had no interest in the estate, preferring the hectic pace of London Society, which he loathed. She'd feared his horses, found it distasteful that he would concern himself directly with his tenants rather than delegate the tasks to others. If Larissa had been born a son, very likely he and his wife would have gone their separate ways, nodded to each other from across the room at the few social events he felt compelled to attend. When Evangeline had died along with their son, he'd felt sorrow, guilt.

And a curious sense of freedom.

Could he put all that aside now for the good of the family?

He was ashamed how badly he wanted to deny it. He had never shirked his duty in any other area of his life.

The matter was still on his mind as he made his way to the schoolroom after breakfast. The maids were just clearing away the last of the dishes there as well, and he took a moment in the doorway to appreciate the sight of his three daughters, happily engaged in listening to Jane read. Abelona had climbed into her lap, her golden curls brushing the shoulder of Jane's dark gown. Calantha crowded in on one side, as if memorizing the pictures on the page. Even Larissa was leaning forward, eyes bright and curious. And Jane, Jane's look was equally bright, as if the old story about the first queen of Britain was the most inspiring she'd read.

Too bad he couldn't find a wife like Jane.

He shut off the thought. If Larissa could not accept Jane as a governess, she would never become accustomed to her as a mother. And, much as he disliked the fact, his daughter was right. Jane had never lived in his world. She couldn't know the duties imposed upon a duchess. She'd face criticism, disdain. He wouldn't dim that bright spirit for the world.

Pasting on a smile, he moved into the room.

Simmons sighted him first, stiffening against the wall as if expecting to be found wanting. Abelona spotted him next. She scrambled to her feet and ran to meet him, white skirts fluttering. "Father!"

Calantha and Larissa rose as well. Of the two, only Calantha looked pleased to see him. Jane's smile said she felt for him.

He led Abelona back to the group. "Good morning, girls, Jane."

Larissa's eyes widened. Apparently, a previous governess or his mother had covered the proper use of a lady's first name. He continued undaunted. "We had some trouble last night. It will not be repeated."

Larissa hung her head. Abelona nodded.

"Betsy says you won't beat Larissa," Calantha reported. "Even though she deserves it."

He'd have to have a word with Parsons about the staff speaking in front of his daughter.

"There will be no beatings in this house," he agreed. "Nor can I condone disrespect for those in authority. Betsy, Maud, Simmons, and Mrs. Kimball are here to care for you. You owe them your obedience."

"What if they tell us to do something horrid?" Calantha asked. "Miss Carruthers once ordered me to eat paste."

"Because you put it in Abelona's hair," Larissa reminded her.

Calantha shrugged. "I thought it would smooth out her curls."

"Girls." Jane's voice hinted of laughter. "I promise never to order you to eat paste or anything else so unworthy."

"What about Brussels sprouts?" Abelona asked, narrowing her eyes.

"Brussels sprouts are entirely wholesome," Jane insisted, "despite their disgusting sliminess."

All three girls shuddered.

"Be that as it may," Alaric said, unsure how the conversation had gotten away from him, "I expect you to treat those who care for you with respect. If anyone gives you an order you feel you cannot obey, bring the matter to me for a decision. Is that clear?"

They nodded solemnly.

"Larissa, I believe you have something to say to Jane."

Larissa looked to Jane, then to him. He crossed his arms over his chest. She swallowed and returned her gaze to Jane. "Please forgive me for trying to frighten you, Mrs. Kimball. I won't do it again."

Jane inclined her head. "I forgive you, Lady Larissa. But I'm not sure the wardrobe feels the same. It's a mess."

Clever woman. Alaric nodded. "Then I'm sure Larissa would be happy to set it to rights."

The way her brows gathered reminded him of her mother in a fit of pique. "That's a servant's job."

"Not today." He helped her rise and pointed her at the door to the governess's quarters. "If you hurry, you'll still have time for an arithmetic problem or two before your constitutional."

With a martyred sigh, Larissa headed for Jane's room.

Simmons followed as if determined to help.

Jane rose. "I should supervise. I have an image of paste sticking my clothes together."

Calantha giggled.

He caught Jane's arm as she passed. "Don't give them ideas."

That grin was saucy. "Or paste, it seems."

"Meet her halfway," he murmured. "Let her practice curtseying for the queen or some other ladylike pastime today."

"Ladylike." The smile had gained an edge. "Conversations about the weather, perhaps."

"Nothing so banal. Embroidery or singing."

Now there was a decided gleam in her eyes. "As you wish, Wey. I'll add singing to the curriculum. You may want to find something to do outside." And with that threat, she strode after his eldest.

CHAPTER EIGHT

Once again, Jane had won the battle, but not the war. Ladylike pursuits indeed, as if sewing a fine hand or trilling an enthralling melody was more important than foundational studies that would help the girls understand the world. But if Wey wanted her to teach them to sing, she would, and heaven help the rest of the household.

Unfortunately, she had no time to begin just then. She started Larissa on the wardrobe, then asked Calantha to help Abelona with her letters. She returned to her bedchamber to find Larissa hanging her cloak on a hook, nose wrinkled.

"A little respect, if you please," Jane told her. "That cloak's been to five countries, besides England."

Simmons, standing on duty against the wall, coughed as if questioning the claim. She was just glad he hadn't pitched in to help Larissa. But then again, he wasn't the most helpful sort, for a footman.

Larissa shook her head. "You wore this old thing so far? It's very plain."

"Needs a bit of gold braid," Simmons said, lip curling in a sneer.

Jane stilled. That could have been an offhand remark, or she might have just discovered who'd been in her trunk. But why would a footman need to paw through her things? Unless, of course, he'd managed to drop the trunk on the way up and had had to throw everything back inside. That certainly sounded like Simmons.

"Braid would be nice," Larissa said, hands stroking the wrinkles from the cloak. "You could sew it along the hem. Did you learn to sew, Mrs. Kimball?"

Still testing her, it seemed. A governess who hadn't come out might have more deficiencies.

"Certainly," Jane said. "I can mend a hem or stitch up a wound quick as you like. But I wouldn't attempt fine embroidery."

Larissa raised her chin. "A lady knows how to embroider."

"Never claimed to be a lady," Jane reminded her. "And mind those boots," she added as Larissa tossed one into the wardrobe. "I'll need them to ride."

"Looks like they've been cross five countries too," Simmons said.

That was enough from him. "Looks like the nursery fire is burning low," Jane countered. "If only we had a footman to carry coal."

With a scowl, Simmons left.

Larissa straightened from arranging the boots, something flashing in her hand. "This is very nice. It looks like a broach Grandmother wears. You should put it on the cloak."

Jane frowned at the cameo in her palm—carnelian on pearl, by the look of it, in a gold filigree setting. Even Jimmy's stepmother had never owned anything so fine.

"That's not mine," she told the girl. "Where did you find it?"

Larissa gestured with her free hand. "It fell out of your boot just now."

Jane's heart sank. There only one explanation for finding something so expensive among her belongings. Someone was attempting to get her discharged. A governess who shouted down ghosts and created unicorns might be tolerated, but a governess who nicked from her employer would be tossed out with the day's trash. But was it Larissa or Simmons who had gone so far?

"Funny thing, that," Jane said. "Perhaps we should see if Her Grace is missing it."

Larissa's eyes widened. "Someone stole it?"

"Can't think of another way it would find itself in my boot," Jane agreed.

Larissa raised her chin. "Stealing is wrong. The thief should be punished."

She wasn't a good enough actress to be putting on such a show. Apparently, Larissa wasn't the culprit. But that didn't mean she wasn't above pinning the blame on Jane.

"Who do you think stole it?" Jane asked.

Larissa frowned as if considering the matter. "No one in the schoolroom. Simmons, Betsy, and Maud are with us all the time, and so are you."

Jane blew out a breath. "Yes, I am, Lady Larissa. I'm glad you realize that. Why don't you hang on to the broach for now? We'll send word we'd like a moment of Her Grace's time and present it to her when she comes."

Larissa nodded, carrying the broach carefully to the worktable where her sisters bent their heads to exclaim over it. Jane stayed behind just long enough to rifle through the pockets of her cloak and peer inside her now-empty trunk. But she found no other bits of jewelry or anything else to incriminate her. She could only hope others would realize, like Larissa, that Jane couldn't have taken that broach.

Her charge was wrong about one thing, though. While Jane was expected to be constantly on duty with the girls, except for her upcoming Sunday afternoon off, Betsy, Maud, and Simmons all left the schoolroom in the course of their duties—fetching clean linens from the laundry, carrying up food, carting more coal for the fire. And while a nursery maid might be remarked upon if discovered in the duchess's chambers, a busy footman might not.

So why was Simmons as determined as Larissa to see her gone?

Alaric had been perusing the budget proposal from the Society for the Discharge of Persons Confined for Small Debts when he spotted Parsons in the library doorway. He was tempted to send his butler away unheard for a time. The charity was one dear to his heart, ever since he'd seen the misery generated when the father of his good friend, Sir Harry Orwell, had been confined to debtors' prison when they were lads.

At Harry's plea, Alaric had accompanied his friend on a visit to the dark, crowded prison. He'd never seen such a place of torment, all hope obliterated from every countenance. While Orwell senior had run up a sizable debt through riotous living, many of the men huddled in the cells near him were being kept from their families for paltry fees incurred through no fault of their own—former soldiers who couldn't pay the tax on land they could no longer work, tenant farmers whose crops had failed and had no way to pay the tithe to their landowners. If he could help return them to their families and productive work, their wives and children would be better for it.

But the look on Parsons' face told him his butler thought more pressing matters were at hand than the suffering of men in prison. He lay down the budget proposal. "Yes?"

Parsons ventured into the room. "We appear to be in the midst of a delicate situation, Your Grace. I have been alerted as to the location of Her Grace's missing cameo."

"Then return it to her," Alaric ordered.

Parsons crept close enough that Alaric could see a decided gleam in his eyes. "That's the thing, Your Grace. I have been informed that the broach is located inside Mrs. Kimball's boot."

Alaric frowned. "Her boot."

"Yes, Your Grace. I would not wish to suggest anything untoward, of course."

"Of course," Alaric drawled.

"But the matter is troubling. Much as she has endeared herself to Lady Calantha and Lady Abelona, perhaps it would be wisest to send her back with that employment agency person and her feline, before she causes more harm."

He saw no wisdom in the idea. Did Parsons really want to start interviewing governesses again, going through one after another while his daughters huddled neglected in the schoolroom? Besides, Jane had earned her place beside them through spiders, unicorns, and ghosts, and he rather thought she was quickly earning a place in all his daughters' hearts.

He rose. "I will deal with this, Parsons. Has the broach been retrieved from the boot yet?"

"No, Your Grace. It was left in place in case it provided evidence."

As if he would ever bring Jane up on charges. He could only fear his eldest daughter had found yet another way to rid herself of a governess she should be proud to call her own.

"Say nothing further about the matter and return to your duties," he ordered Parsons. "I'll resolve this with my mother."

Who smiled at him as he walked into the schoolroom moments later.

"Wey, how delightful. Were you invited for hot chocolate too?"

Cups held rather precariously in their little hands, his daughters all beamed at him as they sat around the worktable, Betsy and Maud busy setting out a platter of biscuits and pouring the dark liquid as Simmons hovered ready to lend a hand. His mother's flounced rose-colored skirts looked out of place among the sturdy furnishings. But Jane looked the most uncomfortable, shifting on the hard wood chair and avoiding his gaze.

She could not be a thief. He could not be so mistaken in her.

He made himself stroll calmly into the room. "Good morning, Mother. I need no excuse to visit my daughters." Calantha nodded. "Mrs. Waxworth said Father saved his excuses to avoid us."

His steps faltered.

"Nonsense," his mother said, cup poised in her hand. "Your father is a very busy man. He rarely has time for social obligations, much less chocolate in the schoolroom." Had she heard the sobriquet the *ton* had given him? The Hermit Duke, they called him, as if attending their glittering events was more important than ensuring the safety and livelihood of his tenants.

"And I will not interrupt you now," Alaric said, edging toward the door to Jane's bedchamber. "I merely came to see personally how Larissa faired on the task she was set earlier."

Larissa paled as his mother's gaze swept her way. "And what task was that? Solving some complicated problem? Embroidering a handkerchief for her trousseau?"

Once more he nearly stumbled. Trousseau? Surely it was premature for Larissa to be so obsessed about preparing for her come out, much less her marriage.

"More on the line of understanding fashion," Jane said with a smile to his daughter.

Larissa drew in a breath. "Yes. Fashion. Thank you, Mrs. Kimball."

That must have taken something to praise her governess. "Yes," Alaric agreed, sidling closer to the room. "Thank you, Mrs. Kimball. I'll just take a look." He whisked open the door and darted inside.

"Wey?" His mother's voice drifted after him as he threw open the wardrobe. "Whatever are you doing in Mrs. Kimball's room?"

He slipped his hand down inside the boots, first one, then

the other, but no broach met his fingers. Straightening, he let out a breath. "Apparently nothing."

Simmons poked his head through the doorway. "May I be of assistance, Your Grace?"

"No, thank you," Alaric said, striding past him. For a moment, he thought Simmons looked disappointed. Was the fellow so determined to serve? Perhaps he found his work in the schoolroom less than challenging.

Everyone else seemed more confused than concerned, for they were all staring at him. "Nicely done, Larissa," he said. "I trust everything is well with you, Mother?"

"Yes, fine," his mother answered with a frown. "And you?"

"Excellent." He moved to join them at the worktable and helped himself to one of the biscuits, waving off Betsy's offer of a cup. "Did you ever locate that broach you were missing?"

Jane and Larissa exchanged glances. What did they know? His mother, however, brightened.

"Yes, as a matter of fact," she said. "Larissa found it for me. It must have slipped off the last time I wore it to the schoolroom."

"Very good news." He smiled at them all as he munched the biscuit. Calantha and Abelona returned his smile, Larissa still looked pasty, and Jane's eyes were narrowed as if she saw right through him.

"Admit it," she said that night when she came to make her report. "You thought I'd stolen that broach."

Parsons, standing by the closest bookshelves, choked on something and hastily turned his gaze to the books.

"Why would I think such a thing?" Alaric asked, spreading his hands.

Jane glanced at the butler. "Oh, I don't know. Perhaps a little bird told you."

The color of Parsons' face seemed to be deepening.

Jane returned her gaze to Alaric's. "I'm no thief, Your

Grace. Even Lady Larissa realizes that."

Alaric eyed her. Her back was straight, her head high, quite the picture of affronted womanhood, with good cause. "Is it possible my daughter borrowed her grandmother's broach to have you blamed?"

The intake of Parsons' breath was audible.

Jane shook her head. "No, not Larissa or her sisters. I have my suspicions, but I won't trouble you. I can deal with the matter myself."

She was apparently the only one of his staff so capable. "A thief in the household must concern me," he countered.

She frowned. "Has anything else gone missing?"

"Not that I have been made aware of." He looked to his butler. "Parsons?"

The man drew himself up. "I can say with certainty, Your Grace, that nothing was misplaced before Mrs. Kimball arrived."

Red flamed in her cheeks, but her voice remained sweet. "And has anything except that broach been misplaced since I arrived, Mr. Parsons?"

"No," he admitted, looking a bit annoyed about the matter. "At least, not to my knowledge."

"And you keep a close eye on the household, I know," Jane said with surprising respect. "So, it was only the broach that I had no opportunity to take or knowledge of its existence, and it just happened to find its way into my boot."

"Ha!" Alaric crowed. "It *was* in your boot!"

Parsons cast him a triumphant glance.

Jane nodded, color still high. "Yes. Larissa found it when she was setting the wardrobe to rights. But I didn't put it there."

He wanted to believe her. Her logic was impeccable. As a new staff member and the governess, she could hardly traipse about the castle unnoticed. Of course, there was always the dead of night, when most would be sleeping, but her nights had been taken up with spiders and ghosts. And where could she hope to sell such a bauble? Even if someone in Weyton, the village across the bridge, could afford a fair price, they'd immediately suspect its provenance.

Besides, she was so very open in all other ways. Why lie now?

"Still after the plate and silver?" he joked.

She grinned. "Absolutely. Though I'm thinking the crystal might fetch a good price too."

He shook his head at her audacity. "Parsons, lock up the crystal as well."

Jane held up a hand. "That was a jest, Mr. Parsons. I have no intention of taking anything from this house."

Even his heart?

He shoved down the thought. The arrival of Jane Kimball was turning out to be the best thing to happen to Wey Castle for a long time. He refused to think beyond that. And he would make sure Miss Thorn knew how much he appreciated Jane when she came to check on her client's satisfaction, for he didn't like thinking about the result should Jane decide that they weren't worth the bother.

CHAPTER NINE

M iss Thorn and Fortune returned the next day. Calantha spotted them from the schoolroom window. In her lavender redingote and creamy wool skirts, hat at a jaunty angle, Miss Thorn still looked more like the lady of the manor than Jane thought she ever would. Mr. Parsons didn't even appear to muster an argument before ushering her into the house, and Simmons shortly brought word that Jane and the girls were wanted in the library.

Jane had kept an eye on the footman after the incident with the broach. Though she suspected him of attempting to see her sacked, she refused to accuse him without more evidence. She knew how it felt to be discharged on someone else's story. She would not treat another that way.

But though Simmons occasionally muttered under his breath about how she was dealing with the girls, he was careful to stay within the bounds of behavior expected between a footman and the governess. Still, she didn't much like his smile as he escorted her and the girls downstairs now. It was almost as if he expected to rid himself of the lot of them.

Wey rose from behind the desk as they entered. In a tailored navy coat and blue-and-green-striped waistcoat, cravat spotless, he looked every inch the gentleman to Miss Thorn's lady. His smile was warm and genuine as they approached.

"Jane, girls," he said. "We have a visitor who wishes to speak to you. Miss Thorn, these are my daughters, Larissa, Calantha, and Abelona, and of course you know Jane."

Miss Thorn, seated on one of the leather-bound chairs before the desk, nodded to the girls and smiled to Jane. Larissa inclined her head with a regal elegance her grandmother would have praised. Calantha's gaze seemed fixed on Fortune as the cat slipped from Miss Thorn's lap to return her stare.

"Oh, a kitty!" Abelona rushed forward.

Fortune darted under the chair. Jane had always known she was a clever thing. She caught Wey attempting not to grin outright and pretended not to notice.

"A cat, to be precise," Miss Thorn said, rising and bending to peer under the chair. "Do come out, Fortune. I'm told the young ladies know their manners."

Larissa glared at her youngest sister. Abelona sank back against Jane's skirts. "I'm sorry. I didn't mean to scare her."

"Creatures don't take well to sudden movements, Abelona," the duke murmured. "You might remember that with your unicorn."

If Miss Thorn wondered about the reference to the mythical beast, she did not comment. Instead, she shot Abelona a look. "Fortune doesn't frighten easily. I'm certain she was only startled. Ah, here she comes now."

Fortune strolled out from under the chair, then paused to delicately lick the white of her front paw. Glancing up, the cat blinked great copper eyes as if surprised to find them all watching. Then she wandered up to Larissa and rubbed herself against the white of her muslin skirts. Larissa was so still, Jane thought she might be holding her breath.

"She likes you," Miss Thorn said with approval. "You may pet her if you like."

Larissa reached down and stroked her hand along the grey fur. Fortune arched her back against the touch. Larissa smiled.

Calantha was trembling in her need to move. "May I pet her too?"

As if in answer, Fortune moved to twine herself around the girl's ankles.

Calantha giggled. "She tickles."

"Me too, me too," Abelona begged.

Fortune eyed her a moment, and Jane feared the little girl was about to be snubbed. But the cat suffered herself to come closer. Abelona gently patted her head.

"I believe," Wey said, voice hinting of amusement, "you had questions for my daughters, Miss Thorn."

She smiled at him. "Answered to my satisfaction, Your Grace." She turned to Jane. "And how are you getting on, my dear?"

So many thoughts crowded her mind, pushed against her lips. Mr. Parsons' stiff-backed manner, Larissa's rigid expectations of order in the schoolroom, the duchess's demands, Jane's suspicions about Simmons. But she glanced up, and her gaze collided with Wey's. His smile seemed hesitant, as if he knew all her doubts and concerns, as if he feared she would leave them.

As if he wanted more than anything for her to stay.

She smiled at her benefactress. "I love it here. Best position I've ever held. Tell His Grace to pay you what you're worth, for I never plan to leave."

Meredith agreed to allow Jane and the girls to take Fortune up to meet the duchess. Her pet snuggled into Jane's arms and cast her mistress only a fleeting glance as the quartet left the library. So much for being needed. Oh, why posture? Meredith had always known she needed the cat far more than Fortune needed her.

"I suspect I will shortly be asked to secure a cat," the duke said with a fond smile toward the door.

"A shame Fortune cannot have kittens," Meredith

replied. "An accident when she was young, I was told. At least she will not be judged on her ability to sire heirs."

The smile that turned her way was cooler, more polished, and she was reminded of his father. Now, there had been a duke—all power, prestige, and pride. She sensed more in Jane's duke, a thoughtful kindness missing from this house for generations.

"I do think he'll be suitable for Jane," she'd told Cowls only this morning before setting out for Wey Castle.

Her elderly butler had put his long nose in the air, as if sniffing for the truth. "Very likely, given the tales told of him. But I shall endeavor to keep in touch with my contacts."

His contacts. She'd never dreamed when she'd asked her childhood butler to come out of retirement and serve in her first establishment that she was getting such a treasure. But Mr. Cowls' ability to ferret gossip from other servants was legendary. He and his brother, who served Lady Agnes deGuis, had a network of former associates, family, and friends throughout London and indeed much of England. There was little they could not shortly discover. It was from him she'd learned the fate of the previous governesses, and the duke's pressing need for a new one.

But what if she and Mr. Cowls were wrong? She could not allow Jane to suffer for it. After all Meredith had endured as a companion to Lady Winhaven, she'd sworn never to see another brought so low. She had not thought Jane to be the type to be taken in by a handsome face and broad shoulders, but it wouldn't be the first time a lady had seen a hero where a villain resided. She knew how easily a lonely heart could be deceived.

She made herself lean back in the chair as if she hadn't a care. "It seems Jane is satisfied with the position. What of you, Your Grace?"

Was that a twinkle in the green of his eyes? "I thought my opinion was of no importance."

"Lesser importance, perhaps," she allowed, "but importance nonetheless. Has Jane Kimball lived up to your expectations?"

Once more his gaze veered to the doorway, as if he couldn't wait to see Jane returning. "She has surpassed them."

Meredith smiled. Yes, kindness, and more. Just what she'd hoped for Jane. "Excellent. Then it does indeed appear as if my work here is done."

He inclined his head, gaze returning to hers. "If you would tell me the name of your bank, I will have my London solicitor Mr. Mayes deposit the agreed upon fee into your account."

Cold rushed past her, and she pressed her arms to her sides to keep from shivering. "Mr. Mayes? Mr. Julian Mayes?"

"The same." He frowned. "Is something wrong, Miss Thorn?"

Very likely she looked as if she'd seen a ghost. She'd certainly tried to act as if Julian Mayes was dead to her. But the duke must never know that.

She gathered herself and rose. "Not at all, Your Grace. But I fear a bank would be inconvenient for me. I would prefer my fee paid directly."

His frown did not ease. Neither did her tension.

"Then where may I have Mr. Mayes bring the payment to you?" he asked.

"I would prefer not to meet Mr. Mayes." Her tone was becoming clipped. Could he hear it as well? Another moment, and he might recall a different dark-haired, lavender-eyed lady associated with the dashing Julian Mayes. "Perhaps you could pay me now."

"I regret that I do not keep cash at hand," he replied. "There is seldom any need here on the island." His gaze roamed over her face, as if trying to see inside her. "Is there some problem with Mr. Mayes in particular? I know his

firm has distinguished itself for solving difficult situations,
but I trust him in more mundane matters as well."

And she could not trust him at all.

Perhaps she should merely decline. It wasn't as if she
needed the money. Lady Winhaven had seen to that,
however shocked Meredith had been to find herself the
beneficiary of her late mistress' will. But surely His Grace
would wonder if she refused.

"I simply see no need to trouble Mr. Mayes," she told him.
"Have someone drop the fee off at my place of business,
forty-three Kensington Road. And now, I really must go."

Before she betrayed herself further.

What was it about the Fortune Employment Agency and
everyone associated with it that always left him feeling as if
the world had tilted? Miss Thorn had seemed redoubtable,
yet one mention of Julian's name, and she was fleeing out
the door and calling for her cat to be returned to her.
Julian had established his credentials as an exceptional
solicitor, handling any number of tricky legal questions
from inheritance to infidelity for his wealthy clients. Surely
Miss Thorn need not fear him.

Unless she had something to hide.

He shook himself. His father had been the skeptical
type, always expecting people to be less than what they
appeared. Very likely that was what had driven him to evict
that family from the island years ago.

"Suspect the worst," he'd advised Alaric more than once,
"and you'll rarely be surprised."

Alaric had no intention in living that way. He'd
rather suspect the best, and he'd only occasionally been
disappointed. All that was required was to temper optimism
with solid facts, well researched.

Yet something inside him had soared to hear Jane declare
herself satisfied with the position. He told himself it saved

him from another painful search for a new governess, that it maintained household order. But he found himself a little embarrassed at how eagerly he looked forward to their evening chat.

As the time drew near, he tidied up the papers on his desk, pulled out Samuel Johnson's dictionary and left it open as if he had been looking for the perfect word, brought a second lamp from the stack to better light the space. It was when he caught himself adjusting his cravat for the third time that he froze.

What was he doing? He didn't have to impress the woman. He was the Duke of Wey. She worked for him! Besides, who could hold a candle to her dashing cavalry officer husband? He was returning the dictionary to the shelf when he heard a movement. He forced himself to stroll out from among the shelves.

Parsons was gliding to his place by the wall, and Jane was waiting by the desk. The two lamps sent amber lights skipping through her dark hair as she turned to watch him approach.

"Your Grace," she said.

"Jane," he acknowledged. "Are you here to tell me the girls want a cat?"

A smile blossomed on her lips, and his smile rose to meet it. "There was some talk," she admitted, "but I discouraged it. The castle really isn't situated to allow a feline easy exit and entrance, particularly in the winter. I doubt Mr. Parsons would want to carry a kitten out to do her business."

Alaric caught his butler grimacing before Parsons returned his gaze to the books.

"Very thoughtful of you," he told Jane. "Then things are going well?"

She shrugged, setting her skirts to swinging. "As well as might be expected. Singing lessons met with approval. Arithmetic still evinces moans. But we progress."

He shook his head. "I feel as if I should apologize again

for my household, Jane. I never realized we were so topsy-turvy until you arrived."

He thought Parsons sniffed his disagreement.

"I'm not sure my arrival helped," she said.

"On the contrary. Thanks to you, we might actually be righting the ship of state."

She looked impressed. "Then perhaps I should go help his Royal Highness next. He's always getting himself into trouble, from what I hear."

"Dreadfully dull fellow," Alaric told her. "Nothing but frivolity morning, noon, and night. You'll be better entertained here."

She glanced up at him from under her thick lashes. "Promise?"

All at once, he was ten years younger, fresh from school and certain the world was his. He could imagine meeting her at her first ball, taking her hand, leading her onto the floor, proud to be partnering the wittiest girl in London. They'd take a turn on the floor, wander out onto the veranda. And, in the moonlight, he could bend his head to hers…

Somewhere beyond the circle of golden light, Parsons shuffled his feet. The image vanished, and with it his ability to act. He was the duke. She was the governess. Duty and honor demanded that he remember that.

Alaric pasted on a smile. "I promise, Jane. Never doubt a duke. Now, I should let you get some rest."

She curtsied, the proper response of an employee to an employer. But that gleam was back in her eyes as she rose. "We have a saying in the schoolroom. Sleep tight, don't let the bedbugs bite. Good night, Wey."

He inclined his head, and she turned and walked out the door. But he rather thought it was his conscience and not the bedbugs that would be biting him tonight.

CHAPTER TEN

WHAT was she doing? Jane's cheeks were still hot as she hurried up the stairs for the schoolroom. She'd been flirting with the duke, pure and simple, as if she'd been at the local assembly and he was no more than a squire's strapping son. But he wasn't the son of a local landowner. He was a duke, the father of her charges, her employer. If Jimmy's stepmother hadn't thought Jane good enough for a cavalry officer, Jane certainly wouldn't be good enough for a duke.

If she had any doubts about the matter, the next day proved her place at the castle. The morning was so cold, ice sketched patterns on the schoolroom windows, so she hadn't the heart to take the girls on a constitutional or for a riding lesson. Instead, she led them marching around the schoolroom to the delight of Calantha and Abelona and Larissa's unveiled contempt. Ladies, it seemed, did not march. She had just settled them with a history text when Mr. Parsons appeared to inform them that they were wanted.

"Lady Carrolton has come calling," he announced. "Her Grace desires that her granddaughters attend her and her friend."

Abelona hopped to her feet, but Calantha and Larissa followed more slowly.

"I told you we needed to practice deportment," Larissa

said with a look to Jane. "We aren't ready."

"It's just a visit from an old family friend," Jane said, rising and setting aside the book.

"Not just any visit," Larissa insisted.

Calantha nodded. "Lady Carrolton is grandmother's *best* friend. She comes by at least once a week. Betsy calls her Lady Quarrelsome."

Mr. Parsons drew himself up. "You can be certain I will speak to Betsy about the matter. I do hope you'll do better about talking out of turn, Mrs. Kimball."

"I never could keep my opinion to myself," Jane told him. "But I'll try."

He did not look comforted as he led them from the room.

Her Grace was entertaining in the withdrawing room, a cavernous space with pearly pink walls, gilded furnishings, and an inordinate amount of pottery. Jane tried not to gawk at the heavenly hosts cavorting about the painted ceiling and focused on their visitor instead. She had thought the duchess had an air of royalty about her, but the woman seated at her right on the pink velvet sofa made the duchess look plebian. Her long face was sculptured and pale, like finest marble. Not a curl was out of place in her elaborately styled white hair. Every inch of her amethyst-colored gown was pressed and stiff. She probably didn't need whalebone to sit so tall.

"Ah, there they are," the duchess said, hands fluttering. "Come make your curtsies, girls. Mrs. Kimball, you may sit over there."

Over there appeared to be against the pink wall on a set of crocodile-legged chairs, one of which was already occupied by another woman a few years younger than Jane. Jane started to move, but Abelona snatched up her hand.

"Don't leave us," she whispered.

Jane twisted to meet her gaze. "I'll be right there if you

need me. Remember what your father said about respect. It applies to Lady Carrolton too."

Abelona sighed but went to sit beside Calantha on the matching pink sofa opposite her grandmother's.

Jane crossed to the wall. The other woman sat, feet firmly planted, both gloved hands tight on the tortoiseshell handle of the square red-leather case on her lap.

"Travels prepared for anything, does she?" Jane murmured as the duchess reminded her friend of her granddaughters' names and ages.

The other woman's gaze darted to Jane, then pointed steadfastly forward. She had honey-colored hair and eyes the blue-green of Lisbon's Tagus River at sunrise. The shapeless navy gown betrayed nothing of her figure.

"Her ladyship is under a physician's care for a number of ailments," she whispered back. "It's important to be ready for any eventuality."

As if to prove as much, Lady Carrolton suddenly began sneezing, tiny little squeaks that nonetheless shook her slender frame. "Ramsey!" she cried between fits as the girls stared at her.

Miss Ramsey rose and hurried to her side, drawing a large square of white silk from her pocket and holding it under the lady's nose. The sound of her blow was far from delicate. Larissa sat unblinking, but Calantha winced, and Abelona looked impressed.

Lady Carrolton sniffed as her companion withdrew the handkerchief. "Thank you, Ramsey. That will be all, but stay close."

"Of course, your ladyship." Miss Ramsey snapped open her case, deposited the soiled handkerchief inside, and closed the case again before returning to her spot along the wall.

Jane shook her head. "And I thought my post was challenging. I'm Jane Kimball, by the way, the new governess."

"Patience," she said, adjusting her navy skirts around the box.

"Yes," Jane agreed. "I imagine you need a great deal of it."

Her mouth quirked. "No, that is yes, but that wasn't my point. My name is Patience, Patience Ramsey. I've been Lady Carrolton's companion for three years now."

"Then your name should probably be saint," Jane told her. "Is she like this often?"

As if in answer, Lady Carrolton began coughing, great whoops that echoed to the high ceiling. Larissa sat farther back in her chair, and Abelona cuddled against Calantha, who looked positively fascinated.

Patience hurried to her ladyship's side. She held a gilded vinaigrette under the lady's nose and gently patted her back. "Easy, now. Breathe."

Lady Carrolton took several deep breaths, and the coughing subsided.

"I must say, my dear, that you bear up well," the duchess said as Patience returned to her seat.

"I try, but it is a constant burden. My dear Lilith is beyond herself with worry."

"What's wrong with the lady?" Jane whispered.

"Everything," Patience whispered back, "and, I fear, nothing."

Lady Carrolton began blinking hard. "Ramsey!"

Patience hurried back with eye drops this time.

And so it went throughout the visit. Lady Carrolton either convulsed over some ill or lobbed pointed comments at the girls.

"Too thin," she said to Larissa. "Have your governess dose you with calf's liver oil."

The look Larissa sent Jane dared her to try it.

"Too quiet," she said of Calantha. "I cannot bear a girl with no opinions of her own."

"She'd love me," Jane muttered to Patience.

Patience's rosebud mouth hinted of a smile again. "Your idea of an opinion may differ from her ladyship's."

"Of that I have no doubt."

"Too pretty," she told the duchess with a look to Abelona. "She'll come to a wretched end, you mark my words. Probably marry a cavalry officer and run off to some heathen country to die of dysentery."

Jane leaped to her feet. "Oh, goodness, look at the time. We must go. So much to do. Terribly sorry, Your Grace. Come along, girls. We must dose you before any of this infects you." She clapped her hands as she rushed forward, and Calantha and Abelona scrambled off the sofa to run to her. Even Larissa moved faster than her usual languid grace. The duchess made some protest, but Patience Ramsey gave Jane the thumbs up as she hustled the girls from the room.

"Lady Carrolton may be a good friend of your grandmother's," she said as she led them back to the schoolroom, "but she is mistaken on several counts. You are most certainly not too thin, Larissa. I predict you'll have a nice willowy figure by the time you come out."

Larissa smiled, then frowned, then did her best to look haughty. Couldn't agree with the enemy, after all. "Thank you, Mrs. Kimball."

"And you are not too quiet," she told Calantha as they entered the schoolroom. "You were only being polite, and I know your grandmother was proud of you."

Calantha smiled as she skipped over to the table.

"Me, me," Abelona said, tugging on Jane's skirts.

Jane smoothed a curl from her brow. "You can marry whoever you please."

Abelona beamed at her.

"She can't, you know," Larissa said, joining them all at the table. "We're the daughters of a duke. We must make advantageous marriages."

"What's advantageous?" Calantha asked.

"Having advantages," Jane explained, seating herself at

the table. "It means your marriage will help your family in some way—bringing in wealth, property."

Calantha wrinkled her nose. "Father has lots of property. Mr. Mayes the solicitor said it was nearly too much for one man to handle."

Small wonder he was so busy.

"I don't want an *advantages* marriage," Abelona said. "I just want my unicorn."

"You'll want that kind of marriage when you're older," Larissa predicted. "Everyone wants an advantageous marriage, even Father. He needs a wife who will give him a son."

Though she knew the truth of it, Jane still felt as if she'd run into a wall.

Calantha frowned. "Why does he want a son when he has us?"

"Because we don't count," Larissa said. "We're just ladies."

Something boiled up inside Jane. "Ladies are important too. How's a duke to get a son without one, eh? Who makes sure this household has food and drink and bedrooms for everyone?"

"Parsons," Abelona said.

"Grandmother," Larissa corrected her.

"Exactly right. Now, no more talk of marriages. After the example you were just given, I think Larissa is right. You need lessons on deportment."

Larissa brightened.

"Right after we finish arithmetic."

The look on his mother's face warned Alaric before he took a bite of the beef at dinner that night. It was just as well. His thoughts had returned with surprising frequency to his recent discussions with Jane and the girls. She'd said she was happy here, but he kept wondering about the gleam in her eyes last night. It was almost as if she'd been flirting with him.

Now he examined the slice of roast he'd taken from the silver platter the footman had offered. Rather blacker than usual. He knocked the tines of his fork against the edge and heard the dry crackle of charcoal.

"Not Cook's usual style," his mother said before taking a long drink.

Neither were the potatoes. He knew they must be near the end of last year's crop, but the mound in front of him was grey and lumpy.

He glanced at Parsons, back straight against the wall. "Is there trouble below stairs?"

His butler kept his gaze on the flowered pattern of the opposite wall. "The kitchen is at sixes and sevens, Your Grace. Someone opened all the doors on the greenhouse, and the produce has suffered."

At least Parsons could not blame Jane for that.

"However," he continued as if determined to cut up Alaric's peace, "the greatest problem appears to be Mrs. Kimball."

Alaric sighed and set down his fork. "What has Jane Kimball to do with the kitchen?"

Parsons moved closer, as if encouraged by his reaction. "Just so, Your Grace. She went so far as to suggest that Cook send fewer sweets and more fruits and vegetables to the schoolroom. She has no sense of the tradition on which this great house was built."

Another adherent to the sacred traditions of the island, it seemed, for all Parsons had been with them less than a dozen years. Planting, tending, harvesting—the rhythms had remained unchanged for centuries. Yet Jane's suggestion made him wonder.

"How many sweets was Cook sending?" he asked.

His mother cleared her throat. "I believe I can answer that. After Evangeline died, I instructed Cook to indulge the girls. I believe she was baking three cakes a day."

Alaric stared at her. "Three entire cakes, every day?"

For the first time that he could remember, his mother refused to meet his gaze. "One for each girl, you see. I'd quite forgotten about the matter, but I agree with Mrs. Kimball that it seems excessive now."

It had been excessive then. He'd had a few friends who had drowned their sorrows in sweets when they were lads. One now struggled with gout, the other with alcohol. He would not want either fate for his daughters.

"Tell Cook we appreciate her efforts to cheer the girls when they needed it most," he told Parsons. "And that we have the utmost confidence in her ability to rise to the occasion now. Let me know if we need to add to her budget or hire someone to help with preparations."

Parsons inclined his head. "Yes, Your Grace. Thank you."

As his butler stepped back against the wall, Alaric turned to his mother. "Are there any other decrees I should know about before Mrs. Kimball brazenly does what's best for the girls?"

Her Grace's smile was rueful. "I may have ordered matching outfits and instructed the maids to dress them identically each day."

So that was the reason they all wore white so often. "Why?"

She scooted forward on the scroll-backed chair. "I never had a daughter. They are so much more fun to dress than a little boy. And they're so adorable dressed identically, like dolls."

"Mother," he said, "my daughters are not your toys."

She flushed red. "Certainly not. I merely mentioned the fact because dear Jane might want to improve their wardrobe, especially Larissa's."

He shook his head as he speared a limp piece of asparagus. "*Dear Jane*, eh?"

"*Mrs. Kimball* seems so formal," she said, returning to her own dinner. "And she is a dear. I'm sure you've noticed."

More than he felt comfortable admitting. Jane was far too much on his mind. He could blame these crises that followed in her wake, but he had the feeling she would have been on his mind regardless.

"And how did today go?" he asked as soon as Parsons let her into the library that night.

That gleam he so admired was in her eyes as she approached the desk. "Quite well," she reported. "Larissa took to multiplication, despite her protests to the contrary. I think we can move on to division shortly."

"Excellent." He motioned her into the chair across from him. "And no more ghosts?"

"None lately, but I won't know about tonight until later. Ghosts don't come out until midnight."

"Learned that in Portugal, did you?"

She shook her head. "Egypt. Those old pharaohs have been moaning for centuries. Kept half the camp awake most nights."

He laughed. It felt surprisingly good, and surprisingly strange. When was the last time he'd had a good laugh?

"You should do that more often," she said, as if she knew his thoughts. "Happiness sits well on you."

Parsons coughed, and she rolled her eyes. "That is, happiness sits well on you, *Your Grace*."

Now Parsons rolled his eyes, as if begging heaven for patience.

"And how did the singing lessons go?" he asked.

"Tolerable."

He shook his head. "And here I spent most of the last two days outside in the cold, on your orders."

"No, you didn't," she said primly. "I'll wager you spent most of the time behind that desk. You're more housebound than your daughters."

Parsons coughed again and added a stomp of his foot for good measure.

"Are you ill, Parsons?" Alaric asked. "Would you care to

excuse yourself for a glass of water?"

"No, Your Grace," his butler managed to choke out.

Jane rose. "It's all right. I should be going. Just know that all is well in the schoolroom, Your Grace. Good night." She curtsied and turned to go.

He wanted to call her back, give her some reason to stay. Life seemed so much better when she was near. But detaining her would be selfish. She had been hired to attend his daughters.

Odd. He never remembered being jealous of his daughters, until now.

CHAPTER ELEVEN

The first real change in their routine came on Sunday. Wey in a superfine wool coat and top hat, his mother in her fur-trimmed pelisse, and the girls in their matching redingotes attended services in the village church on the other side of the bridge. As governess, Jane rode with the family in the landau, while the other servants in their olive livery walked behind. They made quite a cavalcade crossing the bridge that bright morning.

"There's Father's lock," Calantha proclaimed, pointing down the side stream to the west. Jane spotted a square block of a building close to the bank on either side.

"What are you locking up, Father?" Abelona asked, cuddled against Jane's side in the chilly morning air. "Is it scary?"

"No, Abelona," he said with a smile "The lock is a set of gates that closes off the river, to keep our lands from flooding."

"Perhaps we should pray for their efficacy," the duchess murmured, turning away from the sight with a shudder.

"Does it flood here often?" Jane asked Larissa as they walked from the carriage to the duke's private entrance at the side of the church. Like the castle, the building was solidly constructed of golden stone with a square tower at one end topped with a cross.

"Every spring," Larissa said. "Sometimes water fills

people's houses, but we'll be safe at the castle." She put on her polished smile, so like her father's, as they entered the chapel.

Walnut box pews stood in orderly rows, basking in the golden glow from stained glass windows on either side. The center aisle led to a semicircle nave with more touches of gold, from the plates awaiting communion to the lettering on the Bible. The first three boxes on the left had gilded finials as well, and the unicorn crest on the half-doors. Wey, his mother, the girls, and Jane filled the first box. She thought perhaps the other servants would flow in behind, but they found seats farther back. Apparently previous dukes had had larger families.

The vicar was a round-faced balding man who reminded her of her father. He had a better speaking voice, though. It boomed out every prayer and order of the service. Still, his congregation must have grown used to it, for she spotted more than one gazing about distractedly. She managed to catch most of the service while keeping Calantha from rustling the hymnal too often and Abelona from wiggling off the bench. At least Larissa mimicked her father, sitting upright, a slight frown or nod showing that they were attending to each word and giving it appropriate thought. She couldn't help admiring that.

As they left the chapel at the close of services, after Wey had thanked the vicar, the duke turned to her with a smile. "And what do you intend to do with your afternoon off, Jane?"

Her afternoon off. She could imagine riding through the crisp air, coming back to toast and hot chocolate. Sitting with a book before a roaring fire, toes wiggling in the warmth. A shame there was a tall, powerful man in each picture, one she could never have.

She made herself smile. "I think I'll explore the village. You're all right taking the girls back to the castle without me?"

She thought he swallowed as he glanced at his daughters, who were traipsing back to the landau. "We'll manage."

"Good man." She patted his arm and turned for the village.

It took her only a quarter hour to walk the hard-packed streets. Weyton held a cluster of whitewashed cottages, all neat and tidy, plus shops for the blacksmith, cooper, dry goods merchant, and baker. The inn along the river was particularly popular, if the number of people heading in that direction was any indication. Ladies, however, did not go unaccompanied to such a place, for all she'd visited a few with Jimmy and his friends. She was turning back toward the bridge when she spotted Simmons walking toward her. She was ready to scold him for abandoning the girls when she remembered it was his half day off too.

She nodded as she started to pass him, but he caught her arm.

"Ready to bolt yet?" he asked.

Jane pulled out of his grip. His eyes, a dark hazel, were narrowed, and his lips were once more curling into a sneer. Perhaps she should be afraid. He was a good eighteen inches taller than she was and likely outweighed her by two stone of pure muscle. But surely he knew if he accosted her she would take her concerns to the duke, and Simmons would be reprimanded, or worse.

"Not me," she assured him, keeping her smile pleasant. "Takes more than a broach in my boot to scare me off."

"Maybe someone wasn't trying to scare you," he said, holding his ground. "Maybe someone was trying to do you a favor. Ask around—everyone says the House of Wey is cursed. You'd be better off somewhere else."

Did he really believe that, either that he had been helping her by implicating her for theft or that Wey's family was destined for difficulty? "Then why do you stay?" she challenged him.

His look turned hard. "My father was born on the island.

I promised myself I'd return one day. I have business here, some scores to settle. You don't."

"Three little girls who need me?" Jane reminded him. "I call that reason enough. You do right by them and me, and you'll have no trouble from me, Simmons."

He shrugged. "Sorry. If you won't leave, I can't make the same promise. Enjoy your afternoon off, Mrs. Kimball."

He strode off, but she felt as if he took some of the sunshine with him.

Alaric had always enjoyed Sundays, a time for rest, contemplation. While he thought Mr. Dennys' sermon particularly inspiring, focusing on the importance of duty, by evening he found himself ill at ease. It didn't take much to realize why. Jane wasn't going to come report. What a pitiful fellow he was to keep listening for her footfall.

"Father?"

He looked up from the desk, where he'd been attempting to craft a response about the society budget, to find all three of his daughters crowding in the doorway, stockinged feet protruding from under their nightgowns. Dread pushed him to his feet. "Girls? What's wrong?"

Larissa hesitated, but Calantha shoved past her, Abelona on her heels.

"We're just doing what Mrs. Kimball said," his middle daughter assured him. She glanced back at her older sister. Larissa sighed and followed her into the room.

"I told them this wasn't necessary," she complained as they approached the desk.

Abelona scampered ahead, coming around the desk to tug on the leg of his trouser as if to make sure she had his attention. "Mrs. Kimball said to wish you good night." She crooked her finger, and Alaric bent lower. "Good night, Father. Don't let the bedbugs bite."

He smiled at her. "Good night, Abelona."

He straightened to find Calantha fidgeting. "Mrs. Kimball said you might want to see us." Her face puckered, and her voice turned wistful. "*Do* you want to see us, Father?"

"Of course," he told them all. "It was very thoughtful of you to come bid me good night. Allow me to return the favor and escort you back to your rooms."

He was still smiling when he retired to his own suite of rooms an hour later. Abelona had wheedled a story from him, her sisters draped against either of his arms as he read from the big book she'd chosen. Knights on horseback, ladies sallying forth to find their true loves—he began to see why she believed in unicorns. He could imagine Jane telling the tale with more drama, more excitement. It was just like her to think of the girls, and him, even on her day off.

Now, if he could just stop thinking about her.

Perhaps it was his thoughts of Jane. Perhaps it was the sun shining again the next morning. Whatever the reason, Alaric woke, breakfasted, and took his horse Decatur out for a ride early. A few hardier souls had ventured out in the cold to look over fields and check on animals. Most of them waved to him as he passed. Mr. Harden turned his back.

Still, he was in a much better mood when he returned to the house, and even more so when Parsons announced later that Alaric's friend and solicitor, Julian Mayes, had arrived.

Julian had been one of the few local boys he'd known growing up on the island. The Mayes had had an estate to the west on the river, and His Grace had allowed the boys to ride together on occasion. If they stopped to fish or climb trees or swim, no one but their grooms was the wiser. These days, they stole time during Alaric's infrequent visits to London, and Julian found reasons to drive out to the island.

Now he leaned back in the leather-bound chair across from Alaric's desk, looking little different than when they'd ridden the shore together. His hair was still that shock of red-gold that defied taming. His brown eyes still sparkled with intellect and the promise of good fun. Or perhaps it was the grin he aimed Alaric's way. It was impossible not to brighten in Julian's presence.

"What brings you out this way?" Alaric asked as Parsons handed their guest a tall cool glass of lemonade. There was also cake on the nearby tray. He wasn't sure whether Cook was trying to make amends for some of the meals she'd served recently or transferring the need to apply her sweet-making skills to him.

"A lady," Julian said, crossing his booted feet.

Alaric chuckled. "Why doesn't that surprise me? She must be something special to force you out of London."

"I'm afraid you'll have to tell me. It's your Miss Thorn. I can't locate her."

Alaric frowned. "What do you mean? We sent her address."

"You sent an address," Julian agreed, "but I couldn't find her. The address belongs to an empty warehouse. I asked about the area, and no one had heard of the Fortune Employment Agency. Nor have any of my clients and acquaintances among the aristocracy used its services. The woman is a phantom."

Not a phantom. She'd sat in this very room, argued for her client's rights. "What about the *Times*? Surely she advertises in it."

"I checked there as well. The Fortune Employment Agency did indeed place an advertisement for clientele. However, the letter requesting the ad arrived with payment on the front doorstep of the printing office. No one ever saw the owner."

Alaric sank against the back of his chair. "If there is no

Fortune Employment Agency, how did I end up with a governess through it?"

"A very good question," Julian said. "A better one would be who is taking care of your children. That's why I left London to come here. Someone's having you on, Wey, and I fear it's your governess."

Alaric stiffened. "Nonsense. You cannot lay this at Jane's door. She's been nothing but a ray of sunlight to this dreary old castle."

Julian's brows rose. "*Jane?* And waxing poetic? Now you have me worried."

Alaric refused to be rattled. "And you have piqued my curiosity. Why create a fictitious employment agency to do me a favor?"

Julian spread his hands. "It probably wasn't personal. This Miss Thorn saw an opportunity to make a few quid. When she realized you wouldn't pay her outright, she disappeared rather than court trouble."

Alaric shook his head. "No. She was no stranger. She knew things about us, the ages of my children, the number of governesses we'd been through recently."

"Perhaps Her Grace lamented her circumstances to the woman," Julian suggested.

"Have you ever known my mother to lament anything publicly? Besides, there was something familiar about her, as if we had met before." He eyed his friend. "Do you recall a tall, raven-haired woman with a good figure and an imperious personality?"

Julian laughed. "You could be talking about several of the patronesses."

"No," Alaric told him. "I'm certain I knew her from around here."

Julian stilled. "Did she have odd-colored eyes, almost purple, that can look right through you?"

"Then you remember her too."

"I'm afraid I might." When Alaric frowned, he set aside

his glass. "Do you recall Rose Hill?"

"The estate next to yours? Of course. You spent more time there than in your own house."

"Mrs. Rose made the best brambleberry pie. And she had the prettiest daughter for miles."

Alaric chuckled. "Now, that I remember. She used to hang on the gate to the lane as we rode past. We pretended not to notice her."

"And she pretended not to notice us. But I certainly noticed her."

"But how could Mary Rose have grown up into Miss Thorn? I seem to recall she left the area years ago."

Julian stood and began moving about the library, as if building up his case with each stride of his long legs. "She was forced to leave. Her mother only had the use of the estate in her lifetime. When she died, it went to a distant cousin. Odious fellow. Threw Mary out to fend for herself at the tender age of sixteen."

Alaric's hand tightened on the glass. As if he needed another reminder why he must marry again. He could not allow his daughters to face such uncertainty.

"I lost track of her," Julian admitted, "so I don't know where she ended up. She could well have felt the need to change her last name, severing all association with the toad who took her home and her future from her."

"And start an employment agency?" Alaric questioned. "That seems an unlikely pastime for a gentlewoman, no matter how impoverished her circumstances. I'm afraid you're clutching at straws, my lad."

He returned to his seat. "Perhaps I am. But the fact of the matter is that Miss Thorn's disappearance is mysterious. I say we look further into the matter."

Alaric shrugged. "Be my guest. What do you need from me?"

"For one thing, an opportunity to interview your new governess. She might know more than she's saying."

He bristled, then forced himself to relax. Julian didn't know Jane. His work in London had darkened his outlook, until at times he sounded a bit like Alaric's father, cynical. Likely all he could see was that Jane had come with no reference save that of Miss Thorn, who had conveniently disappeared. He hadn't spent time with her, heard her offer advice in her outspoken manner, watched her eyes light with glee. Once he met Jane, he'd know she would do nothing to harm this family.

"Very well," Alaric said, rising and going to the bell pull. "I doubt she knows more of Miss Thorn's background, but I suppose it wouldn't hurt to ask."

CHAPTER TWELVE

J ane wasn't surprised to be summoned to the library that morning. Calantha had reported that Betsy said Cook was in a snit about trimming the number of sweets. What was Jane supposed to do with three cakes every day—feed them to the pigeons that fluttered about the castle turrets? The tempest had only watered Parsons' dislike of her. He'd scolded her again about showing the proper deference to an employer and peer of the realm. She could only hope if Wey intended to advise her as well that she could rely on his good will to keep her position.

She wasn't prepared to find him in company. A tall, slender, well-dressed man rose from the chair she generally sat in to offer her a bow.

"Mrs. Kimball," Wey said, "may I present Mr. Julian Mayes, late of London. He has some questions for you."

Questions? About what? She glanced from the fellow's too-charming nod to the duke's polished look. "Happy to help, I'm sure."

Mr. Mayes stepped aside and motioned to the chair. "Please, Mrs. Kimball, won't you take a seat?"

Trying too hard, this one. That smooth smile, the artfully messed red-gold hair, whispered of hidden schemes. Surely no gentleman traveled in such perfection. It had to be a façade.

She deigned to sit, but she kept her back straight and her

gaze wary.

"You came highly recommended from the Fortune Employment Agency," he said, taking the seat beside hers. "Did you have the opportunity to meet Mr. Fortune?"

Jane smiled despite her misgivings and glanced to Wey. "It's Miss Fortune, and yes, I met her. Silky grey hair, copper-colored eyes."

Mr. Mayes frowned as he glanced between them.

"Fortune is a cat," Wey informed him. "And I believe you were more interested in Miss Thorn, her owner."

"Yes," he said, turning to Jane. "What can you tell me about her?"

Not a great deal, now that she thought on it. She could explain that Miss Thorn preferred her tea with honey rather than sugar, and that two cups of the sweet stuff seemed mandatory before she started her day. Miss Thorn walked every afternoon, always with Fortune in her arms, as if the cat were her guardian or chaperone. Indeed, she was seldom without her pet. She dressed well, spoke well, moved with a grace Jane envied. Somehow, she didn't think Mr. Mayes cared about any of that.

"I owe her a great deal," she said instead. "I had lost my position, had used up what little savings I possessed. I saw her ad in the *Times*, met her at a coffee shop, explained my situation and what I was seeking in a position. She welcomed me to her home, treated me like family, and found me this post."

"I see." His gaze went to Wey, as if they both saw something invisible to her.

"What's wrong?" Jane asked.

Mr. Mayes offered her that smooth smile. "Surely nothing."

"Mr. Mayes thinks perhaps Miss Thorn is an old acquaintance of ours," Wey explained. "If that is true, she grew up near the island. If she still had friends in the area, it could explain how she knew about our situation, our need for a governess."

Jane nodded. "I always thought she was quality."

Mr. Mayes leaned forward. "She said nothing of her background? How she came to start the agency?"

"No," Jane admitted. "Only that she preferred to help ladies in need. I certainly qualified. But she seemed to know that. I just thought she was good at ferreting out the truth. But you don't have to take my word for it. She's in London. I'm sure you could locate her and ask."

"Not exactly," Wey put in as his friend leaned back and slumped as if defeated. "I requested that Mr. Mayes visit her in London to pay her fee. She cannot be found."

Jane frowned. "What do you mean, she cannot be found?"

"I've been to the building that supposedly held her office," Mr. Mayes told her, tone weary, "and the newspaper offices. No one claims to know a thing about her."

Jane sat back, feeling a bit as if the chair was rolling like a ship at sea. "But you met her, Your Grace. She wasn't a figment of my imagination."

He rubbed his chin. "I met her, and her cat. But she seems to have disappeared without a trace."

And with her, any sense of propriety. Jane Kimball, client of the prestigious Fortune Employment Agency, was worthy of serving a duke's household. Jane Kimball, widow of an obscure cavalry officer, with no recommendation and no one to vouch for her, wasn't worth a moment's time.

Panic nearly pushed her to her feet, and she gripped the arms of the chair to prevent herself from rising. Wey believed in her, had supported her. Surely, he wouldn't turn her away without good cause.

And what of Miss Thorn? She had been so organized, so confident, so determined to find Jane the perfect situation. She hadn't had to take Jane in, house and feed her at her own expense. Could she be in some sort of trouble to have disappeared like this? Shouldn't Jane try to help?

She stood, and they rose with her as propriety demanded.

"Gentlemen, we must try to find her. Something terrible must have happened."

Mr. Mayes nodded, handsome face darkening. Wey came around the desk to take Jane's hand.

"Rest assured, we will locate Miss Thorn," he promised. "She did us a favor by sending you to us. The least we can do is ensure her safety and pay her what she's due."

She felt as if the air had cleared and she could breathe again. "Thank you, Wey. I have an idea of how to locate her. We first met at a coffee shop off the Strand, but her home is on Clarendon Square."

Wey stiffened, and Mr. Mayes drew in a sharp breath.

Jane glanced between them. "Is that important?"

"Our family town house is on Clarendon Square," Wey said, gaze moving to his friend.

How odd. Jane frowned. "And you never met Miss Thorn?"

Mr. Mayes quirked a smile as Wey's color heightened. "His Grace is not known for socializing."

Wey raised his chin. "My time in London is frequently taken up by more important matters. Nevertheless, locating Miss Thorn may not be as difficult as we'd thought, Julian. I trust you can take care of the matter?"

"Decidedly," Mr. Mayes said, but Jane wasn't sure about the look in his eyes. "And thank you for your help, Mrs. Kimball."

He bowed again, and she curtsied. But she could not help thinking that Miss Thorn had made a terrible mistake by attempting to evade this fellow.

Had Jane made a similar mistake by confiding in him?

"Singular woman," Julian said after Jane had left. "Rather quiet for a governess."

Alaric started laughing. "Jane is hardly the quiet type."

Julian raised a brow. "Not telling you she'd lived a few

doors down from you? I'd say she's keeping her own counsel."

"She only lived with Miss Thorn a short time. There was no reason for her to know who owned the other houses on the square. There are more than two dozen in the area. And I assure you she's made her presence felt at the castle. Cook may eventually forgive her for improving the girls' diet, and Jane and my mother appear to have negotiated a truce. Unfortunately, Parsons is implacable."

Julian shrugged. "He always was. So, she's doing a good job for you?"

And excellent job, if unconventional. He found it hard to remember life without her in it. Or perhaps he didn't want to remember life without her. "Jane is easily the finest governess we've ever had." He motioned his friend to the chessboard and took his accustomed seat as Julian slipped onto the other chair.

"You moved my pieces," Julian said with a frown.

Alaric held up his hands. "Not I. Jane has some facility with the game. I suggested she take your turn. Feel free to move the pieces back if you'd prefer."

Julian shook his head, brow clearing. "She actually put me in a better position." He moved one of his bishops forward.

Alaric calculated possibilities. Move too soon, and Julian would have him in check. Too late, and he missed the opportunity to put his friend in check.

"I can't help noticing the change in you," Julian said, watching him. "Spouting poetry, defending a stranger on little evidence. Mrs. Kimball is a handsome woman, I'll give you that. But she's your governess."

His face felt hot, though he knew he'd done nothing wrong. "I treat her with the utmost respect, I assure you."

Julian sighed. "Wey, I will give you the same advice I give myself when I think of encountering Mary Rose again. Watch yourself. You have everything to lose and little to gain by an association with a woman you know next to nothing about."

Alaric leaned back. "You think I don't know that? Each day brings us one step closer to flooding, with no assurance the precautions I've taken will suffice. My daughters are near strangers to me, my mother aloof. I would do nothing to harm them or anyone else who depends on me, including Jane."

Julian held up a hand. "Peace. I wasn't impugning your honor or your intentions. All I'm suggesting is that we need to know more about her. I'll look into the matter when I return to London."

Julian's methods of looking into matters were subtle and effective, enough so that the War Office had lately made use of his services. Still, any investigation into Jane's past seemed another violation of her privacy. She'd answered any questions he'd put to her quickly and easily. Yet, how did he know she spoke the truth? She was caring for his daughters, living in his house. If there was any question as to her propriety, he should know. Surely that was his duty as a father. His father would have had the constable after her by now.

"Thank you," he told his friend. "And it goes without saying that you will report any findings directly to me and only me."

"Of course," Julian agreed, and he neatly aligned his queen. "Check and mate."

Julian didn't stay much longer. Now that he had his marching orders, nothing Alaric said could convince him to spend the night at the castle. Alaric saw his friend out, waved him goodbye, and returned to the library.

But their conversation lingered, like smoke in the air. Could Miss Thorn be Mary Rose? The names seemed too connected to be a coincidence. Had she taken the darker appellation after losing her home? Where had she been since leaving Surrey? How had she come to possess a town house on prestigious Clarendon Square? How had she gained the capitol and presence to open an employment agency? Why had she singled out his family? Was Jane a dupe or a willing accomplice?

The matter refused to leave him. Perhaps that was why he questioned his mother over dinner. "What made you decide to favor the Fortune Employment Agency with our request for a governess?"

Her Grace looked up from her Yorkshire pudding. "I had never heard of the Fortune Employment Agency until I received a note announcing the day and time of the interview with Mrs. Kimball. I assumed you had engaged them."

Alaric sat back. "I did not." He glanced at their butler, standing in his usual place along the wall. "Parsons, can you shed light on this mystery?"

Parsons drew himself up. "No, Your Grace. I would have advised a more prominent London agency."

So, no one in the house could offer him answers. He could only hope Julian would be more successful.

He was almost afraid to sit behind the desk that evening, ready for the next dire tale from Parsons, but his butler did not appear in the doorway to announce Jane's latest innovation that threatened household order. The first notice he had of a visitor was the sound of little feet scurrying across the carpet.

Calantha came to stand just in front of his desk, her pale hair a nimbus about her peaked face. Did she know that was where Jane usually stood to give her reports? Very likely. It seemed his middle daughter was a keen observer, especially when no one noticed she was about.

Jane was standing in the doorway, fond smile on her face, so at least he knew Calantha had not escaped the schoolroom.

"Good evening, Calantha," he said, offering her a similar smile. "To what do I owe this unexpected pleasure?"

She dropped a quick curtsey. "Mrs. Kimball said…"

"Calantha," Jane interrupted, "tell your father what *you* want."

Calantha shifted from foot to foot, as if unsure how to proceed. Alaric rose, came around the desk, and went down on one knee beside her.

"There, now. What is it you'd like to say to me?"

Her face scrunched up. "You look silly like that."

"I don't think you came all the way from the schoolroom to tell me that."

"Noooo." She drew out the word as she shifted from side to side. "It's about singing."

He glanced up at Jane. "Yes, I understand Mrs. Kimball is teaching you."

Jane spread her skirts and bobbed a curtsey.

"Yes," Calantha said. "And Larissa and Abelona and I were wondering…" She took a deep breath. "We are going to have a recital this Friday at two and we would very much like you to come." She paused as if she'd run out of breath, then added, "Please?"

"I am honored to accept your gracious invitation," he told her.

"Oh, thank you!" She threw her arms around him, and he held her close a moment. His gaze dimmed. Tears? Ridiculous.

He released her and drew back. "I hope you'll tell your sisters what I said."

Jane laughed. "Try to stop her."

Calantha dimpled. As he started to rise, however, she grabbed his hand. "Father, wait. There's something else I want to ask you."

Again he glanced to Jane, who shrugged as if she were just as mystified.

"Oh?" he said, returning his look to his daughter. "What

would that be?"

"Can you change my name?"

Alaric rocked back. "Your name? What's wrong with your name?"

She pulled away to bunch both fists in her muslin skirts, twisting them mercilessly. "It's so long. Ca-lan-tha. Girls in books have nice short names like Ann and Jane."

So that was the problem. He met Jane's gaze, and she ventured into the library to lay a hand on his daughter's shoulder.

"I always wanted a longer romantic name," she said thoughtfully, "like Guinevere or Calantha."

Calantha blinked at her. "You did?"

Jane nodded.

Calantha's face puckered. "I don't."

"What do you want to be called?" Jane asked, and Alaric waited for the answer. Evangeline had insisted on the romantic names, mouthfuls most of them. Likely she would have found Calantha's request a repudiation of her wishes. He chided himself for being glad for a moment she wasn't here.

"Callie," his daughter said.

Alaric took her hand. "All my life, I've had to be called by titles. When I was a boy, as my father's heir, I was Viscount Forde. Now that I've succeeded to the title, I'm Wey. No one but me ever called me Alaric, for all it's the name I prefer. If you prefer Callie, that's what we'll call you. I'll alert the staff."

"And Grandmother?" she asked hopefully.

"And your grandmother," he promised, rising at last. "Now, sleep well, Callie."

She dropped another curtsey, with surprising grace. "Good night, Father. Don't let the bedbugs bite."

Jane put a hand to her shoulders to nudge her toward the door but glanced back. He was surprised to see tears in her eyes as well.

"Nicely done," she said. "And thank you, Alaric." She hurried out the door as if afraid of being chided. Likely Parsons would have suggested discharging her for such an impertinence.

When all Alaric wanted to do was thank her.

CHAPTER THIRTEEN

A laric. Jane couldn't help repeating the name to herself as she escorted Callie back to the schoolroom to report to her sisters. It suited him. There was something noble, honorable, old-fashioned about the name. She'd probably be scolded for her cheek in using it the next time he saw her, but it would be a small price to pay for the pleasure that had darted across his face at her comment.

"It's not fair," Abelona said when Callie told them about her conversation with their father, nearly verbatim. "Callie gets a different name. I want one too."

"Very well," Jane said. "What do you want to be called?"

"Abby, but Larissa said that's where the monkeys live."

"I think you mean monks," Jane told her, trying not to smile. "What about Belle?"

Abelona beamed. "I like it! Thank you, Mrs. Kimball." She hugged her tight.

"Well, I don't want to change my name," Larissa said with a toss of her head. "I sound like a princess."

"Too bad we're only the daughters of a duke," Callie said. "You'd make a very good princess."

Larissa raised her chin. "I'll be a princess one day. All I have to do is marry a prince."

Not marriage again. Jane had never been so glad to see Betsy and Maud in the doorway. "Bedtime!"

Unfortunately, her charges were still discussing the matter

over breakfast. Belle was of the opinion that all princes lived far away. Callie was certain she'd heard someone say they were all old and sickly. Nothing Jane tried would get them off the subject. She finally sent them to their rooms to change into their riding habits. She didn't much care for the outfits, which were all done in black wool with severe lines more suited to dowagers than young ladies. Perhaps she could prevail on Alaric to let them journey to London when the weather warmed to see about new clothes. That ought to make Larissa happy for a time. And Jane could check on Miss Thorn and Fortune.

She couldn't understand why Mr. Mayes hadn't been able to locate her benefactress. Miss Thorn's place of business on Kensington Road had had a nice placard in the window proclaiming it the offices of the Fortune Employment Agency. Jane had only been there once, but she remembered the elegant desk, the wicker basket in the corner with a blanket and pillow for Fortune. Why abandon the place? Had something terrible happened?

"Borrowing trouble," she muttered to herself as she fastened the frogging on her plum-colored wool riding habit. Mr. Mayes had Miss Thorn's home address now. He'd find her, and all would be well.

Knowing they weren't expected at that time of the morning at the castle stables, she asked Simmons to accompany them in case more staff was needed. But when they reached the space pressed deep in the stone of the wall at one side of the courtyard, with narrow exercise pens beside it, he balked.

"I'm a footman, not a groom," he protested. "I was glad to leave off farming to get away from this sort of work. Besides, Mr. Quayle would lock me in irons if I was to touch one of his horses."

"Aye, I would at that." An older man with grey hair as dark and unruly as a storm cloud came out of the smaller stable leading an elegant sable-coated horse for Larissa.

Jane recognized Mr. Quayle, whom she had met since Belle's unicorn had been brought up to the castle.

"If you'll give us a moment, Mrs. Kimball," he said now, "we'll have things ready for you. I'm afraid the, er, unicorn isn't quite up to riding today."

"I'll speak to her," Belle promised. She turned and headed for the exercise pens, where Jane caught a flash of white. Simmons followed her. It was his duty to look after the girls, but Jane rather thought he was trying to escape the work required of the grooms.

"You may want to ride west today," the master of horse told Jane. "Some interesting doings at the lock."

"Mr. Parsons says it's a folly," Callie piped up as she waited for another groom to turn a black horse for her to mount. "I like follies. Grandmother's friend Lady Carrolton has one."

Mr. Quayle scowled. "It's no whim. Parsons has served inside the castle for too long. He's never had to live through a spring flood."

Jane glanced through the opening in the courtyard to the fields stretching beyond. With the waters of the Thames swirling in the distance, it was all too easy to imagine the acreage covered with water. She must have shivered, for Mr. Quayle hurried to assure her.

"Now, don't worry. His Grace has the matter in hand." The master of horse nodded to the groom bringing out a dapple-grey horse for Jane, her saddle on the broad back.

"Do you want me to fetch Lady Abelona?" Mr. Quayle asked.

"I'll go," Jane said. "Callie, tell Mr. Quayle about your new names."

The master of horse turned to Callie as she launched into her recitation.

Belle had moved around the edge of the stable until she was out of sight. But as Jane turned the corner, it was Simmons's voice she heard first.

"They'll never let you ride her, you know," he was telling Belle as she clung to the fence edging the pen. "She's too much horse for a little girl like you."

"She's not a horse," Belle said stubbornly. "She's a unicorn. You just can't see her horn right now."

Jane smiled at the childlike faith. Simmons snorted. "Unicorn. There's no such thing. They're just humoring you because they think you'll cry."

Belle stomped her foot. "I won't."

He bent to put his face on a level with hers, mouth turned up in a familiar sneer. "You will. Because next time you'll be the one with spiders in her bed."

"Not while I live." Anger fueled each step. Jane marched up to him and seized his ear before he could rise. "Apologize to Lady Belle, at once!"

"Sorry, sorry," he muttered, trying to wiggle out of her grip.

"You'll be a great deal sorrier by the time I'm finished with you," Jane promised. "Go back to the house and tell Mr. Parsons I refuse to see your face in the schoolroom wing again. And if you dare to set foot in that space, we'll just see where the spiders end up."

She released him and took Belle's hand. "Come along, Lady Belle. You can continue to ride a nice pony until your unicorn is ready for you."

She did not so much as look at Simmons as she swept back to the stable yard.

Mr. Quayle regarded her as she returned. "Everything all right, Mrs. Kimball?"

Callie's eyes were wide. "She told Simmons to go away. I heard her."

Jane's face was on fire. "We would appreciate a pony, Mr. Quayle, and the help of a groom as usual."

With a nod from the master of horse, two of the grooms hurried to help.

Jane struggled to regain her composure. It was bad

enough that Simmons treated her disrespectfully. He wasn't the first, and she could take care of herself. How dare he treat Belle and Callie that way? He was nothing but a bully, and she wouldn't have it. If Mr. Parsons thought otherwise, he was in for a reckoning too.

She was merely glad that Belle seemed to have recovered. She chatted away on the back of her black pony, a young groom with hair nearly as dark leading her. Belle pointed out butterflies bobbing across the fields, hawks circling above. Larissa rode along, head up, as if she really was a princess surveying her domain. But Callie kept glancing at Jane out of the corners of her eyes as if she was in awe of their governess.

They found the lock easily enough, near the westernmost edge of the island where a group of men gathered at the shore. From here, she could see the wooden gate jutting out from either side of the stream, meeting in the middle and bowing slightly downstream. Shut now, water trickled through the joining. Two wide beams topped the gates, anchored by chains secured to a capstan. One of the chains had been laid out on the muddy ground, and the workers were all eyeing the fellow who was running his hands down the massive links. He rose just then to tower over them. Jane's heart started beating faster.

"Your Grace," she said, and all the men turned to look in her direction.

"Mrs. Kimball," he said, wiping the grease from his bare hands with a rag he'd tucked into his breeches. "Girls. Lovely day for a ride."

"Father," Larissa said, voice sounding much like her grandmother's, "you're dirty."

"Am I?" He glanced down at the mud speckling his boots and breeches. "Why, so I am." He winked at her. "Don't tell Her Grace."

He sounded almost happy. Perhaps he was merely glad to see the sky for once.

"What are you doing?" Callie asked.

He nodded to the men to continue their work, then moved closer to Jane and the girls.

"Testing the lock," he said, taking the halter of Belle's pony and leading her and the beast away from the workers, with her sisters, Jane, and the grooms following. "As we talked about Sunday, the spring rains can make the river swell. The water covers our crops, fills our tenants' houses." He pointed to the side stream leading back toward the castle. "Many men in the area dug our stream deeper this past summer. When we open the gates, the river will flow into the channel, helping to lower the water level around the island and directing it downstream, away from our lands. At least, that's the hope."

She heard it in his voice. Very likely everyone in the castle would be fine, but he was worried about his tenants, his neighbors. Jimmy would have approved.

She started. That was the first time in days she'd thought about Jimmy. Was her heart starting to heal at last?

Funny. Just telling Jane and the girls about his plans eased the tight muscles in his shoulders, as if a burden had been lifted. But he couldn't rest easy just yet. The true test of the lock would be when the river rose.

"We shouldn't keep you," Jane said. "But it sounds like a grand plan. General Wellington's sappers would be jealous. They were always figuring how to go over or under a moat."

"I imagine they were." He stroked the horse's neck, but he knew he was only delaying their departure a moment. "Enjoy your ride, ladies."

He watched as they turned the horses and ambled back the way they had come.

"Good for their ladyships to see you taking an active interest in the land," Willard said as Alaric joined him near the lock.

"It's their home as well," Alaric agreed. He nodded to the chain. "I think we have it this time. Let's give it a try."

"You heard His Grace," Willard called to the waiting men. "Open the gates."

The mechanism was designed to allow a single man to operate it. Willard had organized the local militiamen to staff it, so it could be opened day or night. The fellow on duty now, a veteran with one wooden leg from the knee down, set the process in motion. Slowly, nearly too slowly for Alaric, the chain tightened on the capstan. Each clank, each purr of the machinery, made him tense anew. But the gates eased open, and the river tumbled in. Maybe this really would work.

Only when he'd seen the gates close again successfully did he feel comfortable leaving his steward and riding Decatur back to the castle. He even gave the gelding his head, letting him run with the wind. The air felt clean, moist, winter's chill gone. It wouldn't be long now. He could only hope they were ready.

Quayle took Decatur's reins as Alaric swung down from the saddle.

"Everything all right with Mrs. Kimball?" his master of horse asked.

Alaric shook his head. "Don't tell me. She doesn't want the girls to ride sidesaddle."

Quayle frowned. "She never said as much to me."

"Then let's not give her any ideas," Alaric told him, giving the horse a pat. "Was there something else concerning you?"

The older man nodded to a groom, who came to take the horse for its rubdown. "Have a look at Lady Belle's unicorn, will you?"

Alaric fell into step beside him. The white horse pranced around the exercise pen as if eager to run. "She looks well. That's not why you brought me here."

"No, Your Grace," Quayle murmured, hand on the top rail of the fence. "We had a little trouble this morning. It's not my place to deal with the indoor staff, so I've never said a word to Simmons when he escorts the little ladies to see me, even if he seems a bit hard on them at times."

He thought he knew where this was going. "I take it Mrs. Kimball had no such trouble."

"Ordered him out of the schoolroom, she did, and I'd have done the same. What sort of man threatens a little girl with spiders in her bed?"

Spiders. A terrified little girl screaming in the night with no one to comfort her. The world quieted. The blue sky seemed to be turning red, but he knew the approaching storm was inside him. He thanked his master of horse and headed for the house.

Parsons met him at the door. "Your Grace, I must speak to you about Mrs. Kimball."

Alaric drew up short. "Is this about Simmons?"

Parsons sighed. "Yes, Your Grace. He's been assigned to the nursery for six months now, brought in on the recommendation of Her Grace. You know why he was hired."

He knew. The Simmons family had been the one his father had insisted on evicting. Culling, he'd called it, as if uprooting a family was akin to selling an extra calf from the herd. When the man's son had approached Willard about a position, explaining that his father and mother were gone and all he wanted was to return to the place where he'd been raised, Alaric had agreed to hire him. Alaric was the duke now. He had every right to soften his father's harsh edicts.

Yet he knew what his father would say now. Alaric had given Simmons a chance, acted from his heart, not his head, and look at the results.

"I remember why Simmons returned to the island," he told the butler. "But being a long-time tenant cannot excuse his behavior."

Parsons frowned. "No one's ever complained about his service before, yet Mrs. Kimball insists that he be given another post. He insists she is incompetent for hers."

"Mrs. Kimball is incorrect," Alaric said, and no one could have missed the triumph that flashed across the butler's face. "Simmons is not to be given another post. He is to be discharged. Pay him what he is owed, and tell him I want him out of the castle by morning."

Parsons stared at him. "But Your Grace…"

Alaric met the fellow's gaze. "Careful, Parsons. You are trying my patience. You are in charge of the indoor staff. Either you knew Simmons was mistreating my daughters and doing nothing, or you failed to see the damage being done under your own nose. Neither inspires confidence in you."

The butler turned white. "Of course not, Your Grace. I will keep a closer eye on all the staff, I promise. I would never want anything to happen to those dear girls."

"Good. Then send Simmons packing, because if I see him before you do, I won't be responsible for my actions."

He was still steaming when he returned downstairs a short while later, having changed out of his dirty trousers and boots. He'd thought about going to his daughters, apologizing in person, but he'd wondered whether that might only make matters worse. He'd followed Evangeline's advice, left the girls to the care of others, mostly women. The one man in the mix had failed them, and he couldn't convince himself it was entirely Simmons' fault.

Until Simmons broke into the library.

He still wore the livery of the House of Wey, but his olive coat was askew, and his shirt was untucked. Parsons and another footman puffed in his wake.

"I won't let you do this," Simmons shouted at Alaric, face florid. "I won't be forced off the island again."

Alaric rose slowly, met the fellow's outraged glare.

"I never understood why my father evicted yours," he said. "But if his lack of judgement was half as grave as yours, then I stand by his decision. And my own."

Parsons took hold of one arm, the footman the other. Simmons shook them off.

"It's that governess. She's lying. Can't you see she's wrapped you around her finger?"

Alaric stiffened, but Parsons succeeded in grabbing Simmons' arm again.

"So sorry, Your Grace," the butler gritted out, tugging the former footman away from the desk. "Come along, Simmons. Don't make matters worse for yourself."

Once more Simmons broke free, rushing toward the desk. Alaric met him, blocking his way forward, hand braced on his shoulder. "My decision has nothing to do with Mrs. Kimball. I will not have my daughters mistreated. You had a duty to them, and you failed. You can walk out of this house of your own volition, or I will throw you out. Choose wisely."

Simmons eyed him, the muscles in his face working. He raised his head. "I'll go, but you haven't seen the last of me."

"Yes, Mr. Simmons," Alaric said, "I have. Because my next act as magistrate for this district will be to have you clapped in irons to be tried at the next assize."

Simmons turned and strode from the library.

"Thank you, Your Grace," Parsons said, face glistening with sweat. "I'll just make sure he leaves." He and the other footman hurried in pursuit.

Alaric drew in a breath. He'd rarely had to discharge staff or agents. The people he'd had chosen or inherited from his father were largely reliable, even-tempered. One or two had needed encouragement to do their tasks efficiently, but never had he encountered such belligerence. The fellow would bear watching.

Because Alaric refused to be derelict in his own duty again.

CHAPTER FOURTEEN

The next few days were surprisingly peaceful in the schoolroom. The girls went about their routine and practiced hard for the recital on Friday. Jane never saw Simmons again, but Callie reported that Betsy said he had been let go. Apparently, he'd made quite a scene, vowing revenge on her, Mr. Parsons, and Alaric. She couldn't regret that she'd refused his service. Percy, the new nursery footman, a gangly lad with brown hair and freckles, seemed utterly awed to be serving the girls. She had to be careful they didn't take advantage of their privilege, for he was wont to do their least bidding with puppy-like adoration.

Mr. Parsons was nearly as helpful. He stopped by the schoolroom several times a day to enquire if there was anything she needed. If even a chair was out of place, he'd glare at Percy, who would rush to make it right. Cook sent up healthful meals, the duchess was pleasant over tea, and Alaric had been everything kind and supportive.

He always looked up eagerly when she came to make her nightly reports. Sometimes they played chess. He had beat her at least twice, but he never pressed his advantage, as if he was loath to let the game end. Another time, he had books waiting on the polished desk, historical and scientific tomes he thought might be of interest to the girls.

"And one I'm sure Mr. Parsons and my mother would approve of—*The History of the House of Wey*." He'd leaned closer, smile playing about his lips. "My grandfather wrote it. I suggest it for nights when you're having trouble falling asleep."

She'd found it far more interesting than that. It seemed the original tower had been built to protect this section of the river from invaders centuries ago, and the Dryden family had been doing its duty ever since. The previous duke had gone to some pains to trace his proud lineage, and she wasn't entirely surprised to see a princess or two among the duchesses. The former Duke of Wey had also delineated crop yields, the number of lambs and foals, and the loyal retainers and tenants of the castle. She saw several familiar names, Quayle and Simmons among them. And she could not help noticing the many years when it was recorded, "Small yields this year. Lost three fields and four lives to the floods."

"It seems you have cause for concern," she told him the next evening. "Can nothing be done?"

"Our best hope is the lock," he said. But he rose to go to one of the larger bookcases, returning with an old map, which he spread on the desk.

"Look here," he said, and Jane came around to stand beside him. "This shows our reach of the Thames fifty years ago. Do you see the island?"

Jane frowned, bending closer to the brittle parchment. The river was braided and curving here, with any number of pieces of land isolated along its shore. "Is that it?"

"No." He bent closer as well, shoulder brushing hers. "Here's our island."

"Truly? It looks so small."

"That's because it has grown in the last half century. By my estimate, deposits from the river have added two feet to the western edge, enough to be noticed. My neighbors, however, have not fared so well."

Jane cocked her head. "Neighbors? Those islands on the map to the west of you—I didn't see them when we rode out that way."

"That's because they no longer exist," he said, sadness lacing his words. "They were swept away by the river. I'm determined that our lands will not suffer the same fate."

She turned to look at him to voice her approval, and the words fell away. He was so close, she could see the fine lines around his eyes, the hint of blue in the jade. Another few inches, and their lips might meet.

As if he knew it as well, he straightened. "So, now you see why the lock is so important to me."

Yes, she did. And she had a feeling she also knew why he was becoming so important to her.

She put the matter from her mind as best she could, but it quickly became apparent her charges had another matter to concern them.

Friday morning, Larissa refused to come out of her room until she'd tried on every gown in her wardrobe, twice. Callie paced the schoolroom mumbling and wringing her hands. Belle curled up in Jane's chair and hid her face in her arm.

"If you're that concerned about singing," Jane finally told them, "I'll just cancel the recital."

"Nooo!" Larissa went down on her knees, wrinkling the blue silk gown she'd finally consented to wear. "Oh, please, Mrs. Kimball, we may never convince Father again."

Jane helped her to her feet. "He's not an ogre, you know. He won't eat you."

"Grandmother might," Callie said with a shudder that set her yellow skirts to swinging.

Belle burst into tears. "I don't want Grandmother to eat me!"

"No one is eating anyone," Jane said sternly. "You are merely to sing for your family, providing them a moment of joy away from the toil of their lives."

Larissa sniffed. "Grandmother doesn't toil."

"Father does," Callie said. "I saw him."

"Go to your rooms and practice your pieces," Jane said, feeling a headache coming on.

By a quarter to two, she was just as jittery as the girls. *Teach them to sing*, he'd said, as if it were that easy. What songs did she know besides the hymns her father had taught her and the bawdy ballads belted out around a campfire by cavalrymen afraid they'd meet their Maker in the morning? Her father had never encouraged her to sing; Jimmy had just hugged her tight when she'd tried to join in. Alaric and his mother would listen to the girls and know her for a fraud.

A piano wouldn't fit up the narrow stairs, so they had no accompaniment. She'd had Percy set up two armchairs from the girls' rooms near the worktable, with ample view of the room. As the time approached, she adjusted the collar on Larissa's gown, tucked a hair behind Callie's ear, and wiped jam off Belle's cheek with the sleeve of her own gown. Three pairs of eyes in white faces gazed back at her. Jane gave them her best smile.

"You will be marvelous, and even if for some reason you aren't, I am still very proud of you."

Their smiles were as weak as their confidence.

Precisely at two, Alaric entered the schoolroom, the duchess on his arm. Percy hurried to escort them to their seats. Alaric sent his daughters a smile as he sat. The duchess inclined her head.

"You may begin," she said. "Larissa first, I think, then Calantha and Abelona."

Apparently, the duchess had decided not to accept the change in names. But it was her decree more than anything, Jane thought, that made her granddaughters exchange panicked glances.

"Actually, Your Grace," Jane said, "we have a program all laid out. Lady Belle will start." She nodded to Belle, who stepped forward and cupped her hands, one atop the other.

"Believe me, if all those endearing young charms,

Which I gaze on so fondly today,
Were to change by tomorrow, and flee in my arms,
Like fairy-gifts, fading away!
Thou wouldst still be ador'd as this moment thou art,
Let thy loveliness fade as it will;
And, around the dear ruin, each wish of my heart
Would entwine itself verdantly still!"

How the little girl had struggled over the big words, hanging on Jane's arm as Jane explained the meaning. Now Jane nodded encouragement as Belle went into the second verse, then glanced at Alaric and the duchess. His smile remained on his face, but it was once more that polite look she was coming to dislike. His mother was turning whiter with each note.

What had she done wrong this time?

Jane Kimball had no ear for music. It could be the only explanation for the tuneless cacophony coming from his youngest daughter's mouth. He'd heard Belle sing from time to time, the little ditties of childhood, so he knew she had some facility. She was clearly singing what she'd been taught.

She finished, and he applauded, earning him a grateful smile from Jane and a grin from Belle. His mother regarded him as if he'd gone mad, but she shifted on the chair and prepared to give her attention to Callie.

His middle daughter fared no better. He knew the song, an old country ballad that bore no resemblance to the tune Callie attempted. Once again, he applauded, and this time his mother managed a nod that might be taken as praise.

At last Larissa stepped forward, and he steeled himself for another few moments of torture.

She glanced at Jane. "I'd like to sing something other than what we practiced, Mrs. Kimball."

"Go right ahead, Lady Larissa," Jane said. "I trust you to

choose something appropriate."

Larissa nodded and faced front again. And when she began to sing, he was certain a trained orchestra accompanied her.

"O my love is like a red, red rose
That's newly sprung in June.
O my love is like the melody
That's sweetly play'd in tune."

And it was in tune. In tune and in time and sung with a sweetness that made him catch his breath. Larissa could have no understanding of such a love, that mountains and seas could not move. He'd never felt such a love himself, yet he found his gaze drawn to Jane. Her lower lip was trembling. As Larissa finished the ballad, Jane wiped at her eyes, and he had to fight the desire to hold her close, to comfort her.

Beside him, the duchess clapped her gloves together with enthusiasm, and he bestirred himself. There was clearly only one way forward now.

He rose. "Mrs. Kimball, my dears, well done. I've never heard such music."

"That's certainly the truth," his mother muttered.

"I'm so impressed with what you've done," he continued, "and I can see that each of you has a gift. It would be a shame not to pursue it further. I will enquire about hiring a voice instructor."

Larissa beamed, and Callie and Belle jumped up and down, even though he was fairly sure they had no idea what he meant. Jane signaled to Percy, who brought in a cart with tea and cakes.

"That bad, were they?" she murmured as they stayed out of earshot of Callie.

"That good," he assured her. "However, I realized I put an undue burden on you when I suggested that you teach singing as well."

"*Hm*," she said, as if she saw right through him, but she went to stop Belle from helping herself to another slice of cake.

That evening, still well pleased with himself, Alaric looked up from reviewing the book of accounts his steward had provided to find his butler paused in the doorway. "Parsons, if you have come to complain about Mrs. Kimball, I will sack you."

His butler's face crumbled, but he recovered quickly. "I merely wished to inform Your Grace that Mr. Mayes has arrived from London. He is seeing to his horse but asked to speak with you as soon as possible. He specified that you be alone. Shall I tell Mrs. Kimball to delay her report?"

Disappointment shot through him, but he nodded. "Send Mr. Mayes to me as soon as he's ready."

Julian strode in a short while later. His normally dapper bottle green jacket showed signs of his travel, the wrinkles pronounced in the lamplight.

"What's happened?" Alaric demanded, rising.

Julian threw himself into the chair opposite the desk. "Nothing good. I came as soon as I had proof."

His stomach tightened. "Proof? Proof of what?"

Julian met his gaze, his own hard and implacable. Here was the solicitor who won difficult cases for his clients. "Proof that your Mrs. Kimball is not what she seems."

He made himself remain still. "Indeed? I find that hard to believe. Is she not the daughter of a deceased vicar from Berkshire?"

"That much is true," Julian acknowledged, though Alaric thought reluctantly. "I'm trying to confirm her past employment with Colonel Travers. He and his wife are on the Continent, and the staff they left behind are disinclined to talk."

Unlike his staff, if Callie's reports were any indication.

"Then I fail to see the problem," Alaric said aloud.

"The problem," Julian said, eyes narrowing, "is that she

has deceived you. She came highly recommended from this Fortune Employment Agency, but her past is considerably murkier. I sent a man to her hometown. No less than Mr. Kimball's mother reports that she was a troubled child, always getting into mischief. My man brought back tales of theft, destruction of property, disrespecting her betters, and seduction."

Cold slithered through him. He'd been wrong about Simmons, and look at the hurt his daughters had endured. Could he have been so very wrong about Jane?

"You're certain we're talking about the same woman?" Alaric pressed. "Jane Kimball, cavalry officer's widow."

"It's the same woman, all right, only she's no widow."

He started. "Her husband is alive?"

"Kimball's dead," Julian assured him. "He fell on the Peninsula along with many of his regiment. But here's the thing. The lady ran off with him when she was only sixteen, and I can't find any record of a marriage. Moreover, the staff at the Clarendon Square house she claimed belongs to this Miss Thorn refused to acknowledge the lady or the employment agency, and the neighbors on either side assure me the house belonged to Lady Winhaven before her death six months ago. Let me tell you, that was a nasty business."

The cold had crept into his heart. "What do you mean?"

"A colleague prosecuted the case. Lady Winhaven had a sizeable income from her mother. Her nephew was fully expecting to inherit. She died under questionable circumstances, leaving everything to her companion instead. The names were hushed up to prevent further damage to the lady's reputation, but I can't help wondering whether your Mrs. Kimball might not be involved."

Alaric shook his head. "Not Jane, I tell you, but there's clearly something wrong here."

Julian slapped his hands down on the arms of the chair. "My sentiments exactly."

Alaric rose. "Have Parsons see to a room for you. I'll speak to Mrs. Kimball immediately."

And assure himself every bad word Julian had spoken about her was untrue. Anything less was unthinkable.

CHAPTER FIFTEEN

Jane's head was high as she descended the stairs that evening to make her report to Alaric. She had wondered about the delay, but Callie reported that Percy had mentioned Mr. Mayes was visiting again. She could only hope she'd have a moment alone with Alaric before the two men started a new chess game.

She had every reason to be pleased. She could only call the recital a triumph, and the girls felt the same way. Even the duchess had been complimentary. And as for Alaric, the kind way he'd listened, his praise to his girls, his teases to her, could only warm her heart. Surely things would improve from here.

Her first hint that something wasn't as right as she'd hoped was Parson's face. He was smiling as she approached the library, and it wasn't a particularly welcoming sight. "His Grace is expecting you," he said as he opened the door for her.

Well, of course he was. She'd been making these reports for nearly a fortnight now. Yet the way Parsons said it, brows lifted and eyes alight, suggested that she ought to be expecting her doom. She moved into the library, keeping her steps steady for all she wanted to rush forward and demand an explanation.

Alaric was seated behind the desk, the lamplight throwing his face in sharp relief. "Mrs. Kimball," he said.

So precise, so cold. Had she done something to offend? She came to a stop at her usual spot. "Your Grace. Thank you again for attending the recital. The girls are in alt."

The tension in him softened only the slightest. "It was my pleasure."

She struggled to continue with her report. "Everything else is going well. We spent some time this afternoon on deportment. Lady Larissa was delighted."

He inclined his head. "I imagine she was. Where did you learn deportment?"

Odd question. She'd already told him her qualifications. "I'm the daughter of a vicar. No one needs to know more about how to behave properly in company."

He rose and came around the desk, and she very nearly retreated. "Will you walk with me, Mrs. Kimball?"

In such a mood, she wasn't sure she wanted to go anywhere with him, but he glanced at Parsons, and suddenly she understood. They might stroll together through the house, where anyone could come upon them, but he could not speak to her alone without tongues wagging.

"Of course, Your Grace," she said, putting her hand on the arm he offered.

He led her out of the library, Parsons trotting behind like a loyal spaniel. Jane tried to stand tall, glide along like a proper lady, but her legs felt a bit shaky. Surely, she'd done nothing worth dismissal. She couldn't think of anything that even warranted a scold. She'd been as good as gold of late.

He said nothing until they had climbed the stairs to the gallery and stopped before a painting. The young lady with hair as gold as Belle's sat regally in her chair, and even though forty years must have passed, Jane recognized the serene features of the duchess. Glancing back, she noticed Parsons below in the entry, watching.

"What's happened?" she murmured to Alaric, facing front once more.

"Mr. Mayes returned from London this evening," he murmured. "He brought distressing news."

"About Miss Thorn?" Jane asked, forcing herself to keep her gaze on the painting.

"And other matters. The staff at the house on Clarendon Square refuse to acknowledge her existence."

Jane frowned. "I'd tell you her staff was merely being close-lipped to protect her, but her butler Mr. Cowls is worse than Betsy when it comes to gossip. Where could she be?"

"I share your concern," he said. "You should also know that I spoke with my mother regarding Miss Thorn. I was under the impression Her Grace had hired the Fortune Employment Agency. She was under the impression I had done the hiring. So, how did Miss Thorn know of our needs, our situation?"

Jane shook her head. "I have no idea. Maybe she was a guardian angel, sent when I needed her most."

"And why did you need a miracle like that, Jane?"

She couldn't tell him about the colonel. It made her feel dirty just remembering. "My husband was gone, my position ended. I wasn't sure what to do, who to ask for help."

"So, you chose a stranger to see to your future?"

Put that way, she sounded daft. Desperate would have been more like it. "She seemed like a good sort. And Fortune believed in her, and in me. She even liked you."

"You would ask me to put my faith in a cat?"

"The cat's probably better odds than me," Jane said.

He sighed as he moved on to the portrait of a scowling fellow who bore no resemblance to anyone, and they were likely all thankful for that. "Jane, you are such a puzzle. I've never met anyone like you. You speak your mind even when it's in your best interest to be silent. You have shown my daughters love and respect even when they treat you badly. What am I to make of you?"

Jane patted his arm. "I'm an unlikely governess, I'll grant you that. But I'll do right by your girls. I promise."

He regarded her, eyes the color of the tree behind the couple in the next painting. "I've been given a report of you as well."

Her heart slammed against her chest. "A report?"

"It isn't good," he said. "I want you to convince me it's a lie."

Convince him? How? She took a step back. "What were you told?"

"You caused trouble in your village."

She barked a laugh. "Well, that's no lie. I never could keep quiet, as you noted."

"What of thefts? Destruction of property?"

She stared at him. "Who told you that rubbish?"

"A reputable source, from your town."

Jane shook her head. "The other Mrs. Kimball, no doubt, my husband's stepmother."

He nodded. "Her name was mentioned."

Jane sighed. "She hates me. To hear her talk, I convinced her Jimmy to run away instead of the other way around. If she intends to accuse me to all and sundry of theft and other things, though, I'd like to see her proof."

"I wouldn't." He caught up her hands. "Jane, you are quickly becoming indispensable to my daughters' happiness. I cannot have rumors of scandal following you."

"Bit late for that," Jane quipped. "I ran away from home, eloped to Scotland to be wed without the banns, and spent years following the drum with a mess of cocky, cantankerous cavalrymen. Those are more than enough ingredients for any scandal broth. And I wouldn't change a moment of it."

He released her. "You wouldn't be the woman you are without it."

If he was anyone else, if she was anyone else, she might have thrown herself in his arms, told him how much he was coming to mean to her, how much she wanted to stay. But he was her employer and a duke. She had no right to tell him anything.

"So, what will you do?" she asked, watching him. "The only people who could confirm my statements are missing or dead. Can you accept me on faith alone?"

That polite smile was firmly in place, and for a moment she was certain he'd discharge her then and there. He had to have realized she was even farther than he'd first thought from the proper lady Larissa wanted for a governess, the submissive servant the duchess demanded, the upright lady he deserved. He had every reason to send her packing.

"I prefer evidence to faith," he said. "But, from what I have observed, you are the woman my daughters need— strong, sure, firm in her convictions."

Jane drew in a breath, relief cresting like a wave over her. "Thank you. Then I'd like your permission to go to London and learn what's happened to Miss Thorn."

Alaric stared at her. He'd been an inch away from including himself as one of the people who needed her. Already, his conscience was shouting at him to rely on Julian's report, his father's admonitions, not the flimsy yearnings of his heart, a little-used organ. He'd extended his trust, a place in his home, and she wanted to leave?

"I could take the girls, if you'd like," she continued, as if she had no idea of the havoc she was wreaking to his ordered thoughts. "We could make it an educational trip, see the sights. The British Museum, the Tower, Hyde Park." The gleam reappeared in her eyes. "Astley's Amphitheatre."

Something leaped inside him at the mention of the famous riding exhibition. By the way her smile curved up, she knew it. What was wrong with him? He wasn't a boy on holiday. He was still struggling to trust her, could feel a dozen misgivings. He couldn't allow her to leave and take

NEVER DOUBT A DUKE

his daughters with her.

Unless he accompanied them.

He dismissed the idea immediately. He had too much to do here. Willard and the tenants had presented a plan for the crops this year, and he should review it, give them his thoughts. His agents in London had sent recommendations for new investments, some of which must be decided quickly to maximize return. Mr. Harden had complained that someone had been sleeping in his barn. Alaric should request volunteer constables and set up a system of rotation to ensure the safety of his tenants. The rains would start any day, the waters rising. He should be here to make sure the lock worked as intended.

"Your Grace?" she asked. "It will only take a week. The girls are sure to enjoy it. And the expense shouldn't be too great; we could stay in the Clarendon Square house you mentioned."

He couldn't help his laugh. "Calculating the price of the silver already?"

She grinned back. "And the plate. Never forget the plate."

Larissa was demanding, Callie pleading, and Belle a wheedler. He could have withstood any of them where his duty was concerned. Yet that grin, that gleam, and he was ready to throw duty out the window.

Dangerous thought. Dangerous feeling. All his life, he'd been taught what was expected of him. He was to lead an empire of estates and tenants, acres and farm shares, horses and cows and sheep, produce and mines. He was to do everything to safeguard them, increase them. He was to do nothing that might hinder their prosperity and wellbeing in any way.

Not even fall in love with an unlikely governess.

Everything in him demanded that he refuse, that he send her back to her own duties, that he order Julian to keep investigating until Alaric was sure of the truth. It didn't matter that he preferred Jane's company, reveled in her wit.

His enjoyment, his pleasure was immaterial. He had never allowed them to take precedence. Just as he'd never allowed his daughters to take precedence, until Jane had appeared in their lives.

"Five days," he said. "To travel to London, see the sights, and return. The girls can ride in the landau, the servants and bags in a second carriage. We can return with Julian, who is visiting. Very likely Her Grace will want to join us."

Her grin widened. "Us?"

He nodded. "Yes, Jane. Us. I intend to accompany you. Someone has to protect the silver and the plate."

Now, if he could just find a way to protect his heart.

CHAPTER SIXTEEN

A nd so, Jane returned to London. The trip could not have been more different. Instead of Miss Thorn and Fortune beside her, she rode with the girls, Alaric, and Mr. Mayes, the solicitor's horse tied behind and the duchess coming in her own coach. While Alaric was pleasant and the girls beyond excited, Mr. Mayes kept a narrow-eyed gaze on Jane, as if expecting her to pull out a pistol and rob them like a highwayman.

She supposed he had reason. He'd been the one to bring the poor report of her, after all. Mrs. Kimball had filled his head with tales of the brazen girl she'd imagined Jane to be. Jane didn't like thinking how he would react if he heard Mrs. Travers's complaints. She could only hope her former mistress would keep her vow to have nothing further to do with Jane.

She thought Mr. Mayes might go about his business once they reached London, but he insisted on accompanying them on nearly every outing. Trying to protect Alaric and the girls, no doubt. At least Alaric agreed to let her off her duties the first full day in London so she could search for her benefactress. He'd even left the girls with Her Grace so he could accompany Jane.

But the white stone town house on the southern edge of Clarendon Square was quiet when Jane and Alaric approached it. Now that she had seen his town house, an impressive edifice set off by itself on the northern edge, she too wondered at the proximity.

"She hadn't lived here long," Jane said as they climbed the stairs for the green-lacquered door. "I remember seeing boxes in unused rooms, as if she was still getting settled."

"Mr. Mayes mentioned the house used to belong to a Lady Winhaven. An earl's widow in Cumberland, if memory serves." He raised his gloved hand to rap with the brass door knocker, which had a rather fierce face of a snarling lion.

Jane beamed at the elderly butler who answered, relief flowing through her. "Mr. Cowls, it's good to see you again. Is Miss Thorn at home?"

The tall fellow blinked bleary blue eyes and trained his gaze on Jane's face. There was no recognition. "All deliveries are to be made at the back," he intoned.

Alaric drew himself up. "We are not tradesmen, sir."

He transferred his rheumy gaze to the duke. "The lady of the house donates to charity only through her solicitor. Good day."

He started to close the door, but Alaric stepped forward, card held between two fingers.

"I am the Duke of Wey," he said, and no one seeing him in his dove-grey morning coat, black trousers, and perfectly tied cravat could have doubted him. "Take my card to your mistress. She will want to see me."

Mr. Cowls accepted the card, squinted at the writing, then glanced back up at Alaric. "I will place your card with the others requiring my mistress' attention, Your Grace, but the lady of the house is not at home."

"When will she be at home?" Jane asked, knowing that many aristocrats used the phrase to mean they refused to receive visitors but were, in fact, upstairs with their feet to the fire.

"I cannot say, madam," he replied. And he shut the door with surprising alacrity.

They tried again later that day and at odd times the next two days, but his answer was always the same. They received a similar story at the coffee shop where Jane had first met Miss Thorn. The owners remembered the lady and her cat fondly but could not guess where they might have gone.

"It makes no sense," Alaric insisted when he took Jane to Julian Mayes's place of business, a neat office near Westminster. "Surely even in London, ladies cannot simply disappear."

"They can if they know the right people," Mr. Mayes told him darkly, gaze still on Jane.

"By the way she was able to uncover things," Jane added, "Miss Thorn knows the right people. Something frightened her into hiding. I'd like to know what."

"So would I," the solicitor assured her.

So would Alaric, Jane thought. The fact that she had arrived on his doorstep with nothing and no one to recommend her had to undercut his confidence in her. Certainly Mr. Mayes suspected her of wrongdoing. But, unless Miss Thorn wished to be found, Jane was on her own.

"Another card for your collection," Cowls said, bending to offer Meredith the duke's calling card. "I believe that is four, now."

Meredith hunkered down in the satin-striped armchair near the withdrawing room's marble hearth, Fortune curled in her lap. "Throw it away or toss it in the fire. I have no use for it."

Her butler made his slow, steady way to the credenza against the yellow wall to lay the card on a silver salver there. "They will only return," he predicted. "Mrs. Kimball seems quite distressed. I dislike having to prevaricate to her."

Fortune wiggled, and Meredith opened her arms so the

cat could drop to the carpeted floor. "It cannot be helped. The duke brought this on when he enlisted the aid of that odious solicitor."

Turning, Cowl gazed off in the middle distance, as if he were seeing something far away or long ago or both. "I always like Mr. Mayes. A shame he never returned for little Mary. It would have been a good match."

Despite her best intentions, she felt the memories stealing over her as well. She'd known Julian Mayes all her life, admired him since she was a girl. How amazing to discover he'd felt the same way.

"But why must we wait to wed?" she'd asked, as eager as any sixteen-year-old for life to start now. "We have pledged our love. I'm sure Mother would allow us to marry."

He'd caught up her hands, holding them against his chest. "I can't support you, not yet. Give me time to make my mark in London. I'm to start work at a solicitor's firm next week. Once I've established myself, I can treat you as you deserve."

She'd believed him, had even thrown his name at her cousin Nigel the day he'd come to take her home. The sniveling weasel had only laughed.

"With no estate and no dowry? Mr. Mayes has far better choices."

"He'll come for me," she'd bragged. "I've written to him. It's only a matter of time."

But he hadn't come. The little time Nigel had given her to remain in her home had passed. In the end, she'd had no choice but to accept the offer of an old friend of her long-dead father, a man she had never met, to come serve his sister as companion.

Twelve years of indignities, cruelty. Twelve years cut off from everything and everyone she'd ever known. Twelve years of utter servitude. After all that, who would have expected Lady Winhaven to bequeath her such a blessing? Now she need bow to no one.

Especially not for the unreliable Julian Mayes.

"Mr. Mayes was not the man for me," she told her butler. The words must have been sharper than she'd intended, for he blinked himself out his reverie. "Do not forget who Lady Winhaven's nephew had represent him when he attempted to contest the will and prove me a villain."

"Mr. Mayes has had his own firm for some time now," Cowls reminded her, moving about the room and straightening pictures and figurines as he did so. "He may not be cognizant of what cases his former mentor has taken."

"No, but it would require little to connect the Mary Rose he knew to the Meredith Thorn who barely avoided being accused of murder. And then where would Jane be? Where would any of my clients be? We are far safer this way."

As if she disagreed, Fortune raised her head and stalked to the door of the room. Sitting on her haunches, she leveled a look at Meredith.

"Quite right," Cowls said in his wheezy voice, addressing himself to the cat. "I never knew Miss Mary to lack for courage. But times change. Might I interest you in a nice saucer of cream?"

Fortune scampered out the door behind him.

Meredith eyed the fire. Surely, she hadn't lost her courage. She was merely being practical. Jane had professed herself pleased with her situation. Why unsettle things by making a sudden appearance?

Or were things already unsettled? Did the duke doubt Jane because of Meredith? Was that why he'd brought Jane to London, accompanied her around the square? Was Meredith doing more harm than good by avoiding them?

Perhaps she should take a chance and call on Jane, just to be certain everything was fine. And she would be equally certain to do so at a time when she would avoid meeting the duke or Julian Mayes.

Miss Thorn's disappearance was the one concern overlaying Jane's delight in seeing the capital in the company of Alaric and the girls. Everything went so well, even with Mr. Mayes' continued surveillance. For one thing, though the duchess kept busy with friends for the most part, the elderly staff at the London house were welcoming and eager to help.

"His Grace stays with us so infrequently," the round-cheeked housekeeper Mrs. Winters confided in Jane, "and never before with the darling girls. It's a real treat to be of use."

For another, the house sat a few blocks from Hyde Park and had its own mews, so they were able to ride or walk every day.

"Though I miss Unicorn," Belle said, eyeing the prancing iron unicorn mounted on the crest on the gates of the park's main entrance.

Most of all, though, seeing London through Larissa, Callie, and Belle's eyes made everything seem wonderful. They gazed up and up at the stuffed giraffe on the top floor of the British Museum, leaned over the railings to watch the great ships pass under London Bridge, and ran through the just-risen daffodils in Hyde Park holding hands. Every day was a new adventure, a chance to see and try and do. She could tell Alaric felt the same way, for that smile his mother so prized hovered about his lips on a regular basis, and never more than when they took the girls to see Astley's.

Astley's Amphitheatre was located on the other side of the Thames, a short carriage drive away. Though the equestrian display generally opened after Easter, the owner had consented to start early with so many lords and their families in town for Parliament. The great dome curved over a dirt-floored arena more than forty feet across, with a stage and painted scenery three stories tall along the back and a pit for the orchestra in between. Four tiers of seats soared around the circumference, crowded with ladies and gentlemen eager for spectacle, more than two thousand people, according to Mr. Mayes, who had accompanied them. With Alaric on one side and him on the other side of the girls, Jane had no concern for the boisterous crowd.

Neither did the girls. They cheered for the juggler, applauded the brave bear tamer, and laughed over the antics of the clowns. Even Mr. Mayes praised Madam Chivka, who rode with the reins in her teeth while twirling flaming batons.

"She should ride for Wellington," Alaric murmured, breath brushing Jane's ear. She shared his smile.

Finally, the ring cleared, and the master of ceremonies stepped to the front of the stage. "Ladies and gentlemen, Astley's is proud to present our wild allies of the Peninsula, the Russian Cossacks!"

The troop came pounding into the arena, whooping and hollering, their dark hair flying under their tall blue hats. Brandishing curved swords, they followed the rim of the space, dirt churning under the hooves of their shaggy mounts. Mr. Mayes gave them a rousing "Huzzah!" Belle shrank back against Jane, Callie watched mesmerized, and Larissa clasped her hands against her flat bosom. Alaric glanced at Jane with a grin that set her stomach to fluttering again.

It was the panorama. It had to be. She couldn't afford it to be anything else.

"But what's this?" the master of ceremonies cried. "Ladies and gentlemen, I have been given terrible news. Napoleon has crossed the Channel!"

Ice raced through her veins even as cries rang out on every side. No, it couldn't be! They'd fought for years, by sea and by land, to prevent that invasion. What would they do? How could she protect Alaric and the girls?

Before panic could do more than raise its ugly head, she realized her mistake. Likely old Boney was still wreaking havoc on the Peninsula, for surely he wasn't the short, stout fellow riding into the arena below, his French Corsairs right behind him. Drawing his cutlass, he charged at the Russians, who turned to meet their enemy. Swords flashed as steel rang on steel.

"It seems our valiant allies are faltering," the master of ceremonies lamented as the Cossacks began to tumble from their saddles, one going so far as to allow his horse to drag him through the dirt. "Can no one help them?"

Callie hopped to her feet. "I will!"

"Me too!" Belle cried, scrambling off her seat.

"Rule, Britannia!" Mr. Mayes shouted, rising as well.

"Shh!" Larissa scolded. "You'll spoil it."

But all around them, others took up the call. Men lifted their voices along with their top hats, ladies waved handkerchiefs. Alaric surged to his feet and added his voice to theirs. Larissa stared at him. Jane pulled her up.

"Look!" Jane pointed to the troop that entered the arena now. "It's the Dragoons!"

The master of ceremonies confirmed it. "But all is not lost. Here comes the Tenth Dragoons, the prince's own unit, with his Royal Highness leading the way."

She thought the muscular fellow in the front looked a great deal fitter than the frivolous fellow Alaric had described, but the others certainly followed him. They flattened the French, until the so-called Napoleon and the pretend prince faced off against each other.

"You can do it!" Callie called to the prince.

"Show no mercy!" Larissa cried.

"Do it for your unicorn!" Belle shouted.

Something touched Jane's hand, warm, secure. She wrapped her fingers around Alaric's and hung on tight.

The two men circled each other, sneering and snarling.

Napoleon tugged on the reins, and his horse reared, pawing the air.

"Coward!" Mr. Mayes called. "Face him like a man!"

The clash of their steel echoed over the cries of the crowd. Then the prince's sword flashed, and Napoleon fell.

The crowd erupted—shouting, cheering, applauding, stomping their feet. As the prince rode the circle, hands up in victory, the French and Russians dragged their men from the dirt.

"I knew he'd win," Larissa said. "Princes always win."

Jane was more aware of the hand cradling hers. Did Alaric know he was touching her? Surely he could tell the hand he held was bigger than his daughters'. She glanced his way, but his gaze was on the ring, and she'd never seen such wistfulness. He deserved to have become a cavalryman, to ride to defend his country. He deserved better than to be shut up in a library, making decisions that would daunt other men.

He deserved a helpmate, a wife, someone who would love and cherish him, encourage him when things became difficult. If only she could be that woman.

Alaric kept Jane's hand in his as he chivied his little band out of the building for the carriage. It was only practical, after all. He wouldn't want to lose any of them in the crowd. Anyone who could afford the price of a ticket flocked to the famed amphitheater. He'd seen street mongers brush shoulders with viscounts. He felt a little like a sheepdog as it was, even with Julian alongside.

"Our coachman will find us," Alaric told Jane. "Stay close."

"Right at your side, Your Grace," she promised.

And she had been. He had never enjoyed London— the crowds, the noise, the demands on his time. He'd had to make an appearance in Parliament, which had only resulted in a throng of petitions to support this upcoming bill, that worthy cause. Julian had brought several issues to his attention. And Society had attempted to impinge on his time. Even now, before the Season had started in earnest, a dozen invitations lay waiting for his reply. A duke in need of a wife was always of interest.

Yet Jane had been a constant source of support. She kept an eye on the weather, reminded him that it hadn't done more than drizzle since they'd left. She arranged activities for the girls, kept him apprised of the schedule, and worked with Mrs. Winters to make sure meals and staff were available as needed.

And yet Miss Thorn's mysterious disappearance cast a shadow over Jane. Try as he might, he could not forget Julian's report. His friend remained wary; Alaric had noticed the number of times Julian frowned at Jane, as if trying to determine which woman graced Alaric's home— the loving, unorthodox governess or the lawless former minister's daughter, determined to take what she could from life.

The last few days should have been proof enough. Jane had been everything Alaric could have asked. Seeing the sights with her and the girls had opened his eyes to wonders he'd forgotten—the roar of the tiger in the Tower Zoo, sunlight shining on the Serpentine, the smell of roast chestnuts from the street vendors. He found himself nearly content for the first time in a long time. It was almost as if they were a family.

He reined in his thoughts. They could never be a family. Jane Kimball was the governess of his children. He owed her protection, respect, fair remuneration. He owed his daughters assurance that he had chosen their governess well. When he convinced himself to marry again, it would likely be to some fair flower of the aristocracy who had been trained since birth for her role in Society.

"That's a very big sigh," Jane said beside him. "Do you

want me and Larissa to go in search of the carriage?"

Julian stepped closer. "No need. It will be along shortly."

"Jane! Jane Kimball!"

Alaric turned to see three fellows striding toward them. Their navy uniforms had a scarlet blaze down the front, and their trousers boasted a gold stripe.

"You were in the panorama!" Callie cried.

"Not these boys," Jane said with a smile all around. "These are the real things. His Grace, Duke of Wey, Lady Larissa, Lady Calantha, Lady Abelona, Mr. Mayes, may I present Captains Montgomery, Fremont, and Holmes of the Twelfth Dragoons. Gentlemen, I serve His Grace as governess to these fine ladies."

They clapped their heels and bowed, the scarlet plumes on their black and red helmets fluttering. Alaric thought he heard Larissa sigh. At least, he hoped it was Larissa.

"Ladies, gentlemen," Montgomery said, russet mustache quivering. "Forgive the intrusion, but when we saw Jane, that is Mrs. Kimball, we had to pay our respects."

"I take it you know Mrs. Kimball well," Julian said with a look to Alaric, as if Jane's association with the cavalry was somehow more significant than having a husband who had ridden for glory.

Fremont nodded, blond hair glinting. "Great gun, is our Jane. Seen her stare down a cannon's mouth without blinking."

A cannon's mouth? Alaric couldn't help glancing at her. Pink was climbing in her cheeks.

"They're exaggerating," she insisted. "I wasn't the one riding neck for leather across the plains screaming like banshees and scaring the French into retreat."

"Indeed," Julian said. "I'm surprised to see you gentlemen here. I thought the Twelfth was called to Badajoz."

Now he even seemed suspicious of the cavalry. The action had been related in the papers.

"They let a few of us come home," Montgomery said.

"Wellington has old Boney on the run, just like in that show, eh your ladyships?"

Larissa and Callie nodded. Belle drew herself up. "I'll send him my unicorn to help. He'll be sure to win then."

"That's the spirit," Montgomery said. He turned to Alaric. "I wonder, Your Grace, would you mind if we borrowed Mrs. Kimball? We'll be back at the front shortly, facing our last moments. It would be good to speak with an old friend."

Again, Julian cast him a look. The cavalryman was doing it up rather brown, but he was right. In a war, a cavalryman knew that any charge might be his last. He ought to give the fellows some time alone with Jane, yet something made him want to keep her close.

"Now, now," Jane answered for him. "I can't go deserting my post. What would Wellington say?"

Montgomery opened his mouth, glanced at Julian, and seemed to think better of his words. "Well, I'm glad to see you're doing so well."

They all bowed with such respect she might have been the Queen Mother. Jane smiled fondly. Holmes, the youngest, face still sporting spots, emboldened himself to speak at last.

"I'm not sure when we'll see home again. Would you wait for me, Jane?"

Alaric wanted to put her safely behind him, inform the upstart he should move along. Jane would not be waiting for anyone but him.

He was only glad the words hadn't tumbled out of his mouth.

"Now, then, Johnny," she said with a sisterly cuff on his shoulder, "what would your dear Elena say? Off you go, and behave yourselves."

"Too late for that," Fremont said with a grin, but they bowed again and took themselves off. This time he was certain Larissa sighed.

NEVER DOUBT A DUKE   167

Callie elbowed Belle. "I think Larissa changed her mind. She doesn't want to marry a prince anymore. She wants to marry a cavalry officer."

Jane flushed, but Larissa shook her head. "No, I don't. Cavalry officers leave their wives behind."

"They do indeed," Jane murmured, gaze following her husband's comrades.

Something tightened inside him. She deserved a husband to support and cheer her, someone who would appreciate her canny insights and unique character.

"There's the coach," Jane said. "Come along, girls." She elbowed her way forward.

Julian caught Alaric's arm before he could follow. "Well? Will you accept that she isn't a proper governess?"

Alaric removed his hand. "No. You may prefer to doubt everyone you meet, but I have better ways to spend my time. I saw nothing out of keeping with the stories Jane has told me."

Julian sighed. "Then I'll just have to keep digging. I can't see you taken in, Wey. You deserve better."

Perhaps. But he couldn't help thinking that what he really wanted was Jane.

CHAPTER SEVENTEEN

Jane was leading the girls on a constitutional around Clarendon Square on a day that threatened rain when Miss Thorn appeared at last. Alaric was meeting with his London agents, and Her Grace was out visiting friends. Larissa had just passed the door of the town house Jane was still sure belonged to Miss Thorn when the green door opened, and out came her benefactress, Fortune up in her arms. The cat's grey fur exactly matched the grey of the poplin skirts peeking out from under the lavender redingote.

"There's Fortune!" Belle cried, and Jane reached out to hang on to her shoulder before the little girl could dart forward.

Miss Thorn didn't look the least surprised to see them, or the least embarrassed about not having recognized Jane and Alaric's previous visits. She swept down the steps, feather in her hat bobbing a greeting. Fortune's little mouth tilted up as if in a smile to Jane.

"Jane, girls," Miss Thorn acknowledged, acting as if she would pass them.

Jane released Belle and stepped into the employment agency owner's path. "You have nothing more to say to us? We were worried about you."

She paused with a tight-lipped smile, hand stroking Fortune's head. "Sorry to have concerned you, but you indicated that you were pleased with the position. That is still the case, is it not?"

Mystified, Jane nodded. "Yes, I love being a governess."

"And we love Mrs. Kimble," Belle piped up.

Right. She had an audience. Larissa was frowning, and Callie had her chin up, as if she were memorizing every word exchanged. Which she probably was. Still, Jane refused to let her former benefactress go until she had some answers.

"You must know disappearing like that would raise questions," she said. "His Grace and Mr. Mayes are certain they recall meeting you."

She stilled. "Are they? How inconvenient. Please assure them there is no reason for a duke or a solicitor to remember a tradeswoman."

"They seem to think you weren't a tradeswoman then," Jane said. "Were you associated with them? Is that how you knew the duke needed a governess?"

She waved a hand. "His Grace's difficulties are common knowledge. Lady Calantha isn't the only one who listens to what others say."

Callie dropped her gaze, coloring.

"I don't believe you," Larissa put in. "My father is respected."

"He's a duke," Belle said with a nod, as if that were that.

"That's enough, girls," Jane said with a look all around. Then she returned her gaze to Miss Thorn's. Something flashed in the lavender—regret, fear? No, surely not fear, not the redoubtable Miss Thorn.

"I'm trying to help," Jane told her. "I don't like people suspecting you. I don't much like them suspecting me either."

She lay a hand on Jane's arm. "Forgive me, Jane. I had no intention of jeopardizing your position. But you are settled. My efforts now must turn to others who are less fortunate."

So that was it. She was washing her hands of Jane. Jane ought to feel relieved that no harm had come to the woman, but she couldn't help feeling like day-old cabbage.

"I see," she made herself say. "Well, then, I suppose this is goodbye." She reached out and rubbed Fortune's head. The cat raised her chin to allow her access to her creamy throat. Jane's throat was tightening.

"Take good care of your mistress, Fortune. Everyone needs someone who cares about them."

"Jane," Miss Thorn started, then her head came up. Jane heard it too. A carriage had entered the square and was coming around the park in the center. She could see the unicorn crest on the side.

Miss Thorn leaned forward. "If you ever need anything, Jane, please let me know. I want only the best for you." Clutching Fortune close, she hurried across the street and disappeared into the park.

Jane wasn't sure whether Alaric had spotted Miss Thorn until she joined him in the withdrawing room that evening. She and Alaric had taken to playing chess for a time after the girls had been put to bed and Her Grace was out at various soirees and events. The chess set here was of warm wood, the grain smooth in her grip. With the only light from the coals in the hearth and the lamp on the desk, the footman hidden in the shadows, she and Alaric existed inside their own private cocoon for a time, away from demands, expectations.

But apparently not suspicions.

He was standing by the hearth when she entered, hands clasped behind the back of his navy coat. His head was down, as if he were eyeing the fire instead of the portrait over the mantel. In the painting, the ethereally beautiful Evangeline late Duchess of Wey, sat with a golden-haired baby in her arms, her other daughters on either side. Did

Alaric's heart give a painful thump every time he looked at it? Jane's did. How sad to have left three daughters behind.

But how odd that the late duchess's portrait was the only one not gracing the walls at Wey Castle.

He turned as she came into the room, inclining his head in a nod. "Jane. Everything ready for us to return to the castle tomorrow?"

Jane nodded, moving for the chessboard on the table along the wall. Unlike its counterpart at the castle, this withdrawing room was more understated, with walls a creamy jade color and few of Her Grace's ornaments strewn about. The wood-wrapped hearth warmed a camelback sofa patterned in spring leaves with several scroll-back chairs opposite. For some reason, the footman hadn't taken up his usual spot by the door.

"I'll have Betsy and Maud put the last things into the trunks tomorrow," she said, standing beside the chair she occupied when they were playing. "The clothes we ordered for the girls will be sent on as they are finished. It will be good to be home."

Even as she said the words, she started. Home. Since running away from Berkshire to be wed, she'd never truly had a home. Now the castle was her place. She felt a smile forming.

His smile did not answer it. "Anything else of import?"

Jane shrugged. "No. We won't resume lessons until we reach the castle."

He picked up a poker and stirred the coals in the hearth. "No last-minute visits?"

Oh. Jane straightened. "I almost forgot. I saw Miss Thorn today."

He refused to look at her. "Did you?"

"Yes. She was just coming out of that house down the square when the girls and I were passing. She's fine, and so is Fortune."

"I'm glad to hear that. Did she have any explanation for

her disappearance?"

Jane shook her head. "Not a good one. She said I was placed. She had work to do elsewhere."

He set the poker aside. "That cannot explain her refusal to see us."

"I agree. But the lady didn't offer another."

"And you?" he asked, meeting her gaze at last. "Have you another to offer?"

Alaric waited, a part of himself fearing to hear what she would confess. He'd ordered the footman to other duties so he could talk to Jane alone. He hadn't wanted to believe his eyes when he'd seen her and Miss Thorn standing on the street, conversing as if nothing untoward had happened. Then, one look at his carriage, and the so-called employment agency owner had bolted yet again. How could he keep fighting against the evidence before him?

Jane merely shrugged. "Well, she's not too keen on you or Mr. Mayes."

That was no answer either. "And why would that be?" he asked, moving closer to the chessboard.

Jane sighed. "If you have something against Miss Thorn, let's just hear it. I find the whole thing confusing."

"As do I," he assured her as he reached her side. "I have no proof that she is anything other than what she claims. But I don't like mysteries."

She cocked her head. "You don't like believing what you can't touch, you can't see or hear. Faith, like love, isn't like that. You must remember with your wife."

"I never claimed to love my wife." He wasn't sure why he was confiding that now, but it seemed important that she understand. "We tolerated each other, but some days I'm not sure we were even friends."

Her face puckered as she straightened. "I'm sorry to hear

that. I always knew Jimmy loved me, even if he loved the cavalry as much. She was a demanding mistress, and, in the end, she killed him, but I don't blame her. Life for him was the saddle." Tears gleamed like stars in the dark of her eyes.

"And life for Evangeline was her daughters," he murmured. "She'd be pleased to see how you care for them."

She dropped her gaze. "I'm not so sure about that."

He put his finger under her chin and tipped her gaze up to meet his. "I am."

She was staring at him as if she didn't know him. At the moment, he wasn't sure he knew himself. Want and need collided against honor and duty, and he didn't know which would win until he lowered his head and kissed her.

She tasted like honey, thick and rich, and he wanted to go on tasting her until he drowned in the touch. Every part of him felt alive for the first time. This was what a marriage was meant to be.

A noise made him raise his head. Jane's eyes were closed, her cheeks pink, her lips full.

But Larissa stood in the doorway, eyes wide and startled. He must have made a movement toward her, for she bolted like a frightened deer.

And he knew he had a lot of explaining to do, to her, to Jane, and most of all to himself.

Jane blinked, feeling as if the world had suddenly shifted under her, or perhaps she had suddenly shifted into another world.

Alaric had kissed her.

She'd been kissed before. Like everything in his life, Jimmy's kisses had been spontaneous, enthusiastic, rather like the attentions of an overgrown puppy. This kiss had been deeper, more powerful, as if she'd jumped feet first into the warm waters of the Mediterranean. She could scarcely think, only feel. She reached up, touched his cheek, wanting only to continue this closeness.

Yet, from out of the depths of her bemusement, she noticed he was staring beyond her. Dropping her hand, she glanced back, but saw no one. Still, she had enough of her wits about her to make sense of his reaction.

"We were seen."

He nodded, cheeks pinking. "By Larissa."

Worse and worse. The girl didn't like Jane as a governess. She would be inconsolable if she thought Jane was even closer to her father.

"Well, at least it wasn't Callie," she joked, "or she'd have reported it to half the staff by now."

He grimaced, stepping back from her. "Forgive me, Mrs. Kimball. I have no idea what came over me."

But was just as determined as ever to retreat before betraying himself further.

"I could make this easy for you," she said. "Tell you it was all my fault, tender my resignation. But *you* kissed *me*. I suspect we need to talk about it."

He ran his hand back through his hair, even as he moved to distance himself from her. "I have no excuse for my behavior, save one. I allowed my admiration of you to overcome good sense. It will not happen again."

Of course not. Loving Jane Kimball, wanting Jane Kimball, made no sense in his world. A cavalry officer's widow, a governess, would never be good enough to act as his duchess. And she certainly wouldn't allow a different kind of relationship. Colonel Travers may have had other thoughts, but she was not the sort to give herself outside marriage. She knew the value of commitment, of partnership. And she'd have no recourse legally otherwise.

"Quite right," she said. "You're not the kind of master to take advantage of the staff, and I'm not the kind of governess to allow it. I suspect the best we can do is go on as if it hadn't happened."

He did not look comforted. "You forget. Larissa saw us."

Jane sighed. "Yes, of course. I doubt an explanation from me would help. And I don't know what I'd even say."

He started for the door. "I'll speak to her. Return to your duties, Jane, and rest assured I won't trouble you further."

For once in her life, she had no answer. She watched him stride out the door, as if determined to flee from what they felt for each other. Perhaps it was for the best. She'd never been one to hide from emotion. She was more likely to embrace it, encourage it, see how far it would take her. She would never make a good wife for a man so controlled, duke or not.

And yet, that control had slipped. Over the last six weeks, she'd watched him grow closer to his daughters, involving himself more in their lives, encouraging and supporting them. He wasn't completely cold, unreachable. He just needed an excuse to talk, to touch.

To kiss.

Yes, she could have made it easy. She could have encouraged him into her bed. But she wanted more. She wanted all of him, a friend, a lover, a husband.

Anything less would never satisfy. It was all or nothing, and it very much looked as if the answer was nothing.

CHAPTER EIGHTEEN

B ounder. Coward. Dastard. Alaric called himself several other names as he went in search of his oldest daughter. What had he been thinking to kiss Jane like that? It was ridiculous, unconscionable.

Some of the finest moments of his life.

He willed his speeding pulse to slow, his breath to come evenly. He knew the excitement of passion—he'd sired three daughters and a son, after all. But nothing had prepared him for the way he had reacted when his lips had met Jane's. He'd wanted to press her close, shower kisses across her cheeks, her mouth, protect her and cherish her all the days of his life. These were not the thoughts an employer should hold for his employee.

Even if he was finding it hard to remember she was an employee.

He shook the emotions away. It didn't matter how he felt about Jane, his admiration of her inventiveness, her optimism, her speaking eyes and ample curves. He had obligations, duties, one of which was to marry again. She was not the woman he needed for his duchess and the mother of his children. Like his mother, that woman would have to reign over Society with grace, aplomb. She must command servants with a quirk of her brow, inspire devotion with a smile. The formidable Duke of Wey needed an equally formidable Duchess of Wey.

Besides, he had no business interjecting intimacies he had no intention of honoring in marriage. That wasn't fair to Jane or himself.

Now, if he could just find a way to explain that to his daughter.

First, he had to find his daughter. He tried the bedchamber she'd been sharing with Belle and Callie while they were in town, but the nursery maids had just realized Larissa had disappeared and begun searching the other chambers nearby. He asked them to stand down, reassured Callie and Belle that everything was fine, and continued on.

But every room he tried was empty of human habitation, every alcove silent and bare. He should have realized Larissa would turn to only one person besides himself and Jane for comfort. His mother must have returned from her evening entertainment sooner than expected, for he found her reclining on the divan in her bedchamber, Larissa cuddled against her side, his daughter's blue flannel nightgown at odds with the cream silk of his mother's lace-bedecked gown.

"Larissa brought me some interesting news," his mother said as his daughter buried her face in her grandmother's shoulder.

"I'm sure she found it more disturbing than interesting," he said. His mother swung her skirts aside, and he ventured to sit at the foot of the long, pink satin-covered couch. "I came to find you, Larissa. I want to explain."

She sniffed, refusing to so much as look at him. "You kissed Mrs. Kimball."

His mother was watching him, and he couldn't tell from her expression whether she hoped he would deny it or confirm it.

"Yes, I did," he said. "We both regret it very much."

Larissa raised her head, the hollowness in her eyes echoing inside him. "You do?"

He nodded. "Sometimes even adults make the wrong

111

111111111

choices. When we realize it, we work to rectify matters."

"And how do you propose to do that?" his mother asked. Her voice had a decided edge. Was she afraid he was going to discharge Jane, or marry her?

"Mrs. Kimball and I agreed the kiss was inappropriate," he told them both. "It will not happen again. She is on her way to resume her duties."

Larissa's lower lip trembled. "So, she won't be punished for breaking the rules?"

It was on the tip of his tongue to deny it, but curiosity stopped the thought. "What rules do you think she broke, Larissa?"

She waved a hand. "Dozens! She breaks them all the time, and no one does anything. Servants are not to speak back to their masters, but she corrects me. People are to respect their betters, but she argues with you. Unmarried ladies are never to kiss a gentleman, but she kissed you!"

He felt as if he walked a tightrope like a performer at Astley's. One misstep, and he would fall to his doom.

"I kissed her, Larissa," he said. "The fault is mine and mine alone. She is your governess, not a typical servant. And as your governess it is her duty to correct you when you make a mistake."

She pouted. "Who corrects her when *she* makes a mistake?"

"That is my role," he told her. "One of the reasons she reports to me every evening is so I can learn about your progress and correct any mistakes she might be making."

Still Larissa's militant look didn't ease. "But she's telling you things about us. We aren't allowed to explain our side of the matter."

"Very well," he conceded. "One of you may accompany Mrs. Kimball each evening, on a rotating basis. You may come tomorrow, Callie the next day, and Belle the day after."

Larissa inclined her head graciously. "Thank you, Father."

Her grandmother patted her shoulder. "There now. Back you go to the others. I'd like a few words with your father."

Larissa scooted off the sofa and offered him a smile before heading toward the door. His mother rose and went to shut it after her. Then she turned to face him.

"What were you thinking? Your father wouldn't have countenanced such behavior."

He refused to wince, though the words were like a lash. "I know that, Mother. You can say nothing to me I haven't already said to myself."

"So it would seem." She returned to the divan and fixed him with a stare. "Can you really put this behind you?"

"I must. Jane is too good with the girls."

"There is that." She leaned against the tilted back of the divan as if wearied by the whole affair. "I will look for another wife for you. I would have started before now, but I wasn't sure you were ready."

"I'm not." He rose to pace the room. "I appreciate the offer, Mother, but I don't want another arranged marriage. Is it impossible that I might meet the right woman, without anyone's help?"

"Not impossible," she allowed, "but unlikely. We are isolated at the castle, and you hate coming to town and attending the balls and such. My friends have any number of eligible daughters. I'm sure one will suit."

He wasn't. Try as he might, when he thought of courting, his stomach knotted. He didn't want another stranger in the adjoining bedchamber, across the table at breakfast and dinner, in his arms on the ballroom floor.

He wanted Jane, and he couldn't have her.

And that sounded like one of his daughters, denied a treat. He wasn't a child. He wasn't even a young man on the flush of his first encounter with a lady. He knew what was expected of him, what his family, staff, and tenants needed. He raised his head but couldn't stop the sigh that came out.

"Very well, Mother," he said, turning to face her. "Consult your friends, see who's available. I will do my best to be civil."

"Civility," she said with a shake of her silver head, "will not be enough. Each of these young ladies has a host of suitors, some as titled and wealthy as you. If you want a second bride, you will have to be charming, witty, every inch the duke your father trained you to be."

He nodded. "Understood. I will do what I must to win a bride."

Even if his heart wasn't in it.

They returned to the castle the next day.

"It's been such a pleasure having you and the little girls with us," the housekeeper said to Jane as they came down the stairs for the carriage. She wrung her meaty hands before her white starched apron. "I hope you'll come again as soon as you can."

Jane had a feeling soon would not be soon enough for Larissa or Mrs. Winters.

Alaric appeared to be in the greatest hurry to leave. He rode one of the town horses home, not even sitting in the carriage with her and the girls, as if they had contracted some dread disease. Neither he nor Larissa had mentioned the kiss, though Larissa had taken great joy in informing Jane that either her or one of her sisters would be accompanying Jane from now on whenever she made her report to their father. She wasn't sure why he felt the need to distance himself. She wasn't about to beg him for another kiss.

Even if she dreamed of another kiss.

She had no idea why she was so fixated on it. It wasn't as if they could marry. He was her employer. He was a duke; she wasn't even related to the aristocracy. She gave herself a good talking to before they reached the castle and settled back into their routine. She schooled herself each time she descended the stairs to make her report. No more intimate chess matches among the bookcases. No more sharing of thoughts, feelings. But then he'd greet her and his daughter, and her gaze would latch onto the lips that had caressed hers so sweetly. Or she'd ask him a question, and he'd shift on the chair, arms braced on the desk, and she'd remember the feel of his arms around her.

Oh, but she was lost.

She was merely glad the girls kept her so busy. Besides the usual lessons in the schoolroom, there was riding and painting. True to his word, the duke had hired a voice master who tutored Larissa and Callie twice a week. An elderly maestro from Spain, he was always gracious to Jane and encouraging of the girls.

Then there were Her Grace's weekly teas. Jane had become adept at murmuring conversations with Patience along the wall while Lady Carrolton and Her Grace exchanged pleasantries and gossip and questioned the girls mercilessly. She wasn't sure whether it was Patience's influence or her own initial defiant act of walking out, but Lady Carrolton never prophesized doom for the girls again. When Larissa and Callie sang a duet, both dowagers seemed quite pleased.

"I think you have the worst lot," Jane murmured to Patience one day as Lady Carrolton had complained about the weather, the government, and her health at such length that even Larissa was regarding her with concern. "Does she go on like that often?"

"Too often for those who know her," Patience said. Then she grimaced. "Sorry. That sounded unkind. I am convinced a vibrant, caring woman lives inside that bitter shell. I just haven't found a way to bring her out."

Lady Carrolton began sniffing then, and Patience hurried to offer her vinaigrette, which she proceeded to breathe over, shuddering each time to the macabre fascination of the girls. She had raised a hand, likely to wave off Patience, when she froze. "What is that?"

Jane squinted, then jumped to her feet. A spider dangled on its silken thread from the high ceiling. Even as she started forward, it dropped to the tea tray. Lady Carrolton stared at it in horror, but Her Grace's look was more concerned, and it was trained on Callie.

Larissa put her arm about her sister. "It's all right. It can't hurt you."

Belle didn't seem so sure, pushing back in her seat and tucking her feet up under her skirts.

Jane had nearly reached the table when Callie shrugged out of Larissa's hold and rose. Jane readied herself for the scream, the dash from the room. Instead, Callie brought her hand down with a mighty whack, setting the tea things to rattling.

Jane jerked to a stop. Callie twisted her hand to eye the carnage on her glove, then glanced up at Jane with a grin.

"You were right, Mrs. Kimball. They are squishy."

Lady Carrolton fainted.

"And then I smashed it," Callie told her father that night when she came with Jane to make her report.

"Very brave of you," Alaric said with a nod.

"You don't have to be brave with spiders," Callie said. "They're squishy. Mrs. Kimball told me so, and she was right."

"She often is," he said. His gaze brushed hers, fleetingly, admiringly, like a caress to her cheek. That feeling of loneliness stole over her again. She had to fight against this melancholy!

It was from Patience that she learned of the upcoming dinner party.

"It would be too much to hope you'd be invited as well," she said, fingers twined around the handle of the box in her lap. "I'll be sitting beside her ladyship and her daughter, of course, but I doubt anyone will say the least word to me.

We companions tend to be invisible until needed."

"If it's a fancy dinner party, the girls won't be attending," Jane said. "No girls, no need for a governess."

"That's just it," Patience said. "I understood from her ladyship that the girls will be expected to attend at least part of the time. His Grace is seeking a mother for them, after all. Perhaps he wants their opinion."

Her body felt heavy, as if someone had slung a sodden blanket over her shoulders. "More likely the duchess wants them on display. Might as well know what you're getting into."

Patience sighed. "Three darling girls and a handsome, wealthy duke for a husband. Most women I know would want to accept."

Jane aimed her gaze at her hands, afraid what her face would reveal. "You'd marry him, then, if given the chance?"

"A fellow like the duke isn't likely to notice me," Patience said. "I'm invisible, remember? And there are moments I far prefer it that way."

Lady Carrolton began gagging. Jane caught Patience's hand as she rose. "If you ever want another position, I may know someone who could help."

Patience offered her a grateful smile before going to see to her mistress.

Jane was still thinking about Patience's words when she took Belle to report to the duke that night. Parsons let them in with his usual proper demeanor. He at least seemed pleased that Jane and Alaric were nothing more than polite to each other. But Belle paid the butler no mind. She ran to climb up into her father's lap. Jane's heart turned over as Alaric bent to rub noses with Belle, who giggled. So much for being cold and unreachable.

Jane took her seat opposite them and waited to begin until he looked up. Once again, those green eyes were kind, trusting. She fisted her hands in her lap to keep herself focused.

"Everything is going well, Your Grace. Larissa and Callie are learning a new song, and Belle wrote out an entire verse today."

Belle nodded, golden curls brushing his paisley waistcoat. "'Heaviness in the heart of man maketh it stoop: but a good word maketh it glad.' Mrs. Kimball says that means we should say nice things to people."

His smile brushed Jane. "Very wise."

"I'm going to say nice things to our new mother," Belle said.

He stiffened. Jane held her breath. *Deny it. Please deny it.*

"Why do you think you're getting a new mother, Belle?" he asked, so cautiously he might have been holding his breath too.

"Callie said that Betsy said that Grandmother's maid said that Grandmother said…" she paused. "Yes, that's right. Grandmother said you needed to marry again. And Larissa said so too." She nodded as if that was the end of the matter.

"Very likely I will marry again," he told his daughter, the fact like a knife in Jane's chest. "But rest assured I will consider you and your sisters before I do."

Jane breathed, but not without a pang. Of course he must marry. She had the luxury of mourning Jimmy all her life, if she wanted. He needed a son.

"Promise?" Belle asked.

"Promise," he said. "Never doubt a duke."

Jane forced her voice to come out. "I understand there's to be a dinner party soon. Do you want the girls to attend?"

"Perhaps someone can bring them while we gather in the withdrawing room before dinner," he said. "Betsy can escort them if you like."

He was keeping her safely away from the others. Probably for the best. Who knew what she'd blurt out? He'd have a lot of explaining to do if she confessed her feelings. Yet she longed to know who would be in attendance, how he reacted to them. If only she could be mouse in the corner, one of the painted cherubs on the ceiling.

Or a little girl with a large propensity to repeat exactly what was said to her.

The night of the dinner party, Alaric stood near the hearth, well aware his back was to the wall. He finally understood the choice of certain ladies to hide behind potted palms, for if his mother had consented to bring a tree into the withdrawing room, he'd have been sorely tempted to take refuge.

Of course, the obvious spot to hide had been the library, and he was almost willing to forego the night's dubious pleasure for work. Several more troubling accounts had come in about thefts of food and clothing, barns broken into. He couldn't help wondering whether Simmons was intent on enacting vengeance. He'd assigned Willard to investigate the matter, which, he supposed, meant he had the luxury of socializing for the moment.

Her Grace and Lady Carrolton had arranged for three of the most elegant young ladies of their acquaintance to be in attendance, along with their mothers and fathers, brothers, and assorted friends. It was a congenial group, conversing easily. After all, it wasn't every day that the Hermit Duke entertained. At the moment, he felt more like King Louis facing the mob.

Unlike the mob, however, they were all lovely, appropriately educated, well bred. They smiled as they responded to his attempts at conversation. But Lady Elspeth, pale hair shining, kept glancing at the door as if she was just as eager to escape. The statuesque Lady Lilith prickled at the least sign he might disagree with her opinions, setting her black ringlets to quivering. And the titian-haired Lady Fredericka eyed him as if she expected him to bolt from the room, which was certainly preferable to standing here on display.

"I recognize that smile," Gregory, Lord Carrolton, said, joining Alaric along the wall. "It's the same one you'd give the dons when they enquired whether you were ready for the exam, and we all knew you'd spent the previous day riding."

Alaric chuckled despite himself. "I hope you'll be as congenial when I refuse to offer for your sister."

His friend glanced at Lady Lilith, who was glowering at Miss Ramsey as she waved the vinaigrette under their mother's nose. "She is an intelligent, devoted woman. But I'd understand completely if you choose not to wed her."

He felt for the fellow. Powerfully built, with a deep booming voice, Carrolton always seemed in command of any situation, except when it came to his mother and sister.

"Is there nothing that can be done for your mother's affliction?" Alaric murmured.

Carrolton sighed. "I've had the best London physicians examine her, and all claim she is perfectly healthy. If it wasn't for Miss Ramsey, I'd be tempted to run off and play pirate with Harry."

Alaric grinned at the mention of their other friend, Sir Harry Orwell, whose home along the coast had once sheltered pirates and smugglers. "Pirate, or spy?"

Carrolton's eyes widened. "Did he agree to work for the War Office, then?"

"You didn't hear it from me."

The girls' arrival prevented further conversation. He had suggested that Betsy bring them, but it was Jane who stood behind them in the doorway. She was wearing a burgundy-colored gown with simple lines that called attention to her curves. Perhaps it was the color that made her face seemed flushed. Regardless, her eyes sparkled with mischief, as if she intended to thoroughly disrupt this staid, lifeless party.

He would have paid good money to see her do it.

He forced his gaze to his daughters in their dainty white gowns, each one with a different-colored ribbon around the waist. At least Jane had allowed them that much originality while they waited for their London clothes to arrive.

Among so many strangers, they hung back. Belle was clinging to Jane's skirts, Callie was half hidden behind her, and even Larissa shifted from foot to foot. He pushed away from the wall and strode to meet them.

"And here are the prettiest ladies of my acquaintance," he told them, smiling down at them. Larissa returned his smile. Callie straightened, and Belle transferred her fingers from Jane's skirts to his black evening breeches.

He lowered his voice for Jane's ears alone. "Thank you."

"My pleasure," she said. "Sure you'll be all right?"

Not at all. "They're my daughters," he said aloud. "I'm proud of them."

All three of them beamed at him.

With a smile of encouragement, Jane faded out the door, and he had to stop himself from following.

He turned instead, putting the girls in front of him. "My lords and ladies, may I present my daughters, Lady Larissa, Lady Calantha, and Lady Abelona."

The gentlemen, mostly fathers or brothers of the debutantes or husbands of his mother's friends, all inclined their heads in greeting. One of the older women raised her quizzing glass and squinted at the girls through it as if measuring every inch. Lady Lilith stepped back, chin up, as if his girls had brought the pestilence. Her mother sneezed in quick succession. Miss Ramsey hurried to offer a handkerchief.

"What lovely young ladies," Lady Fredericka said, venturing closer, her sapphire-colored skirts swaying. "Why, I would be smitten with jealousy if they came out with me."

Callie cocked her head. "Why?"

She bent and tweaked one of Callie's limp curls. "Because you're just so adorable."

REGINA SCOTT

"Larissa and Calantha are taking singing lessons," his mother informed the guests. "They are becoming quite proficient."

Lady Fredericka straightened. "Perhaps you would favor us with a song."

Larissa shook her head, backing away until she bumped against Alaric's leg. He lay a hand on her shoulder in support. "Perhaps another time."

He felt her sigh of relief.

"I'll sing," Belle declared. "I know a song Mrs. Kimball taught us."

"No!" He brought his other hand down on her shoulder even as Lady Fredericka's brows rose, very likely at his strident tone. "That is, I think it would be better if we conversed with our guests. Mother, would you take Larissa around?"

His mother stepped forward, and Larissa all but ran to her.

Lady Fredericka filled the space his daughter had vacated. "I would be delighted to converse with little Calantha, Your Grace. I'm sure we have much to discuss."

He glanced at his middle daughter, who was frowning at Lady Fredericka. She wanted to talk to Callie. Callie, who was known to blurt out every secret, annoyance, or embarrassment anyone in his household had ever uttered in her hearing. Callie, who could very well frighten away any lady who might show interest.

He smiled. "What an excellent idea. Calantha, be sure to speak to Lady Elspeth and Lady Lilith as well. I'm sure they'd love to listen to whatever you care to say."

CHAPTER NINETEEN

"And when Lady Elspeth asked whether I liked the schoolroom, I told her I liked it a lot better since Mrs. Kimball threw out Simmons for putting spiders in our beds," Callie told her rapt listeners, pausing to take a bite of her toast and swallow it. "I liked her, but she won't marry Father. Lord Carrolton said she is pining for her sweetheart at home and only came tonight because her mother insisted. Marrying a duke is better than marrying a second son."

Larissa nodded wisely. The three girls were gathered around the hearth in Jane's room, nightgowns puddled about their feet and toasting forks in their hands. Jane had sent Betsy, Maud, and Percy the footman to bed, wanting only to hear more of what had happened downstairs, with no witnesses to any turmoil it might cause her.

Now she felt a tug of guilt at her delight that the lovely blonde would not be pursuing Alaric. From her brief glimpse in the withdrawing room when she'd escorted the girls, it seemed that all the young ladies invited to dinner were beautiful, graceful creatures. Likely they'd make far better duchesses than she ever would.

Her hopes that Callie would be her eyes and ears after Jane had bowed out had been rewarded with a wealth of information. Lady Elspeth loved another. Lady Lilith's hauteur deterred interest. And none of the girls had liked

Lady Fredericka.

"She pinched me," Belle complained, accepting a piece of toast from Jane.

"She pinched all of us," Larissa said, rubbing at her cheek as if she could feel the lady's fingers even now. "But Father will probably marry her. She's beautiful."

Jane busied herself affixing another piece of bread to the toasting fork. "You never know. Beauty isn't everything."

Callie brightened. "Lord Waterbury said Lady Fredericka had only her beauty to recommend her, so if Father doesn't want a beautiful wife, then perhaps he won't pick her."

"Every man wants a beautiful wife," Larissa informed her. "Plain girls end up spinsters."

The far plainer Callie slumped. Jane set down the fork and aimed her frown at Larissa. "I don't know who's been filling your head with such drivel, but that's quite enough. A man wants a wife who will respect and care about him. If a fellow focuses only on the outside, there's something wrong with him, not the lady."

Larissa tossed her head. "You don't understand. You married a cavalry officer."

"Who could have had his pick," Jane informed her. "Every girl in three counties had set her cap for him. He still chose me."

"That's because you're beautiful," Belle said, climbing into Jane's lap. "Inside and out."

"That's very kind of you," Jane said, relishing the warmth of the little body next to hers. "But I know I'm no great beauty. And neither do you have to be to have a happy life."

Callie nodded, but Larissa looked unconvinced.

Jane let them finish their toast and escorted them back to bed. Larissa and Callie snuggled in right away, but Belle's eyes were wide and bright as Jane drew up the covers on the big bed in the little girl's room.

"I know who Father should marry," she said as Jane brushed a golden curl from her forehead. "You."

Something clutched at her heart. "Dukes don't marry governesses, Belle."

She frowned. "Do they have to marry princesses?"

Jane smiled. "No, but they must marry someone who will do them credit."

"Oh." She yawned. "Well, perhaps you could do Father credit. I'd help."

"I'm sure you would. Goodnight, Belle."

"Goodnight, Mrs. Kimball. Don't let the bedbugs bite."

Jane moved away from the bed and shut the door behind her. Funny. So many times Jimmy and his friends had talked about the Forlorn Hope—a dangerous effort to take a position in enemy territory, a task so difficult and important that most of the men would attempt it in the hope of glory and promotion and die instead. She'd never entirely understood the attraction, until now. A part of her very much wanted to march down to the dinner party and proclaim that Alaric would marry no one but her. How glorious indeed if he should throw down his napkin, leap to his feet, take her in his arms, and declare his love.

Unfortunately, the duchess would probably order Jane from the castle while he shook his head and apologized to his guests for her impetuous nature. Her hopes were forlorn indeed.

Jane did not report to him that night. With the dinner party lasting until nearly midnight, Alaric did not think she would. Yet he missed the sight of her, that conspiratorial smile, the banter they used to share. Jane would have had something to say about Lady Fredericka, Lady Lilith, and Lady Elspeth. He could almost hear her voice as his valet helped him undress.

You don't want a duchess who wouldn't say boo to a goose or sneer at everything you do. Lady Fredericka, now, at least she had backbone. Though she seems to admire the silver and the plate as much as I do.

That was the truth. The lady had fingered her silver fork as if weighing its worth, and he'd noticed her examining his mother's porcelain figurines as if determining how much they might bring at auction. While she had gushed over the girls, her effusions rang hollow, and her conversation to him had revealed nothing more of her character. He could not shake the feeling that in offering for her he would be buying himself a bride.

His mother appeared at the breakfast table much earlier than her usual wont, dressed in a sky blue, narrow-skirted wool gown, hair elaborately curled, and paper in hand.

"Is there something particular you hope to accomplish today, Mother?" he asked as Parsons poured him his second cup of tea.

She smoothed the paper on the linen tablecloth as she sat. "We must discuss your options. I took a moment to compose my thoughts."

And had recorded the composition, it seemed. "Indeed."

If she heard the lack of interest in his tone, she did not show it, gaze fixed on the notes she had made. "I was impressed by Lady Elspeth's decorum," she said, nodding to Parsons as he lay a piece of buttered toast on her plate. "She listened more than she spoke, which is always a congenial trait."

"For those who speak a great deal," he countered, setting down his cup. "I keep imagining us sitting across the table from each other and having nothing to say, for days or weeks."

"Hm, yes, well." His mother consulted the paper as Parsons arranged pots of jam and honey in easy reach. "Lady Lilith seemed devoted to her mother. A devoted daughter-in-law would be quite pleasant."

For his mother. "She refused to look me in the eye," Alaric said with a shake of his head. "I was under the impression I was somehow beneath her."

His mother made a face. "Fine. Lady Fredericka, then. She was far more forthright."

"And expected me to agree with every one of her opinions."

His mother threw up her hands. "Well, if you want a wife who speaks her mind at the least provocation and enjoys a good argument, you might as well marry Mrs. Kimball."

Parsons gasped and turned the noise into a cough before composing himself.

"Parsons," Alaric said, "I find myself hungering for some of that pickled asparagus Cook provided last night at dinner. I don't suppose there's any left."

Parsons drew himself to attention. "I shall endeavor to enquire, Your Grace." He strutted from the room.

Alaric turned to his mother. "You're right. I should marry Jane Kimball, but we both know that's impossible."

She reached for her cup, and he was surprised to see her hand shaking as she lifted it. "Nonsense. Nothing is impossible for a duke."

Alaric leaned back, unwilling to accept so quick a response. "I cannot imagine you introducing her to your friends. 'Lady Gossipful, please meet my daughter-in-law, our governess. Her first husband was a dashing cavalry officer. Alaric can never compare of course, but she was glad to marry up in the world.'"

His mother colored. "I most certainly wouldn't go out of my way to disclose her background. And I would set you against a cavalry officer, no matter how dashing, any day of the week."

He inclined his head. "Kind of you, Mother."

She idly tapped her spoon against the side of the cup, head cocked as if thinking the matter over. "But it isn't entirely beyond the pale, you know. Remember Lord Killibridge? He married the woman who had been his nanny when he was a lad." She shuddered.

He knew what his father would say. Lord Killibridge was

an upstart, a fellow so newly elevated to the title he had no idea of the gravity and responsibility of his position. Alaric had been trained otherwise.

"I have no intention of marrying any of the staff," he assured her. "If I followed my own inclinations, I wouldn't marry at all."

His mother straightened. "You must marry, Wey. Your father and grandfather worked too hard to see our lands given to some stranger or worse, the Crown. I will allow that the ladies last night were not up to the standards I would normally hold for a daughter-in-law. I will endeavor to do better next time."

He hid his own shudder. "As you wish, Mother. But you cannot force me to marry."

"No." She sounded sincerely saddened by the fact. "And I do want you to be happy this time. I can see that Evangeline was the wrong wife for you, but I cannot entirely regret the marriage for it gave me three wonderful granddaughters."

"Yes, it did." He thought, he hoped, that she might leave it at that and returned his gaze to his cup. The amber liquid had never looked less appealing.

"If you decide on Jane Kimball," his mother said, rising to take her leave, "then I will simply have to accustom myself to the idea, and so will the rest of Society. I hope you'll consider that."

How could he fail to consider it? For a moment, he felt as if she were reinforcements, charging over the hill to save his regiment from certain doom. Yet would Society truly accept Jane as a duchess?

The question kept nagging at him as he went to the library after breakfast to review the reports Willard had provided on needs around the island this spring. He had never been fond of the Social whirl, so if some of the high sticklers snubbed him for his wife's humble beginnings, he'd shed no tear. But Jane did not deserve the condescension and condemnation she'd likely receive. And if he and Jane were not welcomed in Society, wouldn't he have isolated her more surely than locking her in the schoolroom? Could she be happy in such a life?

And what of the girls? Would they be treated poorly for his choice?

"The morning post, Your Grace," Parsons announced, moving into the library with a silver salver balanced on one gloved hand. "And Mr. Willard sends word that the river is starting to rise."

A chill went through him, but he accepted the notes from his butler and dismissed the man. Sitting back at the desk, he thumbed through the stack. The thick vellum of invitations from mothers who wanted a duke for their daughters, the pressed sheets with Julian's hand on some matter concerning the estates. One stood out—the writing canted and crooked, as if written in a hurry and with great emotion. The missive was battered, as if it had traveled far. He took his penknife and broke the seal.

Dear Duke of Wey, I understand from Mr. Mayes that you have questions about our former governess, Mrs. Jane Kimball.

He started, gaze darting to the signature at the bottom of the note. Colonel Travers's wife was writing to him. Julian must have reached her at last. He returned to the top of the note to read the rest.

I can only tell you that I thought her a fine model for my daughter until I discovered her in my husband's arms.

The chill he'd felt earlier spread through his body.

Jane Kimball is nothing but an adventuress, out to trap any man who makes the mistake of wandering too close. I discharged her without recommendation, and I suggest you do the same. It is never wise to succor a viper in one's bosom. Sincerely, Mrs. Grace Travers.

The letter fell to the desk as if his fingers had gone numb. He rather thought his heart had suffered the same fate. Jane, an adventuress? It couldn't be.

She had joined his household under suspicious circumstances, something inside him whispered. Insisted on dealing only with him. Allowed herself to be alone with him on numerous occasions. Wormed her way into his daughters' hearts.

And his.

He rose from the desk, to go where, he wasn't sure. He clasped his hands behind his back, paced in and out among the maze of bookshelves. The wisdom of ages surrounded him—with tomes by philosophers who understood the workings of the mind, poets who delved into matters of the heart. None would tell him what he most longed to know. Could he trust Jane?

Of course he could.

He was used to relying on reports, recommendations, the insights of others. Julian had cautioned him against her. Miss Thorn refused to answer questions. Now Mrs. Travers insisted she was no good. He knew what his father would have done—discharged her immediately, voice imperious and face merciless.

He would never be his father.

For once, he was thankful for that. Had he followed his father's advice and viewed everyone with suspicion, he would never have come to know Jane. And that would have been a great loss. Jane was encouraging, positive, honest to a fault. She brooked no response that wasn't in the girls' best interests. She had helped his daughters to learn, to grow. Even his mother had mellowed in her company if she could suggest accepting a governess as a daughter-in-law.

Besides, if Jane was hunting money or a title, she had had him dead to rights. He'd kissed her. She could have demanded income for her silence, even that he marry her. Instead, she had helped him think through options, suggested that they pretend it had never happened. She could not have allowed such an opportunity to pass if she was an adventuress.

It only followed, then, that Mrs. Travers was slandering Jane's good name. The question was, why?

CHAPTER TWENTY

The rain lashed the windows as Jane made her way down to the library the evening after the dinner party. It was Larissa's turn to join her, and the girl moved at a stately pace that was no doubt considered ladylike. Jane tried to match her, for all she'd have preferred to pick up her skirts and move. After all, she might as well pretend she knew how to be a lady.

Alaric was standing at the window, hands clasped behind his back, apparently staring at the rain as the grey day faded into a stormy night. He turned as Parsons announced them.

"Good evening, Larissa, Mrs. Kimball. Please, sit down."

So formal. Was something wrong? Jane took her customary spot, while Larissa perched daintily beside her in the other chair as if concerned the leather seat would swallow her.

"Did you enjoy meeting everyone last night, Larissa?" he asked as he seated himself behind the big desk. Once more the top was cluttered by papers, as if they'd interrupted him in deep study of some important matter.

Larissa folded her hands in the lap of her muslin gown. "Oh, yes, Father. Everyone was very kind and congenial. I hope I have the opportunity to further their acquaintances."

Very prettily said, but part of Jane still hurt for the girl. It was the wish of a matron, not a girl years away from her first Season. Was it truly what Larissa wanted, or was she merely saying what she thought her father expected?

"I'm not sure when we'll have the pleasure of their company again," Alaric said.

"Of course," Larissa said. "The Season will be starting in earnest after Easter. They will all want to go to London. Will we be going up to London too?"

She sounded so wistful. For once, Jane could commiserate. She'd enjoyed London far more than she'd thought possible. She made herself study the closest section of bookshelves, squinting as she tried to make out the titles on the fine leather spines.

"I may need to go to London to attend Parliament," Alaric said. "But only a day here or there. No need to uproot you and your sisters."

Jane turned in time to see Larissa slump in her seat.

"And how are your studies going?" Alaric asked as if he had not just doused her hopes.

Larissa rallied and went on in some detail about the Maestro's singing lessons, her proficiency at watercolor. Jane interjected where she could to include riding, mathematics, and history, as well as her sisters' accomplishments.

Finally, Alaric leaned back. "I'm glad to hear things are going so well. Please give my regards to your sisters, Larissa. Now, return upstairs, if you would. I'd like to discuss some matters with Mrs. Kimball privately."

Jane looked at him askance, but his calm, pleasant demeanor betrayed nothing.

Larissa climbed slowly to her feet. "But you require a chaperone."

"Mr. Parsons will be here to make sure matters do not get out of hand."

The butler nodded with entirely too much conviction.

Still Larissa held her ground. "It's not right. You said we would come with her. You said you wouldn't kiss her again."

Parsons started so badly Jane thought he might fall off

his feet.

"Larissa Mary Elizabeth Augustine," Alaric said in a voice that would have made Jane quake. "I asked you to leave. Go to the schoolroom. Now."

Larissa turned and ran.

"Make sure she reaches the schoolroom," Alaric told Parsons. "Then return here immediately."

With a wary look to Jane, the butler hurried from the room.

"So, are you sacking me or kissing me?" Jane asked.

He shook his head. "Neither. But this is not a discussion Larissa should be privy to. I had a letter today from Mrs. Travers. I imagine you can guess the contents."

She could, and she suddenly understood why he was so distant. "I'm a scheming, wanton woman, and you should send me packing."

"A fair summation."

And what was she to say? He'd only just recovered from suspecting her because of Miss Thorn's behavior. This letter had to reinforce his concerns. Yet how could she counter it? It was her word against that of the hero of the Peninsula.

As if he saw the fears crowding her, he leaned across the desk. "I don't believe a word of it, Jane."

Relief left her shaking in the seat. "Thank you."

He inclined his head, straightening. "I would, however, like to hear what really happened."

Jane licked her lips, straightening. "Even if it does no one credit?"

"Even so."

She sighed. There was nothing for it now. "Very well. The colonel returned from the field to recuperate. He'd taken a ball in the thigh, and I imagine it hurt a great deal. He'd imbibed alcohol to deaden the pain, and in that state decided a widow like me must be lonely for a man's company. He came to my room, pushed his way inside, and tried to offer me his services. When I refused, he attempted to convince me of his skills. I used a maneuver Jimmy taught me to incapacitate him. Then I called the footmen and ordered them to take him to his room. I had my things packed, resignation letter in hand, when Mrs. Travers came to order me from the house. He'd spun a fine tale, you see. It seems I seduced him. Why, I have no idea. He would have made a wretched lover and a pinch-penny one at that."

He shook his head. "I'm sorry, Jane. Your first employer attempted liberties, and I succeeded in them. What a poor opinion you must have of gentlemen."

"I hold a true gentleman in highest esteem," she assured him. "It's the scoundrels who try to take advantage of those they fancy are weaker that get my back up. Colonel Travers acted like a scoundrel. You didn't."

"I'm afraid I cannot see the difference."

He sounded so disgusted with himself. "And that proves my point. I imagine Colonel Travers was sorry that he was caught. You're sorry because you feel you broke a rule. You and your oldest daughter seem inordinately fond of rules."

He spread his hands. "Rules are important. I was taught they are the fabric on which our lives are woven."

She had been taught the same thing. Funny how it had never stuck.

"I'll grant you they have their place," she allowed. "And some are more inviable than others. Taking someone's life for profit is always wrong but telling a mother her red-faced screaming baby is beautiful should never be considered a lie."

That won a smile from him.

"Besides," Jane said, "I don't know any rule against two unmarried adults agreeing to share a kiss. You'll notice I didn't try my maneuver on you."

"For which I must be grateful," he said. His smile quickly faded. "Thank you for your candor, Jane. I'll let you return to your duties."

Duty. He held that concept so high. His care of the estate was a duty, his interaction with his daughters a duty. Commendable, of course. But what of joy? Of love?

Jane rose to her feet, heart pounding in her ears. She'd done outrageous things in her life—elope to be married, travel half the world living in nothing better than a tent, order cavalry officers about, agree to be governess to a duke's children. Some had denigrated her for it, scoffed that she never was and never would be a true lady. What she was about to do was the most outrageous yet. Her father and mother would despair of her. Jimmy, dear Jimmy, would have cheered her on.

"I'm beginning to see my only real duty as caring for this family," she said. "I know you're in the market for a wife. Why not me?"

Jane Kimball, asking to be his wife? Joy leaped inside Alaric, forcing him to his feet. It was on the tip of his tongue to agree when Parsons hurried back in.

"Sorry, Your Grace. Lady Larissa went straight to the duchess, and it took a little finesse to set things right." He glared at Jane as if it were entirely her fault.

His world crashed down around him. The river was rising. His precious lock was about to be tested. His daughters needed a mother, his title an heir. It didn't matter what he wanted, what he needed, who he knew would make him happy. He had duties, obligations. They would always have to come first.

"Thank you, Parsons," he said. "And thank you, Mrs. Kimball, for your kind offer. I will never forget it. But I fear I must decline. Duty, you know."

Her face, always so open and friendly, shut, and he nearly reached out to her. As if she knew his thoughts, she stepped back, away from him. "Of course, Your Grace. I won't trouble you further." She turned and walked out, head high and steps steady. Never let your enemy glimpse your pain, his father would have said. His Grace would have been proud of her.

He drew in a breath. "That will be all, Parsons."

His butler inclined his head and followed Jane from the room.

Alaric sat heavily on the chair, stared at the papers awaiting his attention. Requests from tenants, a demand from Mr. Harden to evict a trespasser from his lands, bills due to come before the House of Lords, correspondence on any number of matters. Duties. Requirements. Expectations. With a sweep of his arm, he scattered them. They fluttered to the floor, where they lay abandoned, just like his dreams.

Stupid! Why had she taken such a chance? Of course he'd refused her. Dukes did not marry governesses or cavalry officer's widows. Even Larissa knew that. Why couldn't Jane get it through her head?

She wasn't some green schoolgirl, wide-eyed at the idea of love and marriage. She'd loved and lost. Alaric was nothing like Jimmy. There was no reason to expect a second love as great as the first.

Or perhaps even greater.

She stopped at the foot of the stairs leading to the schoolroom suite, pressed her back against the silk-draped wall, gulped in a breath as tears started to fall. Her impetuous heart had led her to abandon her family, follow a husband through mud and war. It shouted now that, against all odds, she had found another man to love and cherish. The problem was, he didn't want her.

No, that wasn't right. He wanted her. His kiss proved as much. So did the fact that he had believed her over Mrs. Travers. He might even love her, but not enough. Duty must come first. Like Jimmy and the cavalry, Alaric served another. And he had chosen it over her.

She drew out her handkerchief, dabbed the tears from her cheeks. She had never been one to lament her fate. Most of the time it had been a fate she'd courted. So what if her dreams were thwarted now? Upstairs were three little girls who needed her. She had a position and a calling. Perhaps that would be enough to fill the hole in her heart.

But she doubted it.

CHAPTER TWENTY-ONE

"Why must we ride today?" Larissa whined as Jane finished fastening Belle's riding habit. "It's raining."

It had been raining nearly every moment of the past two days since she'd proposed to Alaric, as if the sun had gone into hiding like her heart.

"It's only a drizzle," Jane said, rising. "Cavalry officers ride in the rain."

Larissa sniffed. "We are not cavalry officers."

"And not likely to be so sure in the saddle if you let a little rain scare you off." She smiled at them all. "We'll only go to the western tip and back. That's not very far. A little air will do you good."

Larissa sighed but followed her from the schoolroom.

Mr. Quayle was complimentary as he had the grooms assist them into their saddles. "Ladies who ride in poor weather will be better suited to handle life's difficulties."

Larissa did not appear to be comforted.

Neither did Belle. She eyed the pony with a frown. "When may I ride Unicorn?"

"When the weather improves," Jane said. "You wouldn't want to splash mud on her pretty white coat."

"Unicorns like mud," Belle insisted.

"I don't," Larissa grumbled.

Still Belle balked. "If I can't ride Unicorn, I want to ride all by myself."

Mr. Quayle frowned. "I'm not sure that's advisable."

Jane went to the pony, ran a hand over its coat. "You've always chosen a reliable mount."

"Of course," the master of horse said, grey head coming up. "It's her ladyship that concerns me."

Belle stood taller. "I can do it."

Jane believed her. That little body held a great deal of determination. "There you have it, Mr. Quayle. If you'd be so kind as to help her up."

The master of horse moved slowly to comply as a groom helped Jane into her sidesaddle. She glanced at Mr. Quayle. "All clear this morning?"

She'd told him the day before that she preferred the girls to ride at times other than their father until they had a little more practice and could do him proud. She knew Alaric was already proud of his daughters. She was the one who wasn't ready to face him after her outburst in the library. She'd even sent the three girls down together to make her report the last two nights, knowing that Callie would repeat exactly what she was told.

"His Grace left this morning to check the river level upstream," Mr. Quayle said. "Mr. Harden, one of the tenants, is managing the lock today, and he won't act unless His Grace or Mr. Willard the steward orders it. You won't run into anyone."

With a grateful nod, Jane urged her horse out of the stable yard, Belle at her side and Larissa and Callie just ahead.

Even with grey skies and hard rain wetting her cheeks, she couldn't help relaxing in the saddle. Green shoots poked up across the fields, and birds called from the thickets along the river.

"Gentle on the bit, Callie," she reminded her charge. "There's no need to keep reining in."

"But he wants to go faster than I do," Callie said, arms

flexed as she tugged on the reins.

"Then hold the reins tight, but still," Jane advised. "He'll understand."

Callie must have complied, for the horse obligingly slowed.

Jane nodded. "Very good. You'll make captain yet."

Callie glanced back at her with a grin.

"I wish you would stop comparing us to the cavalry," Larissa said, voice heavy with a pout. "We are ladies."

"Indeed you are," Jane told her, "and I know no one more judged by how well they sit a horse other than the men of the cavalry. Do you want to be left behind when your father goes fox hunting?"

"Father doesn't hold with fox hunting," Callie reported. "He says it's unkind to the fox and ruins the fields."

He would, and she couldn't help admiring him for it. "Very well. Don't you want to beat the gentleman who challenges you to a race?"

Larissa raised her head in derision, then quickly ducked against the rain. "A gentleman would never ask a lady to race."

"Not if she rides like a slug."

"Have you ever raced?" Belle wanted to know, sitting serenely in her seat.

"Once or twice," Jane admitted. "And always with my husband. He won, of course. Never could top Jimmy in the saddle."

"I'll ride better," Larissa predicted. "I'll practice and practice until there isn't a lady who can match me."

"That's my girl."

Belle shifted on her seat, glancing around. "Where did the birds go?"

Jane frowned. Something was wrong. The birds had fallen silent. Instead, a sharp crack rang through the air, like a giant working a forge.

"What's that?" Callie asked.

Larissa craned her neck as if to see. "It sounds like its coming from Father's lock."

Jane clucked to the horse, and they all moved closer to the copse of alder that hid the gates from view of the road. The noise grew louder even as they approached. Then it suddenly stopped.

Jane pulled up and slid from the sidesaddle, keeping the reins in one hand as she eased closer to the lock. What she saw drew her up hard. Someone had attempted to chop through the capstan. Rain ran in rivulets down the deep cuts. The ax blade was embedded deep in the wood, preventing the gates from being cranked open. Already they bowed inward as the rising river tried to shove its way through.

Jane straightened. "Something happened to the lock gates," she told the girls. "We need to alert Mr. Quayle to send someone after your father."

"You'll be telling no one."

Jane gasped as a male body slammed into hers. The reins whipped from her fingers, and she heard Callie scream.

Jane dug in her heels to keep from falling as Simmons pinned her arms to her sides.

"This is your fault," he said, shaking rain from his head. "You tried to force me off the only home I ever knew, just like the old duke forced my father. Things were never right after that. I came back for revenge, and I won't go until you all suffer."

Jane didn't wait to hear more. As Jimmy had taught her, she brought her knee up to collide with Simmons's frame. He sucked in a breath, releasing her and doubling over. It was the work of a moment to make sure her knee met his jaw as well. He collapsed in the mud.

She whirled to find Callie staring at her, horse turning in agitated circles, while Jane's mount showed white around its eyes.

"Where are Larissa and Belle?" Jane cried, hurrying

toward her.

"The pony ran off with Belle, and Larissa said she would go after her." Callie managed to point back the way they had come.

"Right." Fear hastened her steps. She calmed Callie's horse, then focused on her own. Crooning and standing patiently, she convinced the poor beast to allow her to tug him toward a rock to help her climb back into the saddle. It was some moments before she accomplished it.

As she urged the horse forward, Callie alongside, she glanced back at the lock. The gates were starting to groan against the onslaught of the river. The Thames was rising. With the chain damaged, would they have any way to stop the flood?

The rain picked up as Alaric rode toward the stables. He'd seen enough upstream to know they were in for it. He could only pray the lock would work.

"Beastly day," his steward said, wiping water from his face. "I've never seen so much mud."

Too much mud, too much water, too much work—the rhythm of his life. It seemed as if the entire world had darkened since he'd turned Jane away. She refused to see him. Though he'd enjoyed talking with his girls the last two nights, he couldn't help wishing Jane had come with them. He had to find a way to mend this rift between them, without giving her hope that they could ever wed. Surely he could find a way to converse with her, spend times with the girls with her, travel to London and see Astley's again without remembering the feel of her in his arms.

He must have groaned aloud, for Willard rode a little closer. "I'll change horses and go straight to the lock, Your Grace."

"I'm coming with you," Alaric told him. He urged the

horse along as fast as was safe to reach the stables, where he ordered a fresh horse.

Quayle didn't argue, passing the reins to a stable boy. "Check on Mrs. Kimball and the girls on your way to the lock. They rode that direction a while ago. I would have expected them back by now."

He felt as if the icy rain had dribbled down his back.

"Mrs. Kimball and the girls rode out in this?"

"Yes, Your Grace. Do you want me to send someone with you in case there's trouble?"

"No time," he said, swinging up into the saddle of the horse a groom had just brought out. "Have the grooms saddle up and follow Willard."

Quayle and Willard nodded as Alaric called to his mount and galloped from the yard.

The horse only lengthened its stride as they cleared the buildings. They pelted down the track, trees and fields flying on either side, mud churning up behind. Peering through the rain, he tried to make out another set of riders, but nowhere did he see the dear little trio led by the dark-haired woman who had stolen his heart. All he could do was send up a prayer for their safety.

He was nearly at the lock when he heard a call. Reining in, he saw Jane and Callie cantering toward him. His heart leaped, then sank again.

"Where are Larissa and Belle?" he asked as soon as they came abreast. Jane's riding habit was sodden, the hem crusted with mud as if she had slipped from the horse. Callie was shivering, hair clinging to her skin.

"We're going after them," Jane said. "The pony ran away with Belle, and Larissa went after her. But you're needed here. There's trouble at the lock. Simmons damaged it to punish us. The gates are closed, and the river is trying to force its way through."

He should go after his daughters. Their lives might depend on it. Yet if he didn't manage to open the gates, all their work to save the fields would be for nothing. People could lose their lives along with their livelihoods. Duty and love battled inside him.

Jane reached across the space and lay her hand on his. "Open the gates. Callie and I will save Larissa and Belle."

All along she'd asked him to trust her—with his home, with his daughter's schooling, with his heart. All along, he'd fought her. Giving in had never felt so right.

"Go," he said. "I know you'll take care of our girls." He leaned across the space, pressed a quick kiss to her lips, then put his heels to the horse's flanks and urged the beast into a gallop once more.

CHAPTER TWENTY-TWO

Jane watched him go, heart swelling. She'd blamed him for putting his duty before his daughters, before her, yet how could she love a man who would do less? When it came to the choice of gratifying his own wishes or meeting the needs of others, he always thought of those who depended on him first. In every way, he was a hero.

Callie shivered beside her, recalling her to her own duty now. Somehow, she thought the pony Belle had been riding would make for the known, which meant back toward the stables at either the home farm or the castle. But Alaric had surely just come from that direction. He hadn't seen Belle or Larissa. There was only one other direction they might have gone. She directed the horses away from the lock onto the road that led toward the northern edge of the island.

The rain was pounding down now, wind bending the grass and peppering drops against her face. The icy grey river streamed relentlessly along, sucking at the roots of the alders, pulling at the shore. She sent up a prayer for safety, for Belle and Larissa, for Alaric, and for her and Callie.

"There!" Callie pointed, and Jane made out two horses standing beside the bulrushes. She urged the horse closer, heart pounding.

Belle and Larissa sat huddled on the ground, the older girl's arms around her little sister. Both clutched the reins of their mounts, which milled about behind them. Keeping her own reins in hand, Jane slid from the sidesaddle and hurried to them.

"Are you hurt?"

Larissa shook her head, rain running off her hair. "I fell, but I'm all right."

"*You* fell?" She glanced from Larissa to Belle for confirmation.

Belle nodded, smile bright though her teeth chattered. "I stayed on the pony, Mrs. Kimball. I only slid down to help Larissa."

Jane breathed a prayer of thanks as she helped both girls to their feet. Larissa did seem unhurt, for she stood and walked without limp or grimace.

"We couldn't find a way to get back in the saddle without the grooms," Larissa said.

"We knew you'd come," Belle added.

Jane brushed a wet curl from her cheek. "Smart thinking. Now, we just need to get everyone home."

Putting Larissa back in the saddle wasn't hard. Jane cupped her hand and boosted the girl up. Belle she could just lift into place. But with no rock or fallen tree to climb up on, getting Jane reseated was another matter.

"Ride ahead," she told Larissa and Callie. "I'll walk with Belle until I find something to help me mount or a groom comes along."

The girls nodded and headed off.

Belle hunched in the saddle. "Can't I go with them? I'm cold."

"I know, sweetheart," Jane said, leading the horse forward. "But even though you were very brave, I don't want you to have to ride as fast as Larissa and Callie. We'll be home before long. Think of sitting in front of a nice warm fire."

"With toast?" Belle asked.

Jane smiled. "Of course. What do you think we should put on it?"

As Belle debated the merits of jam, honey, or cinnamon and sugar, Jane walked as quickly as she could, always with an eye out for a rock or hump she could use to mount. Her wool riding habit soaked up the rain, sending her sagging skirts deeper into the mud. Cold settled into her bones.

She had never been so glad to hear hoofbeats approaching. Mr. Quayle rode out of the rain, more gallantly than any cavalry officer. He was down in a moment and helping her mount. Together, they started back toward the stables at a quicker pace.

"Has His Grace returned?" Jane asked.

"Not yet. But don't you worry for him. I sent Pat and Eddie out to help, and Mr. Willard was with them." He urged his mount closer. "Have a care, Mrs. Kimball. Some folks seem bent on blaming all this on you."

Blaming her? What had she done? Numb inside and out, Jane accompanied him back.

It seemed half the household had come from the castle in concern. Betsy and Maud had Larissa and Callie in hand. Percy was begging for a horse, so he might go after Belle. Mr. Parsons alternated between demanding answers and ordering the remaining stable boys about. Mr. Quayle swung down and went to help Belle.

"You'd be better served to look to your own charges and leave mine alone," he said, thrusting the shivering Belle at him.

Mr. Parsons stepped back from the wet bundle in obvious distaste. "Percy, see to her ladyship."

Mr. Quayle handed Belle to the footman and turned to help Jane down. Mr. Parsons put out a hand to stop her before she could join the girls.

"Not so fast, you. Lady Larissa tells me you caused all this."

Jane glanced at Larissa, who stepped closer to Betsy's warmth even as she raised her chin.

"I told Mrs. Kimball it was too wet and cold to ride,

but she wouldn't listen. She never listens to me. She didn't listen to Mr. Quayle either. He told her Belle shouldn't ride alone. Belle might have been hurt because of her."

"Mrs. Kimball wouldn't hurt me," Belle protested, nearly limp in the footman's arms. "She loves me."

"I highly question that." Mr. Parsons's voice was colder than the rain. "And you mentioned something about the river?"

Larissa nodded. "Father's lock is broken. She said so."

Gasps rang out all around, and Maud and Betsy clasped their charges closer. Mr. Quayle strode for the stable, calling for the stable boys to ride to the home farm and move the horses there to higher ground.

"Did you have anything to do with this?" Mr. Parsons demanded.

Jane stared at him. "Of course not! Simmons struck the capstan that holds the chains to open the gates. His Grace is out there attempting to fix it now."

The butler took a step closer. "Lies. Simmons left the island days ago."

"He didn't!" Callie piped up. "He was there, at the gates. I saw him. He said it was Mrs. Kimball's fault."

Jane cringed. Everyone knew Callie reported exactly what she heard.

"It's a mistake," she said, struggling to keep her voice calm as faces hardened against her. "Why would I want anyone to damage a lock meant to keep us all safe?"

Mr. Parsons cut his hand through the air like a knife. "Enough. The lock is immaterial. You willfully endangered the lives of Lady Larissa and her sisters. You have refused to listen to advice and council, disobeyed His Grace and the duchess at every turn. You leave me no choice but to discharge you of your duties and demand that you leave at once."

"No!" Callie cried. She yanked herself out of Maud's grip and ran to Jane. "Don't leave, Mrs. Kimball. I love you!"

"Put me down!" Belle cried, kicking in Percy's arms. "I love her too."

Jane gathered Callie close, mind and heart in turmoil. "Don't worry, sweethearts. Your father will have something to say about this."

"You continue to forget that I run this household," Mr. Parsons said. "I'm sure His Grace will side with me when I explain the matter to him. He has known me far longer than he's known you, and he will not countenance behavior that puts his daughters at risk. Betsy, Maud, return their ladyships to the schoolroom and await further instructions."

Jane released Callie to an apologetic-looking Maud. Larissa hesitated.

"I didn't mean for her to leave," she told Mr. Parsons. "Can't you just punish her? I'm sure she'll learn her lesson."

"I wish I shared that belief," Mr. Parsons said with a nod to Betsy. The nursery maids and footman hurried the children from the yard.

Jane stood alone, bereft. That was it? She was merely to leave? She felt as if the air had vacated the yard, her lungs.

"Do not bother collecting your things," Mr. Parsons said as if intent on heaping coals on her head. "They will be forwarded to Miss Thorn. Let's see if she can find you another position after this."

Very likely even Fortune would not be so accommodating. Two positions and no references? Jane was clearly damaged goods.

"You're making a mistake," Mr. Quayle warned Mr. Parsons as he came out of the stable leading a horse.

The butler drew himself up. "The inside of the house is mine. Your realm is the stable. See that you stay there." With a look of disgust at Jane, he turned on his heel and strode back into the castle courtyard.

Mr. Quayle grabbed a blanket off the horse and draped

it about Jane's shoulders. "I don't care what his nibs says. You're welcome to stay in my stables as long as you like."

That would be easy. Likely she could appeal to Alaric to override the butler's edict, but to what purpose? Larissa might never respect her. Mr. Parsons would forever look for opportunities to discharge her. And she would have to watch from the schoolroom while Alaric courted and married someone else.

All her life she'd had to fight—for the right to her own opinions, for a place at Jimmy's side, for food and water at the crowded campaign camps, for a position of dignity as a widow. Perhaps it was time she stopped fighting.

She pulled the blanket off her shoulders. "Thank you, Mr. Quayle, for everything. I think it best if I go. Might I prevail on you for a carriage to take me off the island? I believe the mail coach to London stops at Walton-on-Thames. I might just be able to catch it."

Alaric heaved one last time, and the gates burst open, water rushing down into the channel. The grooms and tenants who had helped him pull the chain by hand straightened, clapping each other on the back.

"That's done it," Willard proclaimed.

"Three cheers for His Grace!" someone called, and shouts echoed against the wind.

Alaric inclined his head in thanks as he moved to where the remaining groom stood with arms folded, regarding the pitiful lump of humanity at his feet. Simmons sat hunched, muttering to himself. He'd been on his feet when Alaric had ridden up, looking as if he wanted to lash out at someone. But even he knew the penalty for striking an aristocrat. That hadn't stopped him from speaking out instead.

"Your father caused this," he'd said as Alaric had hurried to the gates to inspect the damage. "He turned my father out with no warning. Da and Mum died in the cold, friendless."

"So you think to return the favor, for everyone on the island?" Alaric had shaken his head. "The important thing now is to get those gates open. We'll have to compensate for the broken capstan by pulling the chain by hand. If you hope to avoid the noose, I'd put your back into it."

A look had flickered across the footman's face, and he had put his hand to his back. "Sorry, Your Grace. I must have injured myself. You'll have to do it yourself."

He'd started. Muscles bunching, he'd braced his feet and pulled as hard as he could. The capstan turned. The gates inched open. But not fast enough. The river was already overtopping them, bending them under the pressure. They'd stick, or worse, burst free and spill water onto the shore. Instead of keeping the island from flooding, he'd be dooming the lands across from him as well.

The arrival of the grooms and Willard had saved them all. With them had come many of his tenants—from older men whose grey hair gave testimony to their years of service to young fellows eager to prove themselves. They'd brought Mr. Harden, who Simmons had struck down to keep him from his duty. Together, they had opened the gates. Already the channel was filling, the waters lowering at the western edge of the island. Now they would have to wait to see if it was enough. In the meantime, he remanded Simmons into the care of two of his grooms to be taken to the local jail on charges of vandalism, theft, trespassing, and attempted murder.

"I'm sorry I didn't recognize the danger sooner, Your Grace," Willard told him as the grooms rode away. "Like you, I thought perhaps Simmons had refused to leave, but I never thought he'd do something like this. Makes me wonder about the fires this past summer."

"And the difficulties we kept having at the castle," Alaric agreed, looking to his horse.

NEVER DOUBT A DUKE

"I'll stay and make sure the channel keeps filling," Willard offered. "You go after your girls."

The others were ready to help as needed. With a nod of thanks, Alaric set out once more.

The ride back to the stables felt endless. He had faith that Jane would locate the girls, but part of him feared to find one or more of them hurt. At the very least they would be cold and frightened. He urged his horse faster.

Mr. Quayle met him as he rode in. "The gates?"

"Open," he said, swinging down. "The waters are receding. Let's hope they stay that way. The girls?"

"Safe and in the castle," he said, following Alaric as he started for the house. "But there's trouble. Your starch-rumped butler sacked Mrs. Kimball."

He jerked to a stop. "What?"

Quayle nodded. "Claimed all this was her fault. Nonsense. I agreed it was fine for them to go riding, even Lady Belle. None of us had any idea Simmons was on the loose. She doesn't deserve to be sent packing."

"And she won't be," Alaric said, striding for the house. "Not while I live."

Mr. Quayle called after him, but Alaric would not be stopped. Jane had done nothing wrong. He would stake his life on it. If anyone was leaving, it would be Parsons.

He found his daughters with the nursemaids in the schoolroom. They'd changed out of their wet habits and into nightgowns that fluttered about their stockinged feet as they ran to him.

"Father, Father, Mrs. Kimball went away!" Belle cried.

"Mr. Parsons wouldn't even let her collect her things," Callie said, face puckering. "She'll need her nightgown. She was wetter than I was because she walked with Belle while we rode ahead."

She would have. Jane ever did what was best for her girls.

Larissa was white. "I don't want her leave. She's not a very good governess, but she cares about us."

"About all of us," he assured her. He gathered them close a moment. "Don't worry, girls. I'll see that she returns."

"How?" Callie asked, damp curl brushing his chin. "Betsy said that Mr. Parsons said that she would be lucky to catch the mail coach to London."

Belle nodded. "Mail coaches go very fast."

He could go faster. Decatur and some of the other horses might be spent, but Belle's unicorn could catch the mail coach, rain or no rain. Yet what would he say to Jane? *Come back, the girls need you.*

Come back, I need you.

Come back, I love you.

"Father?" Callie asked, tugging on his sleeve. "Don't you want Mrs. Kimball to come back?"

More than anything in the world.

He straightened. "I'll see what I can do. For now, mind Betsy and Maud." He strode from the room.

His mother met him on the stair. "I just heard. Are the girls all right?"

"Fine," he said. "I'm going after Jane. Parsons discharged her."

She nodded. "Terribly high-handed. I'll speak to him. What are you going to do?"

"Ride after her. Tell her how much she means to this household." He drew in a breath and met Her Grace's gaze. "And Mother, I intend to ask her to marry me."

He waited for the disappointed look, the resignation to her social ruin. His mother snapped a nod. "Good."

He reared back. "Good? I was under the impression you would take her only under duress. What of your position in Society?"

She looked down her nose. "Who would dare question that?"

No one seeing her now. "And what of the skills you expect in a good duchess?"

His mother waved a hand. "Skills can be taught. Jane is

clever; she'll learn. What's more important is she makes the girls happy. She makes you happy. Now, go! Bring home your bride."

CHAPTER TWENTY-THREE

J ane sat in the mail coach, squeezed between a massive merchant and a fat farmer, as the carriage raced for London. The space was so tight she could barely move. The air was thick with the smell of sausage someone had eaten for breakfast, the mingled cologne of her seatmates, the lemon verbena perfume of the farmer's wife across from her. The drumming hooves matched her heartbeat.

She tried to count her blessings. She was safe and relatively warm, thanks to the cramped quarters. Mr. Quayle had loaned her a wool coat and the money for inside passage, so at least she wasn't riding out in the elements like the few other hardy passengers on the top of the coach.

"Least I can do," the master of horse had said as he'd put her in the duke's own carriage for the trip to Walton-on-Thames. "And I'm sure we'll see each other again so you can return the coat."

She wasn't nearly so sure. In fact, the future had never looked bleaker. She was leaving Alaric, the girls, and her heart behind. Even if Miss Thorn found her another situation, she didn't have the stomach for this business. And yet, what choice did she have? She didn't possess Patience's temperament to sit with the sickly, nor any experience to commend her to another sort of work. She was eminently suited to serve as provisioner for the cavalry. A shame her gender prevented her from signing up.

Outside came a yell. The farmer and his wife peered out the window.

"Someone's trying to catch the coach," she reported.

The merchant pulled his satchel closer. "Must be a highwayman. He should know better than to try to stop His Majesty's mail."

The call came again, louder, and the hair stood up on Jane's arms. It couldn't be!

A white-coated horse thundered past, the rider's greatcoat streaming out behind him like wings, and she caught enough of a glimpse to see the hair sticking up off the horse's forehead like a horn.

"Stop this coach!" Alaric shouted.

"This is the mail," the driver shouted back. "We stop for no one."

"I am the Duke of Wey. Stop, or I'll see you before the king."

"Duke of Wey," the merchant said with a snort. "Duke of no way, more like."

The farmer's wife nodded. "What sort of duke rides about in the rain, chasing coaches?"

Hers did.

Jane pressed her hand to her chest, as if she could still the hope rising inside her. He'd come for her, come after her. That had to mean something.

She thought for a moment the coachman would refuse, but then the mighty vehicle slowed, came to a stop. The passengers exchanged glances.

Alaric leaped from the unicorn and wrenched open the door. "Jane Kimball, come out!"

Now they all stared at her.

With an apologetic look, Jane shoved past her seatmates and climbed from the coach. The gentlemen on the top of the carriage gazed down at her, as if expecting some sort of farce to play out. She was a little afraid they were about to get their money's worth.

"We can't stop long," the coachman warned Alaric. "We have a schedule to meet."

"This will only take a moment," the duke promised. His hair was blown back from his face, his cheeks red. His eyes gleamed green against the grey of the day. He took Jane's hand in his.

"Forgive me, Jane, for being blind and stupid. Please come home with me."

She wanted to kiss him; she wanted to push him back and escape before her heart hurt any more. "It's impossible. I'm a horrid governess. You must see that."

"You're an unusual governess," he allowed. "But I think you'd make the perfect wife and mother."

Jane stared at him. That tender smile, the gentle squeeze of her hand said he truly was asking her to marry him. She couldn't believe it. "Really?"

His smile deepened. "Never doubt a duke."

Still she hesitated. So much stood against them—Larissa, Her Grace, Parsons and the rest of the staff, Society's expectations, his need for an heir. Yet surely, if they believed in each other, they could overcome the rest.

"Go on, miss!" the farmer's wife urged. "Say yes. He's a duke!"

"More than a duke," he promised Jane. "I'm the man who loves you."

Jane bit her lip to keep from crying. She'd never thought to hear those words again, to feel the emotion singing through her. She wrapped her arms about him.

"Yes, Alaric, yes! I will marry you."

The entire mail coach cheered.

"Best wishes, Your Grace, miss," the coachman said, gathering the reins. "Give His Majesty my regards." He saluted them with his whip, then shouted to the horses and started down the road at a high rate of speed. The men on the outside waved their hats at her.

As if he feared she'd change her mind, he held her hand

as he positioned Belle's unicorn for mounting. "You'll have to ride up with me, and we won't go as fast returning. This brave beast gave her all."

She touched the horse's neck with her free hand. "But what a run. Only a unicorn could do so well."

The horse blinked her eyes against the rain. It was almost as if she'd winked at Jane.

Alaric put his hands on her waist and lifted her to the saddle. Then he swung up behind her. His arms bracing her, he turned the horse and headed back toward the island.

"We have a lot of people to convince," she told him, warmth percolating into her from his body so close. "It's not every governess who marries a duke."

"No one's opinion matters but yours and mine."

Jane shook her head. "Spoken like a duke. What about the girls? What about Her Grace?"

"Callie and Belle adore you. And Mother all but ordered me to bring you back."

Jane laughed. "Because she didn't want to go looking for another governess, I warrant."

"Because she expects me to marry you. She told me so herself."

"I wish Callie had been there to confirm it," Jane muttered.

Now he laughed. "Don't worry, Jane. I'm a duke. I am allowed to make decisions."

Jane leaned her head back against his chest, fancying that she could hear his heart beating. "Up until now, your decisions have been entirely about your duty. You'll pardon me if I find the sudden change suspicious."

His arms tightened around her. "I admit to selfish reasons for wanting to marry you. I love you, Jane. I want you at my side, not up in a schoolroom far out of reach. But the decision doesn't just benefit me. It gives the girls a mother who cares about them, who will be engaged in their upbringing, who will make sure they don't turn into the pretty dolls my mother seems to prefer."

"You're right there. You couldn't keep me out of the schoolroom. I intend to see our girls more than once a day. No offense meant."

"None taken. You reminded me I have a duty not just as a duke but as a father. I will take a greater part in my daughters' lives as well."

Jane cuddled closer, relishing the feel of him around her. "Very well. You've made your case. I already agreed to be your bride. There's just one thing."

"Name it."

"You get to win over Larissa."

Alaric rode into the courtyard of the castle, head high. He rather felt like a conquering hero, returning the fair princess to her rightful place. He still couldn't quite believe Jane had agreed to his outrageous request. But, meeting her gaze, he knew he'd made the right decision.

Two footmen came out to greet him. He dismounted and lifted Jane from the saddle. "See that this fine steed receives a good rub down and an apple," he said to one of his staff, laying a hand on the unicorn's flank. "She saved my life today."

The footman's eyes widened, but he took the reins and led the horse toward the stable yard. Alaric turned to the other. "Gather Mrs. Kimball's things and move them to the best guest chamber."

"Oh, Alaric, no," Jane protested. "That isn't necessary."

"My bride has no need to sleep in the servants' quarters," he said.

The footman's brows shot up, but he hurried to obey.

Alaric was looking forward to his next duty, but Parsons was not in his usual spot in the entry hall.

"Afraid to face me, the scoundrel," he said.

Jane gave his hand a squeeze. "Let him be for now. You

need to talk to Larissa."

He shuddered, and she laughed. "Now who's afraid?"

"Guilty. Perhaps we could wait until after dinner."

"You just called me your bride in front of the footman. By dinner, the entire island and half the county will know the Duke of Wey is marrying his governess. Larissa deserves to hear it from you, before Callie reports it."

He could not argue that. Taking a deep breath, he went to confront his daughters.

He found them in his mother's sitting room, listening to Her Grace read from the *Book of Ruth*. The landowner who took pity and married a widow. Rather appropriate. If Boaz had felt half for Ruth what Alaric felt for Jane, it would have been a happy union.

They all looked up as he came into the room.

Belle scrambled to her feet. "Did you find her, Father?"

"I did. Your unicorn led me to her. I am pleased to report that Mrs. Kimball is back in the castle and changing into dry clothes even as we speak."

Callie rose as well. "But Betsy said Mr. Parsons sacked her."

Belle frowned. "Why would Mr. Parsons put Mrs. Kimball in a sack? She wouldn't like that."

Alaric motioned them back into their chairs and went to sit on the floor among them. Interesting that Larissa hadn't said a word. She was frowning, but over Jane's return or his informal posture, he wasn't sure. Very likely dukes were not supposed to recline on the carpet.

"Sacking means discharging, Belle," he explained. "Mr. Parsons told Mrs. Kimball she could not work here anymore."

Callie nodded, setting her pale curls to swaying. "Which is why Grandmother sacked him."

Alaric's look veered to his mother. Her Grace raised her chin. "I never liked that man. Entirely too full of himself. He had no right to discharge dear Jane."

Belle nodded too. "I want Mrs. Kimball to work here. I love her."

"Me too," Callie said.

Alaric turned to his oldest. "What about you, Larissa?"

She shifted on her seat. "Mrs. Kimball isn't a very good governess. But I like her anyway."

"Then why did you tell Mr. Parsons it was all her fault?" Callie demanded.

Alaric frowned as Larissa squirmed. "Is this true, Larissa? Did you lie about Mrs. Kimball?"

Larissa lifted her chin. "I didn't lie. It was her fault. If she hadn't yelled at Simmons, you wouldn't have sacked him, and he wouldn't have wanted to punish everyone by breaking the lock." She slumped, hands worrying before her gown. "I truly like Mrs. Kimball, Father. I just wanted her to learn her lesson. You must follow the rules."

"Ah, yes." Alaric glanced at his mother, who also squirmed. "The rules. Who makes the rules, Larissa? Who says they must be obeyed?"

She blinked. "Everyone."

Callie nodded. "Miss Carruthers, Miss Waxworth, Miss Durham, Lady Fredericka, Grandmother."

"And Mother," Larissa murmured.

So that was the problem. Even from the grave Evangeline was exerting her influence over her daughter.

"I grant you there are rules that keep people safe," Alaric said carefully. "Those are important to follow. There are also guidelines to polite behavior. We should generally follow them so that everyone feels welcomed and valued. But sometimes, doing the right thing means breaking the rules."

Larissa frowned. "Like when?"

"Like when you insist that your son marry a woman he doesn't love for the good of the family," his mother put in. "The right thing to do is to let him find someone he can love, who still fits in well with the family."

Alaric gave her a grateful smile. "Like when you become so busy with your duty you forget you have three daughters more precious to you than life. The right thing to do is make sure they know it."

Belle wiggled out of her seat and climbed into his lap. "I love you, Father."

"Me too," Callie said, pasting herself against his side.

Larissa slid off her seat and put her arms as far around him as she could reach. "Me too," she whispered.

He held them close a moment, marveling at the gift he'd been given, a gift he might have overlooked but for Jane.

"I love you too, girls," he said, throat tight. "And I love Mrs. Kimball, that is Jane. I've asked her to be my wife and your mother."

His mother beamed, eyes tearing. Belle and Callie pulled back and exchanged delighted glances.

Larissa sighed as she disengaged, and he readied himself for a fight.

"Oh, how marvelous," she said, smile forming. "We'll have a mother, and we can get a *real* governess."

CHAPTER TWENTY-FOUR

Jane glanced up as Alaric entered the library. She was afraid to admit how much she was looking forward to discovering the treasures around her. The poor man would think she'd agreed to marry him for his library!

The smile on his face told her everything she needed to know.

"You did it," she said, moving away from the bookcases to meet him.

"We did it," he corrected her, taking her hands. "The girls already fell in love with you, just as I did. They needed no convincing to accept you as their mother."

Jane cocked her head. "Even Larissa?"

"Even Larissa," he insisted. "It seems she can see you as a mother much easier than a governess."

Jane laughed. "I always knew that girl was smart. So, what now?"

He released her hands. "Now I have to hire a butler."

Jane raised her brows. "You sacked Mr. Parsons? I would have liked to see that."

He chuckled. "Mother beat me to it. I take it he's already left the castle. You will never have to see him again, Jane."

She couldn't help the relief that thought engendered, though she did spare a moment to pity the fellow for his overzealous ways.

"I have a suggestion," she said to Alaric.

"Someone else Miss Thorn represents?" he asked.

"No," Jane said. "Someone who cares about you and the girls. We'll move Mrs. Winters here."

His smile broadened. "You are going to make an exceptional duchess."

Her cheeks heated. "As to that, only time will tell, but I intend to do my best to make you proud."

He gathered her close. "And I intend to do my best to make you happy, Jane. Whatever you want, you have only to ask."

"In that case," Jane said, turning up her face, "I've been wanting to ask for another kiss since the day you gave me the first one."

His mouth quirked, as if he fought to stay solemn. "It would be my pleasure."

He lowered his lips to hers, arms cradling her against him. In his touch, she knew herself loved, cherished. Home.

After all, one should never doubt a duke.

Meredith Thorn sat in the coffee shop on the corner of Bond Street and Piccadilly, one hand stroking Fortune's back, the other holding a letter from Jane.

"The Duchess of Wey," she murmured to the cat. "Who would have thought?"

Fortune raised her head to eye her, blinking copper eyes.

"Oh, you knew all along, did you? A shame most people don't have your sense."

The shop bell rang as a young lady entered. Neat grey redingote wrapped about her and simple hat on her honey-colored hair, the woman moved into the shop with the grace of a willow swaying in the breeze. She glanced right and left, as if suspecting spies in each direction, then hurried toward Meredith.

"Miss Thorn?"

Meredith inclined her head. "Miss Ramsey, I take it."

Patience sank onto the chair. "Yes. I haven't much time. I'm only given a half hour off every other week."

"As much as that?" Miss Thorn picked up her cup of coffee. "However do you fill the time? I take it you'd like a more generous position."

"Please," Patience said with a sigh. "And somewhere I could do something more useful than carry handkerchiefs."

Meredith glanced down at Fortune. The cat sprang up onto the table and stalked up to Patience.

"Oh, what a beautiful creature." She extended her hand as if for a kiss. Fortune sniffed at the worn leather glove, then rubbed her back under the long fingers.

Meredith smiled as she set down her cup. "Yes, I think we can find something for you. Sir Harold Orwell's aunt is seeking a young lady to help with her scientific experiments. She is in town at present. Let's pay her a call." She gathered up Fortune and rose.

Patience scrambled to her feet. "Now?"

"Certainly," Meredith said. "No time like the present. With any luck, we'll have you settled by tea. We can discuss terms on the way. Fortune will have to approve of Sir Harry, of course."

Patience put a hand to her forehead, but she accompanied Meredith to the door. "I thought it was his aunt who needed help."

Meredith raised an arm to hail a hack. "It never hurts to consider your options, my dear. Now, come along. We mustn't keep your baronet waiting."

Julian Mayes slipped back into the shadows of the alley off Piccadilly. It had been her, his Mary Rose; he was certain of it. Had she any idea how he'd searched for her after learning her cruel cousin had turned her out? He'd once pledged undying devotion, offered to plan his life around her desires. Why hadn't she reached out to him, then or since? Her expenses were being met somehow, if that fashionable gown was any indication. And Wey had said she was indeed living in Lady Winhaven's former residence on Clarendon Square. Renting from the heir, perhaps?

Yet why change her name? If she had married, she'd be Mrs. Thorn, not Miss Thorn. And why go into trade? He could not credit her employment agency was overly successful if she had no permanent business address, no client he could find save Jane and the young woman she was with now.

Then there was the way she'd disappeared, just when he began searching for her again. He was thankful to have spotted her now. He'd been passing the coffee shop twice a day for weeks in the hope of catching her.

Now she hailed a hack, young lady in tow, before he could renew their acquaintance. But this time, he resolved, she would not escape him. He called for a coach himself and set off in pursuit. Wey had sent word he intended to marry his Jane. Against all odds, against all reason, love had triumphed. His suspicions had proved groundless, just as Alaric had predicted. For the first time in a long time, he felt the brush of hope.

Now to renew his acquaintance with Mary.

D ear Reader ~
      Thank you for reading Jane and Alaric's story. When Jane rode onto the page with all her wit and wisdom, I couldn't stop myself from giving her a well-deserved happily-ever-after.

If you enjoyed the book, there's several things you could do now:

Sign up for a free email alert at **https://subscribe. reginascott.com** with exclusive bonus content so you'll be the first to know whenever a new book is out or on sale.

Post a review on a bookseller or reader site to help others find the book.

Discover my many other books on my website at **www. reginascott.com.**

Turn the page for a sneak peek of the second book in the Fortune's Brides series, *Never Borrow a Baronet*, in which Patience Ramsey gets her wish for a more meaningful position as she agrees to pose as a baronet's fiancée to keep others from discovering his secret life.

Blessings!

Regina Scott

Sneak Peek:

NEVER BORROW A BARONET
Book 2 in the Fortune's Brides Series by Regina Scott

Essex, England, March 1812

M y, but life could be unpredictable.
Patience Ramsey peered out of the window of the elegant coach, gaze on the greening fields they passed, hand stroking the fur of the grey-coated cat in her lap. Raised in the country, spending the last three years as companion to the sickly Lady Carrolton, she had become accustomed to routine, solitude. A genteel lady fallen on difficult times could expect nothing more. At least, that had been her impression until she'd met Meredith Thorn of the Fortune Employment Agency, and Miss Thorn had introduced her to Miss Augusta Orwell.

"Gussie," the tall, spare daughter of a baronet had proclaimed the moment they'd met at the family's London town house on Clarendon Square. "Everyone calls me that. Well, everyone I like. And I like you. You have presence."

Patience still wasn't sure why the older woman had said that. She had never noticed a particular attitude when she looked in the mirror. Her long, thick, wavy hair could not claim the glory of gold nor the biddable nature of brown, and it was hardly visible in the serviceable bun behind her head. Her brown eyes could never be called commanding. And while her curves might be a tad more noticeable than Gussie's, she was in no way approaching the status of an Amazon. Besides, a presence was not required to serve as a companion. Lady Carrolton would only have seen it as an impertinence.

But, before she was even certain she would suit in the new position, she had resigned her post with Lady Carrolton, packed her things, and boarded the Orwell coach for the journey to the Essex shore.

"As soon as we reach the manor, I must show you my laboratory," Gussie said beside her now, continuing the rather one-sided conversation she'd begun when they'd left the inn that morning, having spent the night after leaving London. "I'm itching to try the gypsum I purchased in town. It will be just the thing for scrofulous eruptions. I know it. I don't suppose you have any we might test the preparation on."

Patience hid her shudder from long practice. If she could humor her previous employer, who had been convinced she suffered from every illness imaginable, she could surely deal with the irrepressible Gussie. After all, were not the peacemakers called blessed?

"Unfortunately, no," she told her new employer. "But perhaps we can find some poor soul in need of help."

Across the coach, Miss Thorn cleared her throat. *She* had presence. That raven hair, those flashing lavender eyes. And she had an enviable wardrobe. Today it was a lavender redingote cut away so that the fine needlework on her sky blue wool gown showed to advantage. Nearly all Patience's clothes were grey or navy—Lady Carrolton had insisted on it—and none draped so neatly around her figure as the fashionable gowns Miss Thorn wore.

Then again, Gussie had insisted on having Patience fitted for new gowns and purchased accessories before they had left London. The dresses should arrive in a week or two, to be finished by the local seamstress, and the jaunty feathered hat, ostrich plume curling around Patience's ear, sat on her head now. The entire wardrobe had seemed an extravagance, but Patience had learned not to question the vagaries of the aristocracy.

"I believe we agreed that you would not experiment on Miss Ramsey," Miss Thorn said, looking down her long nose at Gussie.

Gussie waved a hand. "Of course, of course. It is merely my enthusiasm for the task speaking." She turned to Patience. "You must tell me, dear girl, when I overstep. I want ours to be a long and happy association."

How different from Lady Carrolton. Her constant complaints, her bitter spirit, had tried Patience in ways she had never imagined. She would be ever in the debt of her friend Jane Kimball, soon to be the Duchess of Wey, for suggesting that Patience might have the opportunity to change her circumstances.

She and Jane had sat together along the wall every week while Lady Carrolton took tea with her long-time friend, the Dowager Duchess of Wey, at the castle belonging to the duke's family. Jane had served as governess to the duchess's three granddaughters. Patience could only admire her dedication to the little girls. That and Jane's bravery. Patience had been taught that silence was a virtue, that one should never state one's opinions in company. Nothing stopped Jane from speaking her mind, not fear of losing her position, not concern that she might be deemed impertinent or a rudesby.

"If you ever want another position," Jane had said on one occasion when Lady Carrolton had been particularly difficult, "I may know someone who could help."

Even though something had leaped inside her at the

thought, Patience hadn't accepted Jane's offer that day. Lady Carrolton had been kind to hire her when she had never worked before, had no reference other than the supportive words of the vicar. Surely she owed the lady loyalty, forbearance. Do unto others as you would have done unto you.

And then had come that terrible day when Lady Carrolton's daughter, Lilith, had lashed out.

"How dare you presume to advise my mother on her medications?" she had spat, pale blue eyes drilling into Patience. "You have no education, no family of merit, absolutely nothing to recommend you. If you dare to contravene my suggestions again, I will see you up on charges. How well will you fare sitting in jail with no one to plead your case?"

It had been all Patience could do to hold back her tears until she had left the withdrawing room. All her selfless service, all her care, and this was her thanks? She had a gentlewoman's education, little different from Lady Lilith's. Her father and mother had been good, kind people who hadn't deserved their deaths of the influenza. She had only been trying to help her ladyship over the illnesses that plagued her. It seemed none of that mattered in the Carrolton household.

There had to be some place she might earn respect, some work where she could find purpose and honor. A position under an employer with integrity, an ounce of human kindness, and an unwillingness to berate those around her.

Miss Thorn had been all understanding. Patience had thought it might take some time to find a new situation, especially as, once again, she had no reference. But she hadn't been in Miss Thorn's company more than a quarter hour before the woman had whisked Patience off for an interview with Miss Orwell. And Gussie had only asked a few questions before declaring Patience perfect for the role as her assistant.

Now, here she sat, leaving her former life behind, riding into a new bright future.

She hoped.

"Such a lovely creature," Gussie said, eyeing Fortune, Miss Thorn's cat, as she cuddled against Patience's chest. "I don't suppose she has any scrofulous eruptions."

Miss Thorn put her nose in the air. "Certainly not. And you may not experiment on her either. Surely you remember our agreement."

Miss Thorn had been very precise in her terms. Patience was to receive her own room, generous compensation, and a half day off every week in her role assisting Gussie in developing salves and lotions to improve the skin. The work could be no messier than tending to the ailments of a quarrelsome lady and with so much more purpose! Miss Thorn had even insisted on traveling out to the Orwell estate to make sure everything was as Gussie had portrayed it. She had been determined that the matter be settled quickly and precisely, and Patience was rather glad of it.

If everything happened quickly, she had no time for regrets or second thoughts.

"Of course I remember our agreement," Gussie said with a sniff. "I remember everything. You might take note of that Miss... Thorn."

Patience's benefactress turned toward the window, but not before she saw her cheeks brighten with pink. Embarrassment? Impossible. Surely nothing could discompose the indomitable Miss Thorn.

As if she thought otherwise, Fortune roused herself and leaped across the space to rub her cheek against her mistress' arm. Miss Thorn glanced down at her gratefully.

Gussie nudged Patience. "Look there, up that hill. That's your new home."

Patience turned to the opposite window. Though the sun was nearly at the western horizon, the air felt suddenly warmer, the day brighter. The fields had given way to fens and marshes, their grasses undulating in the breeze from the water. Close at hand rose a promontory studded with trees and topped by a sturdy, square manor house. The red brick glowed in the spring sunlight; the multipaned windows gleamed. She drew in a breath and caught the scent of the sea.

The proximity to the waves was even more obvious as they rolled across the causeway that led toward the promontory. To her right lay miles of tide flats, brown and muddy; to her left, the twisting maze of creeks and channels that made up the marshes.

"It floods on occasion," Gussie said with a nod to the track. "I can remember springs when we didn't see another person until after Easter."

Patience's stomach dipped, but she managed a polite smile. Since her parents had died, she had always been alone. The isolation of the house would make no difference.

They followed the drive to stop in front of the stone steps leading to the front door. A manservant in a navy coat and breeches came out to open the carriage door and then went to help the coachman with the horses. Patience followed Gussie and Miss Thorn up the steps, through tall white columns and the wide, red-lacquered front door into a spacious, dark-wood-floored entry hall. More white fluted columns held up the sweeping stairs leading to the second story, and opened doors in all directions invited her to explore the house further. But the portraits hanging from the high ceiling against the creamy stuccoed wall, life-sized and rich in their gilded frames, stopped her movement. Miss Thorn paused to eye them as well. In her arms, Fortune twitched her tail as if finding the portraits equally compelling.

"My grandfather," Gussie said as if she'd noticed them staring at the swarthy fellow standing with his hand on a globe as if he owned the world. "He earned the baronetcy through some effort that pleased the Crown. A merchant, they say, making his fortune on the high seas. A pirate, if you ask me."

Patience blinked. So did Fortune.

"That is my father," she continued with a nod to the next gentleman, who was seated beside a green baize table. "Nearly gambled away our entire fortune before his untimely death. My brother attempted to take up the challenge. He was killed in a duel over the accusation he had cheated at cards before we ever had the opportunity to have him painted."

Patience swallowed. Fortune turned her face away.

Gussie's censorious look eased into something warmer as she motioned to the final portrait of a man standing gazing out a window that looked very much like the ones on either side of the front door. "And then there's Harry. I raised him as my own. They say heredity will out."

Patience frowned. This fellow boasted a shock of mahogany hair, curling against his brow; blue eyes that gave no quarter; a solid chin that brooked no disobedience; and shoulders broad enough to take on any challenge. It seemed Sir Harold Orwell had inherited his forefathers' chiseled good looks. How sad if he had inherited their less attractive attributes as well.

Through one of the many doors came a small fellow in the navy livery that must belong to the house. White hair, short cut, sat like a wreath about his head, leaving his dome bare. His round face was as wizened as a winter-nipped apple, and nearly as red. He hurried up to Gussie. "Your ladyship. I regret that you have guests."

Miss Thorn turned from their perusal of the portraits. "Invited guests, sir." Fortune drew back as if just as insulted by the comment.

He inclined his head in their general direction. "My apologies, madam, but I was referring to the other guests. The ones who arrived earlier this afternoon."

Gussie frowned as she removed her hat and offered it to him. "Other guests? What other guests?" Suddenly, her eyes widened, and Patience would only have called the look horrified. "Cuddlestone, no! Please tell me it isn't so."

He sighed, so gustily that his chest deflated. "I wish I could, your ladyship. They claim to have been invited to stay for Easter. Sir Harry had already left. I could not in good conscience send them away before consulting with you."

"You could, and you should," Gussie insisted. She rubbed her forehead. "I will not allow this."

Miss Thorn took a step forward, holding Fortune protectively close. "Is something wrong, Miss Orwell?"

As if in answer, there was a cry from above. Patience looked up to find a lady about her age on the landing. She rushed down before Patience could register more than pale blond hair and big eyes.

"Gussie!" She enfolded the lady in a hug. "You've returned! How marvelous. And with company." She pulled back and aimed a happy smile all around. Every bit of her trembled with obvious joy, from the ringlets beside her creamy oval face to the pink satin bow under her bosom, to the double flounces at the bottom of her white muslin skirts.

Gussie drew in a breath as if overwhelmed to find someone even more effusive than she was. "Yes. Miss Thorn, may I present Miss Villers. I imagine her brother is about somewhere."

"Taking a walk in the garden," Miss Villers confessed. She inclined her head to Miss Thorn, who returned the gesture, and beamed at Fortune. Then she turned expectantly to Patience, who smiled dutifully. Would Gussie even think to introduce her? In the Carrolton household, she had become used to being overlooked. Good companions, as Lady Lilith had enjoyed saying, should be invisible.

"And you must meet Miss Ramsey," Gussie said. "She's going to marry my Harry."

Learn more at
www.reginascott.com/neverborrowabaronet.html

OTHER BOOKS BY REGINA SCOTT

Grace-by-the-Sea Series
The Matchmaker's Rogue

Fortune's Brides Series
Never Doubt a Duke
Never Borrow a Baronet
Never Envy an Earl
Never Vie for a Viscount
Never Kneel to a Knight
Never Marry a Marquess

Uncommon Courtships Series
The Unflappable Miss Fairchild
The Incomparable Miss Compton
The Irredeemable Miss Renfield
The Unwilling Miss Watkin
An Uncommon Christmas

Lady Emily Capers
Secrets and Sensibilities
Art and Artifice
Ballrooms and Blackmail
Eloquence and Espionage
Love and Larceny

Marvelous Munroes Series
My True Love Gave to Me
Catch of the Season
The Marquis' Kiss
Sweeter Than Candy

Spy Matchmaker Series
The Husband Mission
The June Bride Conspiracy
The Heiress Objective

Perfection

And other books for Revell, Love Inspired Historical,
and Timeless Regency collections.

ABOUT THE AUTHOR

Regina Scott started writing novels in the third grade. Thankfully for literature as we know it, she didn't sell her first novel until she learned a bit more about writing. Since her first book was published in 1998, her stories have traveled the globe, with translations in many languages including Dutch, German, Italian, and Portuguese. She now has more than forty published works of warm, witty romance.

Alas, she cannot have a cat of her own, as her husband is allergic to them. Fortune's Brides came about because her critique partner and dear friend Kristy J. Manhattan is an avid fan of cats, supporting spay and neuter clinics and pet rescue groups. If Fortune resembles any cat you know, credit Kristy.

Regina Scott and her husband of 30 years reside in the Puget Sound area of Washington State. Regina Scott has dressed as a Regency dandy, driven four-in-hand, learned to fence, and sailed on a tall ship, all in the name of research, of course. Learn more about her at her website at *www. reginascott.com.*

Made in the USA
Coppell, TX
30 August 2020